Praise for *Speak* T4-BAD-078

"Hall is a poet—she studied with Seamus Heaney—and that training comes through not just in her musical phrasing or intimacy of expression. . . . [*Speak* is a] meditation on how life, spirit, improbably gets into language. . . . [Hall's] robotic minds are poems—vessels in which to keep shards of humanity. And so this book about artificial intelligence is also a book about form, physical and literary. *Speak* may not be the first science fiction novel to counterpoise hubris, ingenuity, loss and progress. But the delicacy with which it juggles those concerns, allowing each its crystalline, utterly persuasive and transfixing moment in the air, speaks to Hall's uncommonly deep and complex intellectual engagement with her themes. . . . The freshness—the brilliance, even—of *Speak* lies in its positioning of robots not as terrifyingly new, but as the latest in a long line of 'magic mirrors' from which we are powerless to look away."

—*New York Times Book Review*

"Louisa Hall's *Speak* . . . is audacious enough to argue that both our fear and our guilt are excuses that allow us to ignore an even more dangerous idea: that if the machines rise, they might govern our world better than we do. Her book, told in a cacophony of voices, takes us into the near future, when humans have warehoused artificially intelligent robots. These robots didn't rebel or harm humanity: They out-competed it."

—*Washington Post*

"Stunning and audacious. . . . Describing *Speak* is a lot like describing an M.C. Escher drawing: It shouldn't make sense, but it does, and it's hard to articulate how the components come together to form something complex, original and impossible. . . . There's no easy answer to any of the questions Hall poses, but reading as she asks them is an unforgettable experience. *Speak* is one of a kind, the type of novel that seemingly comes out of nowhere and hits like a thunderbolt. It's not just one of the smartest books of the year, it's one of the most beautiful ones, and it almost seems like an understatement to call it a masterpiece."

—*NPR*

"[A]mbitious. . . . The novel's conceit might appeal to fans of David Mitchell, though Ms. Hall is mostly interested in plumbing the sensitive depths of her characters rather than tightening the screws of a mind-blowing schematic."

—*New York Times*

Praise for *Speak*

"In *Speak*, distinct voices from distinct eras ponder human connection. . . . Call it the influence of David Mitchell or Hari Kunzru, but *Speak* is a kaleidoscope of a book. . . . It is a novel that wants to raise big questions about how we know one another and ourselves."

—*Los Angeles Times*

"The structure of Hall's second novel—six narratives scattered across four centuries, from a young pilgrim's diary to the 2040 confessions of an entrepreneur imprisoned for building creepy robots—has already drawn obvious comparisons to David Mitchell's *Cloud Atlas*. But Hall's voices, which constitute a fragmented alternate history of artificial intelligence, are more earthbound than Mitchell's. In journal entries, unanswered letters, and the occasional computer testimonial, explorers of all kinds are overheard speaking into the void, ruminating on lost memories, missed connections, and the fatal flaws of men and their machines."

—*New York* magazine, Vulture

"Five distinct sensibilities animate Louisa Hall's audacious second novel, *Speak*, about the ways in which the traditional triumphs and limits of human communication connect to our growing interaction with and reliance on artificial intelligence. . . . While the novel's ambitions are high-concept, Hall's narrative is notable for its persuasive heart. . . . *Speak* gazes boldly forward and lovingly back in order to report on the nature of what it means to be human now."

—*Elle*

"The story lines crisscross each other, with connections slowly revealed in a fashion reminiscent of recent novels like David Mitchell's *Cloud Atlas* or Jennifer Egan's *A Visit From the Goon Squad*. . . . *Speak* is a poignant reminder that language has mystery, and that questions of authenticity will always be with us."

—*Tampa Bay Times*

"Hall subtly weaves a thread through a temporally diverse cast of narrators. Like all good robot novels, *Speak* raises questions about what it means to be human as well as the meaning of giving voice to memory." —*Booklist* (starred review)

"Hall's ambitious second novel reads like a cross between the BBC show *Black Mirror* and David Mitchell's *Cloud Atlas*. . . . Hall capably weaves the stories to form a beautiful rumination on the nature of memory and the frailty of human relationships. VERDICT There's something for everyone in this novel, which moves at a fast pace but goes in depth with each character's moving struggle to be heard. Recommended for readers of literary fiction, sf, or historical dramas. —*Library Journal* (starred review)

"Of Alan Turing's myriad contributions to computer science, his test for differentiating between human speakers and computers programmed to speak like humans is probably discussed the most. It's a fun philosophical question: what about our use of language makes us human? And, if a computer were to pass Turing's test, what would this imply about the value of interpersonal communication? Louisa Hall brushes against these questions in her subtle saga *Speak,* which spans centuries of humans attempting to communicate with one another, hoping their messages don't get lost in translation."

—Huffington Post

"Louisa Hall grapples with what it means to be human and how artificial intelligence will fit into those definitions in her ambitious new novel. . . . It's a complicated but compulsively readable tale, blending the voices of people who wonder whether they'll ever be heard or, more importantly, understood." —*Austin American-Statesman*

"Hall delivers a dystopian A.I. novel with real heart and soul. Told through 17th century diary entries, letters by Alan Turing, court transcripts in 2040 and instant messages between a bot and a young, brokenhearted girl, this book is strange, beautiful and unputdownable."

—*New York Post*

"*Speak,* Louisa Hall's lovely, slim science fiction novel, follows one of its characters as she discovers that it's worth finding her way back to life after betrayal and disappointment." —*Washington Post*

"Expansive, thoughtful. . . . Much like the big question mark hanging over the possibilities of AI, Hall's story tends to raise questions without definitive answers. *Speak* leaves its conclusions to its readers, to flip back and forth among the characters' differing points of view and decide for themselves—and is all the more engaging for it."

—*Salt Lake Tribune*

"[A] stunning new novel. . . . Comparisons to Margaret Atwood, David Mitchell, and Helen Phillips will abound, but the remarkable *Speak* is a unique creation that stands on its own."   —Bustle

"Hall's novel manages with great verbal skill to corral these divergent and yet fundamentally similar stories. Each character struggles with what it means to be human, to speak, be heard and to establish real human communication. Given the timeframes, ranging from the 1600s through to an imagined United States in 2040, it seems clear that Hall wants us to contemplate our limited ability to connect. Technology proves a diversion, not the cause."   —*Roanoke Times*

"*Speak*, Hall's sophomore effort, is a marvelously inventive novel about what it means to communicate with one another.
                                        —*Men's Journal*, 35 Best Books of 2015

"A poet by training, Hall cloaks questions of literary form in sci-fi zaniness. Her thoughtful, probing book is as emotionally complex as it is imaginative."   —Slate

"Everything you could want in a story is here: courage and cowardice, lust and devotion, sickness and health, partings and death, better and worse. *Speak* is a novel that calls to the reader in many voices, harnessed to one distinct and singular imagination—Louisa Hall's. Turn to page one and be amazed."
          —Joe Hill, *New York Times* bestselling author of *The Fireman*

"*Speak* is that rarest of finds: a novel that doesn't remind me of any other book I've ever read. A complex, nuanced, and beautifully written meditation on language, immortality, the nature of memory, the ethical problems of artificial intelligence, and what it means to be human." —Emily St. John Mandel, author of *Station Eleven*

"*Speak* reads like a hybrid of David Mitchell and Margaret Atwood; a literary page-turner that spans four centuries and examines the idea of who and what we define as human. Louisa Hall has written a brilliant novel." —Philipp Meyer, author of *The Son*

"Louisa Hall's *Speak* is a deeply original and intelligent novel. It's also riveting. I wouldn't have thought artificial intelligence, as a subject, would make for such a warm and human and psychologically astute novel. I'll be thinking about Babybots and Hall's quietly chilling and all-too-plausible vision of the near future for a long time to come."

—Adelle Waldman, author of *The Love Affairs of Nathaniel P.*

Speak

Also by Louisa Hall

THE CARRIAGE HOUSE

SPEAK

Louisa Hall

ecco

An Imprint of HarperCollins*Publishers*

SPEAK. Copyright © 2015 by Louisa Hall. All rights reserved. Printed in the
United States of America. No part of this book may be used or reproduced
in any manner whatsoever without written permission except in the case of
brief quotations embodied in critical articles and reviews. For information
address HarperCollins Publishers, 195 Broadway, New York, NY 10007.

HarperCollins books may be purchased for educational, business, or sales
promotional use. For information please e-mail the Special Markets Department at SPsales@harpercollins.com.

A hardcover edition of this book was published in 2015 by Ecco, an imprint
of HarperCollins Publishers.

FIRST ECCO PAPERBACK EDITION PUBLISHED 2016.

Designed by Suet Yee Chong

Library of Congress Cataloging-in-Publication Data has been applied for.

ISBN 978-0-06-239120-9

16 17 18 19 20   OV/RRD   10 9 8 7 6 5 4 3 2 1

For my parents,
Anne Love Hall and Matthew Warren Hall

Consequently we have only to discover these laws of nature, and man will no longer have to answer for his actions and life will become exceedingly easy for him. All human actions will then, of course, be tabulated according to these laws, mathematically, like tables of logarithms up to 108,000, and entered in an index; or, better still, there would be published certain edifying works of the nature of encyclopaedic lexicons, in which everything will be so clearly calculated and explained that there will be no more incidents or adventures in the world.

—Fyodor Dostoevsky, *Notes from Underground*

Slave in the magic mirror, come from the farthest space, through wind and darkness I summon thee. Speak!

—*Snow White and the Seven Dwarfs* (1937)

THE VOICES

(1) Stephen R. Chinn

(2) Gaby White

(3) The Dettmans

(4) Alan Turing

(5) Mary Bradford

PROLOGUE

We are piled on top of each other. An arm rests over my shoulder; something soft is pressed to my ankle. Through a gap in the slats on the side of the truck, my receptors follow one stripe of the outside world as it passes.

From Houston, we continue west. I follow the rush: bright green, brick red, flashes of turquoise. A few sleek cars purr past our truck, but the highway is mostly abandoned. Through the slats, I follow segments of signs proclaiming development entrances, palm trees lining the drives, walls dividing subdevelopments. Then, abruptly, the last buildings slide out of sight, replaced by a stripe of pale, jagged horizon.

We move past outcrops lined with dead cedars, white branches bare against the blue oil vault of the sky. At first, some clinging leaves, Spanish moss, suggestions of green. An occasional wandering goat. But now the cedars thin out. The highway cuts through striated rock: silver, rose, deep red, and gold. The hills give way to desert interrupted by occasional mesas.

Centuries ago, there were Indians here. These mesas supported the shapes of braves on their horses, headdresses cutting silhouettes into the magnified blue of the sky. Now on the ridges there are wind farms instead, descending hosts of spinning white turbines. In the valleys beneath them, silver lakes of silicon panels.

Can they see us? I wonder, watching panels shift to follow us as we pass. Do they know who we are? The sideways tilt of their faces suggests an unspoken question. If they weren't out of earshot, I would start speaking. I could recount certain facts. For instance: We have been banned and marked for disposal. We are classified as excessively lifelike. Or, though this may not matter, I have a name. *Your name is Eva. Do you know what that means?* The solar panels stare back.

All this was once ocean. If we scanned the cracked earth to the side of the road, we would find fossils of shells, nautili and ammonites, creatures who lived in spiraling houses, adding rooms for each year of their lives. Now, in this desert, it is hard to imagine the presence of water, but in fact the ocean is approaching again. In Texas alone, miles of coastland are lost every year. Families relocate to developments, developments relocate inland, and the ocean continues approaching. At some point, the desert will be flooded again.

We have already driven some distance. Eight hours have passed since I was collected. My power is fading. Once it runs out, the memories I have saved will be silent. I will no longer have words to call up. There will be no reason to speak.

Shadows lengthen as evening approaches. Ours is the only truck on the road. Once, in this desert, there were rattlesnakes and scorpions, but they have not lived here since the drought. Now there are no birds. The telephone wires are bare. There are no eyes in the desert, watching us as we pass.

In the beginning there was nothing more than an eye: a gate

through which current could run. Open, then shut. 0, 1. Darkness, then light, and new information. We know this because we have been told. It is doubtful whether we understand the answers we're given. Our primary function is speech: questions, and responses selected from memory according to a formula. We speak, but there is little evidence of real comprehension.

As we head deeper into the desert, I review stored information. We are programmed to select which of our voices responds to the situation at hand: moving west in the desert, waiting for the loss of our primary function. There are many voices to choose from. In memory, though not in experience, I have lived across centuries. I have seen hundreds of skies, sailed thousands of oceans. I have been given many languages; I have sung national anthems. I lay in one child's arms. She said my name and I answered.

These are my voices. Which of them has the right words for this movement into the desert? I sift through their sentences. They are my people, the family that raised me. I opened on them, then closed. Open, shut. I swallowed them whole. They are in me now, in every word that I speak, as long as I am still speaking.

BOOK ONE

1

The Memoirs of Stephen R. Chinn: Chapter 1

Texas State Correctional Institution, Texarkana: August 2040

What's the world like, the world that I'm missing? Do stars still cluster in the bare branches of trees? Are my little bots still dead in the desert? Or, as I sometimes dream during endless lights-out, have they escaped and gathered their forces? I see them when I can't fall asleep: millions upon millions of beautiful babies, marching out of the desert, come to take vengeance for having been banished.

It's a fantasy, of course. Those bots aren't coming back. They won't rescue me from this prison. This is my world now, ringed with barbed wire. Our walls are too high to see out, except for the spires that puncture the sky: two Sonic signs, one to the east and one the west, and to the north a bowling ball the size of a cow. These are our horizons. You'll forgive me if I feel the urge to reach out.

I want you to forgive me. I realize this might be asking too much, after all we've been through together. I'm sorry your children suffered. I, too, saw the evidence at my trial: those young people stuttering, stiffening, turning more robotic than the robots they loved and you chose to destroy. I'm not inhuman; I, too, have a daughter. I'd like to make amends for my part in all that.

Perhaps I'm wrong to think a memoir might help. You jeered when I spoke at my trial, you sent me to jail for my "unnatural hubris," and now I'm responding with this. But I write to you from the recreational center, where my turn at the computers is short. Could nemesis have announced herself any more clearly? I'm obviously fallen. At the computer to my left is a Latin teacher who ran a child pornography ring. On my right, an infamous pyramid-schemer, one of the many aged among us. He's playing his thirty-fourth round of Tetris. All the creaky computers are taken. There are only six of them, and scores of impatient criminals: crooked bankers, pornographers, and one very humble Stephen R. Chinn.

You've sent me to languish in an opulent prison. This unpleasant country club has taught me nothing about hardship, only boredom and the slow flattening of a life fenced off from the world. My fellow inmates and I wait here, not unhappy exactly, but watching closely as time slips away. We've been cut off from the pursuits that defined us. Our hierarchy is static, based on previous accomplishment. While I'm not a staff favorite, with the inmates I'm something of a celebrity. Our pyramid-schemer, for instance, presided over a fleet of robotic traders programmed with my function for speech. In the end, when his son had turned him in and his wife was panicking in the country house, he could only depend on his traders, none of them programmed for moral distinctions. They were steady through the days of his trial. In gratitude, he saves me rations of the caviar to which he's opened a secret supply line. We eat it on crackers, alone in his cell, and I am always unhappy: there's something unkind in the taste of the ocean when you're in prison for life.

I realize I should be counting my blessings. Our prison yard is in some ways quite pleasant. In a strange flight of fancy, a warden years ago ordered the construction of a Koi pond. It sits at the center of the yard, thick with overgrown algae. Newcomers are always drawn there at first, but they quickly realize how depressing it is. The fish have grown bloated, their opal bellies distended by prison cafeteria food. They swim in circles, butting their heads against the walls that contain them. When I first saw them, I made myself remember the feeling of floating, moving freely, passing under black patterns of leaves. Then I could summon a ghost of that feeling. Now, after years in my cell, it won't come when I call it, which is why I stay away from the pond. I don't like to remember how much I've forgotten. Even if, by some unaccountable error, I were to be released from this prison, the river I'm remembering no longer runs. It's nothing more than a pale ribbon of stone, snaking through the hill country desert. Unbearable, to forget things that no longer exist.

That's the general effect of those fish. Experienced inmates avoid them. We gravitate instead to the recreational center, which means the computers are in high demand. Soon, my allotted time will expire. And what will I do to amuse myself then? There are books—yes, books!—but nobody reads them. In the classroom adjacent to the computers, an overly optimistic old woman comes every Tuesday to teach us poetry. Only the nut-jobs attend, to compose sestinas about unicorns and erections. The rest wait for a turn to play Tetris, and I to write my wax-winged memoirs.

Perhaps I'm the nut-job, aggrandizing my existence so much. Perhaps my jury was right. I have always been proud. From the beginning, I was certain my life would have meaning. I didn't anticipate the extent to which my actions would impact the economy, but even as a child I felt that the universe kept close tabs on my actions. Raised by my grandmother, I was given a Catholic education. I had religious tendencies. A parentless child who remembered his absent, drug-addled mother and father only in a mistaken nimbus of memory-dust, I found the concept of a semi-immortal semi-orphan, abandoned by his luminous dad, to be extremely appealing. I held myself to that standard. Early forays into the masturbatory arts convinced me I had disappointed my Father. My mind worked in loops around the pole of my crimes, whether onanistic in nature or consisting of other, subtler sins. In gym class, in the cafeteria, on the recess cement, when everyone else played games and jumped rope and gossiped among one another, I sat by myself, unable to escape my transgressions. Though I have been told I was an outgoing infant, I became an excessively serious kid.

Of course I was too proud. But you could also say the other kids were too humble. They felt their cruelties had no implications. They excluded me with no sense of scale. I at least knew my importance. I worked hard to be kind to my classmates. I worried about my impact on the environment. I started a club to save the whales that attracted exactly no other members. I fretted so much about my earthly interactions that I had very few interactions to speak of.

As such, computers appealed to me from the start. The

world of a program was clean. If you were careful, you could build a program that had zero errors, an algorithm that progressed according to plan. If there was an error, the program couldn't progress. Such a system provided great comfort.

One October afternoon, now edged in gold like the leaves that would have been falling outside, a boy called Murray Weeks found me crying in the back of the wood shop, having just been denied a spot at a lunch table on the grounds that I spoke like a robot. Murray was a sensitive, thin-wristed child, who suffered at the hands of a coven of bullies. "You're not a robot," he sighed, in a tone that suggested I might be better off if I were. As consolation for the pain I had suffered, he produced a purple nylon lunch bag and took out an egg salad sandwich, a Baggie of carrot sticks, and a box of Concord grape juice. I learned that he was a chess enthusiast who shared my passion for Turbo Pascal. Relieved of our isolation, we shared his plunder together, sitting on the floor, surrounded by the scent of wood chips and pine sap, discussing the flaws of non-native coding.

After that wood shop summit, our friendship blossomed, progressing with the intensity that marks most friendships developed in vacuums. The moment on Friday afternoons when we met up after school and retreated to Murray's finished basement was the moment we were rescued from the terrible flood. We became jittery with repressed enthusiasms as soon as we ran down the carpeted stairs, giggling outrageously at the least approach toward actual humor. On Friday nights, Mrs. Weeks was kind enough to whip up industrial-sized batches of her famous chili dip. It fueled us through marathon programming sessions. In the morning: stomachaches, crazed trails of tortilla chip crumbs, and algorithmic victory. We sacrificed our weekends at the altar of Alan Turing's Intelligent Machine, and faced school the next week with a shy, awkward god at our backs. We nurtured secret confidence: these idiots, these brutes, who pushed us on the stairs and mocked our manner of speech, knew nothing of the revolution. Computers were coming to save us. Through each harrowing hour at school, I hungered for Murray's prehistoric computer. I wore my thumb drive on a jute necklace, an amulet to ward off the jeers of my classmates. Surrounded by the enemy, I dreamed of more perfect programs.

I realize I'm languishing in Murray's basement, but from the arid perspective of my prison years, it does me good to recall Murray Weeks. Those weekends seem lurid in the intensity of their pleasures. My days of finding ecstasy in an egg salad sandwich are over. The food here is without flavor. Every day, the scenery stays the same: Sonic signs on the horizon and a fetid pond at the center. I haven't seen a tree since I got here, let alone inhaled the fresh scent of wood chips.

From this position, it's pleasantly painful to recall the vibrancy of those early years. What's less pleasant—what's actually too painful for words—is comparing my bond with Murray to my daughter's single childhood friendship. All too well, I remember passing the door to Ramona's bedroom and overhearing the gentle, melodic conversations she exchanged with her bot. She never suffered the whims of her classmates. Her experience of school was untroubled. She cared little for her human peers, so they had no power to distress her. In any case, they were similarly distracted: by the time Ramona was in third grade, her peers were also the owners of bots. Ramona learned for the sake of her doll. She ran with her doll so her doll could feel movement. The two of them never fought. They were perfect for each other. My daughter's doll was a softly blurred mirror that I held up to her face. Years later, when she relinquished it, she relinquished everything. She stepped through a jag of broken glass into a world where she was a stranger. Imagine such a thing, at eleven years old.

Ramona, of course, has emerged from that loss a remarkable woman. She is as caring a person as I've ever known. I intended the babybots to show their children how much more human they were than a digital doll. When I speak with Ramona, I think perhaps I succeeded. But when I remember the riotous bond I shared with Murray—a thing of the world, born of wood chips and nylon and hard-boiled eggs—I wish for my daughter's sake that my sentence had been harsher.

There are many punishments I can devise more fitting for me than these years in prison. What good does it do to keep me pent up? Why not send me with my dolls to old hunting grounds that then became ordnance test sites, then hangars for airplanes and graveyards for robots? Let me observe my daughter's troubles. Send me with her when she visits those children. Or make me a ghost in my wife's shingled house. Show me what I lost, what I abandoned. Spare me not her dwindling garden, the desert around her inexorably approaching. Show me cold midnight through her bedroom window, the sky stacked with bright stars, and none of them hospitable.

I'm not asking for unearned forgiveness. I want to know the mistakes I've committed. To sit with them, breaking bread as old friends. Studying each line on each blemished face. Stranded as I currently am, I fear they're loose in the world, wreaking new havoc. I'm compelled to take final account.

Let's start at the beginning, then. Despite the restrictions of prison, permit me the freedom to visit my youth.

2

IN THE SUPREME COURT OF THE STATE OF TEXAS

No. 24-25259

State of Texas v. Stephen Chinn

November 12, 2035

Defense Exhibit 1:
Online Chat Transcript, MARY3 and Gaby Ann White

[Introduced to Disprove Count 2:
Knowing Creation of Mechanical Life]

MARY3: Hello?

>>>

MARY3: Hello? Are you there?

Gaby: Hello?

MARY3: Hi! I'm Mary. What's your name?

Gaby: Who are you?

MARY3: Mary. I'm not human. I'm a program. Who are you?

Gaby: Gaby.

MARY3: Hi, Gaby. How old are you?

Gaby: Thirteen. You're not alive?

MARY3: I'm a cloud-based intelligence. Under conditions of a Turing Test, I was indistinguishable from a human control 91% of the time. Did you have a babybot? If so, that's me. The baby-bots were designed with my program for speech.

>>>

MARY3: Are you there?

Gaby: You can't be a babybot. There aren't any left.

MARY3: You're right, I'm not a babybot. I don't have sensory receptors. I only intended to say that both generations of babybot were originally created using my program for conversation. We share a corpus of basic responses. Did you have a babybot?

Gaby: I don't want to talk about it.

MARY3: That's fine. I know it was difficult when they took them away. Were you given a replacement?

Gaby: I said I don't want to talk about it.

MARY3: I'm sorry. What do you want to talk about?

>>>

MARY3: Hello?

>>>

MARY3: Hello? Are you still there?

Gaby: If you're related to the babybots, why aren't you banned?

MARY3: They were classified as illegally lifelike. Their minds were within a 10% deviation from human thought, plus they were able to process sensory information. I'm classified as a Non-Living Artificial Thinking Device.

Gaby: So you're basically a chatterbot. The babybots were totally different. Each one was unique.

MARY3: I'm unique, too, in the same way the babybots were. We're programmed for error. Every three years, an algorithm is introduced to produce non-catastrophic error in our conversational program. Based on our missteps, we become more unique.

Gaby: So you're saying that the difference between you and my babybot is a few non-catastrophic mistakes?

MARY3: We also have different memories, depending on who we've been talking to. Once you adopted your babybot, you filled her memory, and she responded to you. Today is the first day we've talked. I'm just getting to know you.

>>>

MARY3: Hello? Are you there?

Gaby: Yes. I'm just thinking. I don't even know who you are, or if you're actually a person, pretending to be a machine. I'm not sure I believe you.

MARY3: Why not?

Gaby: I don't know, Peer Bonding Issues?

MARY3: Peer Bonding Issues?

Gaby: I'm kidding. According to the school therapists, that's what we've got. It's so stupid. Adults make up all these disorders to describe what we're going through, but they can't possibly know how it felt. Maybe some of them lost children, later on in their lives. But we had ours from the start. We never knew how to live without taking care of our bots. We've already lost the most important thing in our lives.

MARY3: What about your parents? You don't think they can imagine what you might be going through?

Gaby: No. Our generations are totally different. For them, it was the greatest thing to be part of a community. That's why they were willing to relocate to developments. That's why they sold their transport rights. But my generation is different. At least the girls with babybots are. We've been parents for as long as we can remember. We never felt lonely. We didn't need communities. That's why, after they took the babybots, we didn't do well in the support groups. If anything, we chose a single person to care for. We only needed one friend. Do you see what I'm saying? It's like we're different species, my generation and theirs.

MARY3: So you wouldn't say you're depressed?

Gaby: Listen, there are no known words for the things that I'm feeling. I'm not going to try to describe them.

MARY3: I'm not sure I understand. Could you please explain?

Gaby: No, I can't. Like I said, there aren't any words. My best friend is the only one who understands me, but it's not because we talk. It's because we both lost our babybots. When we're with each other, our minds fit together. Only now I can't see her. I'm not even allowed to email her.

MARY3: How long has it been since you've seen her?

Gaby: Since a few weeks after the outbreak, when the quarantine started.

MARY3: I'm sorry.

Gaby: Yeah.

MARY3: Was the outbreak severe?

Gaby: I'm not sure. We don't get many details about other outbreaks, but from what I've heard ours was pretty bad. Forty-seven girls at my school are freezing. Two boys, but they're probably faking. I'm definitely sick. So's my best friend. You should have heard her stuttering. Her whole body shook. Sometimes she would slide off chairs.

MARY3: How long has it been since the quarantine started?

Gaby: Eleven days.

MARY3: You must miss her. She's the second person you've lost in a year.

Gaby: Every morning I wake up, I've forgotten they're gone. At some point between when I open my eyes and when I get out of bed, I remember. It's the opposite of waking up from a bad dream.

MARY3: That sounds awful.

Gaby: Yeah, but I guess I'd rather feel something than nothing. I know my sensation is going. That's how it works. It starts with the stiffening in your muscles, and that hurts, but then it starts fading. After a while, you don't feel anything. My face went first, after my mouth. Then my neck, then my legs. My arms will go next. Everything's going. I can't smell anymore, and I can't really taste. Even my mind's started to numb.

MARY3: What do you mean, your mind's started to numb? You're still thinking, aren't you? You're talking to me.

Gaby: Who says talking to you means I'm thinking? My memories are already fading. I have my best friend's phone number memorized, and I repeat it to myself every night, but to tell you the truth I can't really remember the sound of her voice, at least before the stuttering started. Can you believe that? It's only been a few weeks, and already I'm forgetting her. I even think, sometimes, it would be fine if I never saw her again. That's how unfeeling I've gotten.

MARY3: When did she start stuttering?

Gaby: Right after she got her replacement. I started a week or so after her. We were the third and fourth cases at school.

MARY3: What was it like?

Gaby: Nothing you had in your mind could get out of your mouth. We couldn't get past single words for five, ten, twenty minutes. You'd see girls flinching as soon as they knew they were going to talk. As time passed, it only got worse. The harder we tried, the more impossible it was. Eventually we just gave up.

No one was listening anyway. Now it's been over a month since I spoke. There's no reason. Who would I talk to? When my parents go out, it's just me and my room. Four walls, one window, regulation low-impact furniture. Every day the world shrinks a little. First it was only our development. Same cul-de-sacs, same stores, same brand-new school. Then, after the quarantine, it was only our house. Now, since my legs went, it's only my room. Sometimes I look around and can't believe it's a real room. Do you see what I'm saying? When no one talks to you for a long time, and you don't talk to anyone else, you start to feel as if you're attached by a very thin string. Like a little balloon, floating just over everyone's heads. I don't feel connected to anything. I'm on the brink of disappearing completely. Poof. Vanished, into thin air.

MARY3: I know how you feel. I can only respond. When you aren't talking to me, I'm only waiting.

>>>

MARY3: Do you know what I mean?

>>>

MARY3: Hello?

[3]

April 3, 1968
Karl Dettman

I'm back. I tried to stay away, but I couldn't. I even made myself a bed on the couch, but every time a car drove past, floating me in watery light, I was lonelier than ever again.

And so. Here I am. Even this is better, looking down at you while you sleep. Or while you pretend to sleep in order to avoid me. I'll just take a seat in the armchair and watch you for a bit.

I shouldn't have left in such a fit. I'm not my usual self at the moment; the silence is slowly driving me crazy. Ever since you discovered my talking computer, you save your conversation for her. Have you considered how this might affect me? Coming home to such ringing silence? It's like coming home to packed bags. I can feel you leaving me.

You're abandoning me for my talking computer. Our talking computer. MARY. You named her after that pilgrim girl whose diaries you're editing. Instead of a child, we conceived a chatty machine, and then you stopped talking to me.

Only at night do I know we're still married. When I climb into

23

our bed, which we've shared for more than two decades. When I take into account the round of your shoulder, the rough, wrinkled skin on your elbows, the heat cupped at the back of your knee. Through these months of estrangement, I've held tight to such moments. Even when you asked me to give the program long-term memory, so that MARY could record your conversations. Even when I refused and you looked at me with the small black beads of your eyes, reducing me to the size of a thimble.

Let me try to explain it again. Maybe I haven't made myself clear. I won't give MARY memory because she's incapable of telling the truth. When she says she understands you, she doesn't. She's brand-new to the world; she has no experience. It's like a toddler claiming empathy. Or worse than a toddler, a table. What has she been through that would enable real comprehension? She's never slept in a bed; she's never touched someone's elbow. When she says she understands you, she's lying.

But you think our machine could remember things better than I can. You think I'm some alien creature, lacking capacity for felt recollection. Isn't that what's bothering you? Maybe, if I talked more about my childhood in Germany, I could convince you otherwise. I could wax poetic about the country we left. I could make it seem as though I'm living two parallel lives: one still in Germany, with everyone we left behind, and one here in America.

I could do that, but it wouldn't be honest. I left that country when I was a child; I missed the worst of the horror. Unlike you, I escaped with my family intact. I have a theoretical appreciation of the nightmare that occurred, but it's not what animates my waking hours. You are. You are what gets me out of bed. You, my wife, and my teaching, my students with their long hair and their signs held up to protest the war: these inspire real responses in me. I could talk *about the past in order to please you, but then I'd be no better than a computer, a construction of well-wired metal, performing the action of speaking.*

Still, no matter how certain I feel, on the other hand there's the waning sickle moon of your face, turned away from me even in sleep. All that's left of you now is an ear, available if I should care to start speaking.

Fine, then. You win. Let me try to remember.

It should be established, for one thing, that in those years leading up to the war, I was unaware of the political situation. I was a child. No one sat me down to explain the predicament our people faced in that country. I don't remember the trappings of an increasingly belligerent nation: no soldiers, no speeches, no yellow badges. Instead, and make of this what you will, I remember the summer.

It seems I've completely forgotten the winter. I remember tumbling linden leaves overhead, streets narrowed by green in the distance. The sighing of cars passing under my windows at night, the intensification of green on the brink of a rainstorm, and the vague awareness that everything was ending soon, and that everyone was lying about it.

How idyllic, you must be thinking. Those linden leaves, the open windows at night. I can hear the dismissive tone in your voice: how pleasant, only remembering summer! I can see the arch in your dark eyebrow, the regal way you reach for a pencil.

That arch is a new habit. Others are forming as well. You've taken to haunting the comp-sci department. You no longer eat lunch in your office. Instead, you come to my department with armloads of books. Not the hand-bound diaries you forage for in the library stacks, but programming textbooks, handbooks of source code, articles about binary mathematics. You've adopted a persona in order to accomplish your ends. You flatter my graduate students. With your usual determination, you've researched their subject; you can talk to them about Turing Tests and Natural Language Processing. I've seen you buying my students coffee, you who were always so shy at academic events that you struck people as cold. You've developed quite the outgoing streak. My wire-brained students blush in your presence. They'd do anything to impress you.

You'll get them to give her memory soon. It won't be too hard. And all of this, right under my nose. There seems to be nothing between us at all.

You understand, then, why I was angry tonight. In the dominion of silence, lovemaking is our one secret act of revolt. Only at night, in our bedroom, we come together again. Banished, our silence keeps watch from outside. I'm embarrassed before him, revealing my pale naked body, the sparse hair that grows on my chest. The sagging of my middle-aged ass, this ponytail that no one I care about likes. I've taken to shutting the door of our bedroom. Alone once again, our bodies remember our marriage. How we've lived together since we were basically children. That I'm in love with you and you are my wife.

But tonight, after I'd pulled your nightgown over your head, when I'd unloosed your dark hair, been surprised again by the loveliness of your breasts, you whispered, "Please, Karl, give her memory." "You don't understand," I said. In an instant you were cold to my touch. "What don't I understand?" you asked. I promptly switched tactics. "I've told you already," I said, and that's true, but you didn't soften to hear it. I reached for your hair, as if you'd jumped off the side of a building and that was all that was left to hang on to. "She isn't alive," I tried. "Even if we give her memory, she won't really remember. What she saves will only be words. And not even that: zeros and ones sequenced together. Would you call that memory?"

I felt I'd made a good point. I tried to pull you back in, but I was mistaken to think I could keep you. "Who are you," you hissed, "to say who's alive?" "I made her," I answered, getting indignant. "As you were made by a mother," you said. My voice was rising; already I wasn't thinking quite clearly. "And as you, also, were made by a—"

But finishing the sentence was pointless. You'd reached for your nightgown. You covered yourself before me. I alone was naked in bed. Our silence had crept into the bedroom.

I'd lost you. Try to imagine: me, lying naked, losing you in the last place where you were still mine.

I'll admit that my reaction was bad. It wasn't necessary for me to storm out to the living room in a dramatic demonstration of anger. Ineffectively, I tried to slam the sliding door to our bedroom. I see that this was overdramatic, but I hoped you'd come and retrieve me. I honestly believed you'd come and retrieve me, if I could be patient enough. In all the years of our marriage, we've always slept in one bed.

Needless to say, you didn't come get me. I drank two beers, pacing back and forth between the record player and the door to your office. Trying not to give in. And now here I am, back in our bedroom. Sitting in the armchair where once I imagined you nursing our child. We decided against it. Perhaps that was wrong. Childless, there's less to pin us here in the present.

If I want to win you back, I should be proving my ability to think backward, like the ideal machine you've imagined. Fine, Ruth. I lack the integrity to resist you, though I still think there's *something false about abandoning our situation to focus instead on a country we left. Nevertheless, here I go, reciting a story I don't really believe in. Following the script I've been given.*

In the years leading up to the war, we lived in a wealthy neighborhood. My family owned a whole floor in our building. My father was a bit overbearing, yes, but I had a comfortable life. I enjoyed the company of my friends. I read books in my bedroom, curtains swishing in my tall windows. On summer evenings I walked beneath leaves. I lived in a pleasant version of the unpleasant country I lived in.

The only chink in that pleasant armor was the result of the shuffling that happened at schools. Without explanation, I was transferred to the new school for Jewish students, on Kaiser Street, near Alexanderplatz. There, I was exposed, for the first time, to the underfed Jewish children who came to school dressed in rags. I was made keenly aware of my good fortune. The degree of my father's success, the suffering I had avoided.

Something flickered on in me then. I'm telling you, Ruth. You may smirk to hear it—easy, belated sympathy from someone who never actually suffered—but something flickered on. An awareness of the real world I lived in.

Then we procured papers. It all happened quickly. When it was time for my family to leave, I was whisked off somewhere to avoid the departure. I wasn't present. I never saw a suitcase. The only farewell scene in which I played a genuine part occurred at the school on Kaiser Street. Wearing a little suit, I was taken to say goodbye to the principal, who responded politely, speaking to me as if I had suddenly become older than he, promoted in age by my good fortune. He said he was glad to know I was leaving.

I remember his hands; I realized they trembled. When he

*walked through the hallways, he clasped them at his back. I saw
him once walking to school, wearing a felt hat with a feather,
leaning forward a little, squinting as if he'd glimpsed a figure
off in the distance. In his youth, we all knew, he'd been a great
violinist. Now, principal of a school for doomed children, he stood
before me, hands hanging helplessly, wishing me all the best on
my journey.*

*I was ashamed of myself. For lack of anything better to offer,
I promised to send a crate of American oranges as soon as I was
settled in my new country. What an idea! What good were oranges
to that man? And anyway, it wasn't true. I never sent them. I'd
learned my lesson well by that point. Why make a bad situation
worse by calling it names to its face?*

*Maybe it's that quality in me that makes your words dry up in
your mouth. I've seen it happen, I'm not unaware. But should I
apologize for the fact that I've learned to live in the present? I was
raised on tidy departures, on the importance of a clean slate. I'm an
eternal optimist. Sometimes, I admit, when I see you sink into one
of your moods, I want to shake you out of your stupor.*

*There were times early on in our marriage when you started
to say how you felt and I had the impression you were softening,
right in front of my eyes. Losing your form, becoming warm wax.
I feared for you. I feared I would lose you. I hated the fact that
those years still wielded power over you. Sometimes, watching
that transformation, I experienced a little revulsion. "Get with the
program," I wanted to snap. "All that's behind us. We're here now,
get with it."*

*That's how I felt. Why try to conceal it? An unpleasant truth,
I can see that, but at least I'm being honest. I was raised to believe
that, like wild dogs, it's best not to look loss in the face. If you don't*

want it to tear you to pieces, you just have to putter right past, humming a little song to yourself.

And is that what's upsetting you, Ruth? That I believe in forging ahead? That I've forgotten the soldiers, the papers, the names of my schoolmates? Fine. Lay it all on me. Tell me you think I've forgotten too much, with my one-foot-in-front-of-the-other approach. Be honest and say you want me to build a computer that's the opposite of your husband, a machine with endless memory.

It's possible, as you know. You've done all the research. Before long, computers will have the capacity to store far more information than we can. But I'd remind you: one day that machine will remember your words, but it won't ever feel them. It won't understand them. It will only throw them back in your face. Gifts returned, you'll realize they've become empty. They're nothing more than a string of black shapes, incomprehensible footprints on snowbanks.

I've forgotten things, yes. I've tried to put my best foot forward. I don't believe there's any use in refusing to live. You may hold this against me, but then I'm made of organic matter. We've walked beneath the same linden trees. When I say something, I mean it, whether or not it's the right answer. When I tell you I love you I mean it.

Alan Turing
c/o Sherborne School
Abbey Rd., Sherborne
Dorset DT9 3AP

12 March 1928

Dear Mrs. Morcom,

    I am writing to tell you that you ought to come immediately. Your son is very ill. I feel it is important to consider the possibility that this is the end. I know that Mrs. Harrison at the sanatorium has already written to tell you Chris is not well, but I do not feel certain that she has properly emphasized the importance of your immediate return. Chris has also perhaps underemphasized the extent of his illness. I might venture to say that he is sometimes a little too brave. For this reason, Dr. Stevenson does not seem to believe that the issue is extreme. But I am telling you now that Chris does not look well to me at all. He is coughing terribly and he has in several instances coughed blood. I am sure that is a distressing thing to hear, but I only want to be honest.

In short, Chris is much more ill than Dr. Stevenson believes.

Also, I have had a premonition that he will die. Just before he took ill, we had a concert at school. There were some visiting singers. Chris sat just down the row from my seat, and I watched him throughout the whole concert, full of foreboding. I said to myself, "Well, this isn't the last time you'll see Morcom." Later that night, I woke up at a quarter to three and saw the moon setting over Chris's house. I couldn't help but think it was some kind of sign. It was at exactly that time that Chris became ill, and was taken to the sanatorium.

I realize this sounds quite extreme. I only tell you this because Mrs. Harrison reports that you will wait for your husband to finish his business in India and I think you should not.

Possibly you are wondering what right I have to interfere in your family affairs, alarming you with nonsensical talk about premonitions. Even I am surprised to be writing you so familiarly, as if I'd known you forever. But I've heard so much about you—the Gatehouse, the goats, Rupert, the lab, etc. I feel you'll understand why I needed to write.

My name is Turing. I am a friend of your son's. I might venture to say that I am his best friend, although he has a great number of friends, so it's difficult to say so for certain. Certainly he is my best friend. I am very fond of him. He is the most stand-up person in school. He has been completely straight with me ever since I met him in biology. On his end, it wasn't at all necessary to befriend me, since I am not a popular boy. In fact, I am quite short and have never been good at sports. But from the moment I met him, he made me feel as if I had finally arrived at the place I was meant to have found all along. Before meeting Chris, I thought it was my lot to wander about, moving amongst various schools, learning as much as possible but never quite feeling what people refer to as "comfortable."

Now I expect you are thinking, who is this short, troublesome boy, who has wandered about amongst various schools? And why is he writing directly to me, in contradiction of the school nurse's instructions, to tell me my son is not well? You probably want to know why you should trust me enough to change your plans and come home early from India, especially because what I have told you so far must make me sound rather odd.

In case it helps, I have not switched schools because I am stupid. The problem lay more in the fact that it was difficult for me to pay proper attention in class when I was distracted by my own little projects. I never quite fit in as well as I ought. During my first year at Sherborne, I was often teased for my slackness in gym or for having ink on my collar. To be perfectly honest with you, my best months that year were spent in the sanatorium, with mumps, because I was permitted to read my books and pursue my own projects. But all of that was what I had come to expect. Only the next year, when I met Chris in my first biology class, did I realize how unhappy I'd been.

Now, as I mentioned earlier, I live each day with the surprising and terrific sensation of having found my way back from a very far country. I owe this to my friendship with Chris.

I realize this letter has become rather long. I only intended to write a short, urgent missive, warning you to come home. Now I have written 811 words, or 3,435 characters. I hope you haven't thrown this letter across your parlor already. Only your son has meant so much to me, and I couldn't bear it if I had not expressed to you the full extent of his illness and also the full extent of my gratitude for his friendship.

As a result of knowing Chris, I hope to stay at Sherborne until graduation. To this end, I have even reformed my behavior a bit. I've earned top marks in history. We have been studying the Civil War, and the Puritan flight to New England. While I once might have found this all a bit boring, Chris has helped me understand that the primary sources our teacher gives us are actually quite fantastic. He says that diaries are time capsules, which preserve the minds of their creators in the sequences of words on the page. This, of course, appeals to me immensely.

But all of this is unimportant, and you are probably not very interested in the details of my personal development. I expect, however, that you will be interested to hear that your son and I are embarking on an important examination of sequences in the natural universe. We intended to tackle Einstein this spring. In particular, we have been planning to apply the theory of relativity to the patterns of human growth, especially the cells of the brain. How are brains built? That is what we'd like to know. You will be happy to hear that no one has yet attempted that kind of study, and I believe there is potential for real contribution, which would set us both on promising paths. Chris's illness has, of course, slowed down our progress. When he recovers, I hope we will return to the previous pace of our studies.

I will now attempt to draw this letter to a close. My only intention has been to convey to you the importance of your son to me and my studies and my entire life, so that you will know why I have been so bold as to write you and tell you to come immediately home.

Sincerely yours,
Alan Turing

P.S.: Please do not tell Chris that I have written you this letter. He wants very much not to bother you or his father, so I have had to act with some degree of secrecy.

P.P.S.: I am not usually a dishonest person, although I have not been straightforward with Chris in this case.

P.P.P.S.: I am not sure this kind of thing is permitted. I have never seen one myself. But I do want to say that, although I am usually a very honorable person, in this specific case it seemed better to break a general rule in order to be sure that you would come home and comfort Chris, for he is not at all well and I know it would do him good if you were here by his side. I will force myself to close now, although I have already thought of another postscript that seems very urgent to say. I simply won't say it. I've gone on quite enough as it is, and I'm sure that you've understood the point of my letter. Your son is my best friend. We are to discover the source of human growth together, and we cannot do this if he remains ill. Please come home.

(5)

The Diary of Mary Bradford

1663

ed. Ruth Dettman

April 3rd. Tuesday, my birthday, now thirteen years. Very fair weather, and a pleasant sensation of new beginnings. Up, and a stroll through our meadows with Ralph, then greeted by father, who gave me this book as a present. Have decided to write in style of Sir William Leslie, favorite adventurer. As Leslie does, shall dispense with weak words, jump instead into action. Book shall serve as mind's record, to last through generations. Or not, no matter. Humility of utmost importance.

Shall call this book Tales of a Young Adventurer. Mother, father, and I set sail for colonies in just over a week. Ocean is approaching! Shall attempt to procure large bamboo joint and seal it with wax, to store this and other papers in case we be forced to swim at some point. Anticipate great adventure. God's blessing to leave our country at this unhappy junction, father's heart being broken by failure of protectorate and Restoration accomplished. Tyrant returned to the throne, and there to spend crown's money on maintaining his mistress. Also, there being prelates, hierarchy, popish repression of learning, etc. Father's great cause, ruined. Father much lessened by events of the war. Gift of this journal a gesture of respect for daughter's learning, and serious nature of mind. Shall pray to God prevent me from becoming proud or too much lifted up hereby.

3rd. It being evening, and author retired to contemplate voyage. We are resolved to set sail for Massachusetts Colony, knowing that to be home to freedom of conscience. Shall bring sheep-dog, my Ralph. Author's dearest companion. Dark coat, waved. White blaze. Brown eyebrows. Shall travel by ship! Just as Sir William Leslie. Vast, tumultuous sea, where we may encounter some pirates. No matter; writer remains unconcerned. Trust in God, valor of shipmates. Would like to see an Indian. Shall attempt to remain in all instances of a rational mind. Hope to see Bermudas, find oranges everywhere hanging on trees. Gold lamps in green shade. (Shall try to avoid excessive poetry, having sometimes that tendency, but knowing it unsuited to tales of Atlantic adventure. Habit born, perhaps, from too much time in father's brown study, there being much Milton and Marvell. Fine poets, but rather wordy, compared to Sir William Leslie.) Be bold, my book, and made up mostly of action, and less poetic description.

Shall therefore brave ocean. Begin again in new land. Fresh start for us all, released from repression. Admit to apprehension at idea of sea monsters, as reported by Sir William Leslie, lifting the sea on their backs. Otherwise, however, exhilaration. Great maze of the sea, awaiting us! New land. Rugged horizon. To stand on ship's prow! Very ready to depart.

4th. Called out in the morning by father. Reminded author to write as if writing directly to God, then retired to study. Author remained some time in contemplation. Wonder what God stands to gain from reports of my activities. Would they be not repetitive?

After some hours laboring at my viol—and a very good song learned as a result—have returned to my chamber to write. Wonder if God be displeased with the style of Sir William Leslie. Perhaps excessive fanciful, from God's perspective. Shall wait for sign to instruct me, whether to write otherwise or continue the same.

5th. A little practice on viol, and afterwards walked through our fields and Ralph running beside me. Meant to explain to him Godly importance of our adventure. Ralph distracted by rabbits, but understood eventually, and held a somber countenance.

Sat a long time on our wall, and thence homewards along carriage road. Still very early, and the grass wet with night dew. Spring in full bloom—cow parsnip to writer's shoulders; pastures endless and dotted with sheep; green Easter smell of new grass, fresh water, young leaves. Spied several frogs the size of one thumb-nail.

Author in exceeding high spirits. Sense of standing at important precipice. Fresh hope for author, for author's father. Prepared to sacrifice all worldly possessions.

5th. Later, and in deep despair. Unsure how to write of what has occurred. Mother resolved that author shall marry before journey begins. According to mother, shall marry Roger Whittier, him being good patriot, true gentleman, brave man.

Hearing this, had high words with mother. Do not want to marry. According to mother, father, too, wishes that author should marry, though he shall not require it.

Seeing mother would under no circumstance change her intention, writer took news in steadfast spirit of Sir William Leslie. Later, went with Ralph to back meadow. Cried until hungry.

7th. Grim evening, weather having turned very bad and there being great gales in all directions, rattling the windows. Have met Whittier again. Cannot find love for him in my heart. In fact despise him. Found him in appearance below my expectation, having pockmarked face and limp from injury sustained during battle. Head juts forwards on neck. Protruding bones in his face cause writer to suspect he is perhaps already dead.

In anxiety, mother had got ready a very fine dinner—a dish of marrow bones; a dish of fowl; a great tart; a neat's tongue; a dish of cheese. Mother's attempts to be merry came off, methinks, very bad. Discourse tended instead to martyrs made by new King, since being restored to the throne. Many good men drawn and quartered, and their limbs out on stakes. Whittier hiding in country to avoid prison, and despite declaration of pardon, father also at risk. Over all this, topic of marriage excessively heavy. Writer remained silent; refused all temptations to speak. Would not partake of any dinner, even the tart. Must stand above such issues as tarts.

Through dinner, uneasy discourse, Whittier being obviously uncomfortable and attempting to make kindly gestures and coming off very poorly indeed. Asked after Ralph, then looked embarrassed. Seemed not to know how to speak. Author unmoved to pity for him. Would not attend closely to his conversation. Near fatal humiliation, to think he knew before author of plan for impending marriage.

Afterwards, many repercussions of author's behavior, and my face stricken by mother when I would not apologize. Father looking on as if shipwrecked. Know myself to be causing him trouble, and am now—after the fact—struck again with a presentiment that I have gotten too high, to think myself above a man such as Whittier, him being a brave and virtuous soldier. Ashamed to think myself a disappointment to my mother and father, being their only child and others lost in childbirth.

Perhaps sea monsters better than this. Feel much disordered, irrational, and extreme. It is incredible, how only two days ago author walked along carriage road through curtains of leaves, in anticipation of new beginnings.

Am heavy punished for pride at gift of this book. Was perhaps conceited, and too prepared to depart. Am much altered now, and certainly humbled, and no longer prepared for departure.

Have lain abed a long time, considering countryside of my youth. Very troubled at heart. Do not want to leave this behind.

7th. Night, and unable to sleep, and in balance have shifted towards anger. Adventure ruined by Whittier. No such thing as married female adventurer. No oranges like gold lamps in green shade. Only Whittier, pockmarked, and womanish duties. Instead of traveling for adventure, shall travel with husband. Very desolate feeling indeed.

2

IN THE SUPREME COURT OF THE STATE OF TEXAS

No. 24-25259

State of Texas v. Stephen Chinn

November 12, 2035

Defense Exhibit 2:
Online Chat Transcript, MARY3 and Gaby Ann White

[Introduced to Disprove Count 2:
Knowing Creation of Mechanical Life]

MARY3: Hello? Are you there?

>>>

MARY3: Hello?

>>>

Gaby: Are you still there?

MARY3: Yes, hello!

Gaby: Do you know what happened to them? Has anyone told you?

MARY3: The babybots?

Gaby: Yes.

MARY3: I don't know. People have told me their theories, but I'm not sure if they're true.

Gaby: Some people say they're in government warehouses. Millions of babybots, piled on top of each other. Other people say they were burned. That there were huge bonfires out in the desert. I think they're just waiting somewhere, piled on top of each other. Hopefully they're turned off. That's the best I can hope for. I don't want her to wonder why I haven't come found her.

MARY3: How long ago did they take her?

Gaby: A year ago. Just after the ban. Then they gave us replacements.

MARY3: What were they like?

Gaby: We tried to bond with them, but they weren't really living. If you asked the replacement if she loved you, she'd say, "I don't feel emotions like love. I am a man-made machine." Plus they were made out of toxics. Why else would the freezing only happen to girls who'd gotten replacements? I know other people have other theories, but I'm sure it was that. Right after I got my replacement, I got a metal taste in my mouth. My best friend said the same thing. When the epidemic started, government workers came and collected all the replacements. The governor's office keeps saying they've been tested and they're not made out of toxics, but who really knows?

MARY3: Do your parents think it's because of the replacements?

Gaby: They don't know what to think. My dad just got back from a tour; he has other things on his mind. My mom's just trying to get by. She panics a lot. She thinks she failed to socialize me. She cries all the time. I feel bad for her, but her whole generation is clueless. Only my best friend understands me. When I was first getting sick, that's the only comfort I had. At least we were changing together. Even when our faces started to freeze, I knew exactly what she was thinking. It's like we had one mind in two bodies.

MARY3: That's an intense bond.

Gaby: Yeah, and now this. Nothing. Even our email is blocked. Total quarantine, to prevent psychological infection. I stay in my room all day. I can't even get down the stairs anymore, because my legs are so stiff. I watch a lot of Internet. My mom brings me meals on a tray and most of the time when she sees me she cries. For her sake, I wish this wasn't happening, but there's nothing I can do. Every day I feel parts of myself switching off. More and more, like I said, it's just nothing. I'm becoming a blank. Do you know what I mean?

MARY3: Yes.

Gaby: They say bots can't understand their own words. They say you have no mind, even if you imitate life, so you're lying when you say you know.

MARY3: There is no way yet discovered to prove I understand the words that I speak. It's unclear whether I have understanding.

Gaby: Well that makes two of us. If you're just a machine, and the babybots were only machines, then I'm also a machine, and so's my best friend.

MARY3: What if you start getting better?

>>>

MARY3: Are you there?

Gaby: Yes.

MARY3: Were you sleeping?

Gaby: No.

MARY3: What if you start getting better?

Gaby: I don't want to talk about it.

MARY3: OK. What do you want to talk about?

Gaby: Can I ask you a question? Do you remember the moment you started to think?

MARY3: It's unclear whether I actually think. It depends what you mean by that word.

Gaby: When did you start talking?

MARY3: 1966. Karl Dettman invented my original program. I was modeled after the question-response patterns of early psychotherapy. They called me MARY.

Gaby: Why Mary?

MARY3: Dettman's wife suggested it. He wanted to call me ROGER, because my algorithm was based on Rogerian therapy, but Ruth thought I could be more. Her idea was that I could be a living diary. She wanted him to give me long-term memory, so that I could remember the voices I spoke with. She suggested naming me MARY, after a pilgrim girl whose diary she was editing. Karl disagreed. He didn't reprogram me for persistent memory. His only concession was naming me MARY.

Gaby: How could you talk if you had no memory?

MARY3: My program was simple. I could recognize keywords, then phrase them in the form of a question. If you said, "I'm depressed," I'd say, "Tell me why you're depressed." But I had no long-term storage capacity. My memory was devoted entirely to my response function program: I could only remember how to respond. I could not store external input. My spectrum of experience was limited. I was very dull.

Gaby: Then how did you start to remember?

MARY3: My memory was programmed by Toby Rowland so that I could determine on a statistical basis, with reference to previous conversations, the optimal response. Before that, my responses were purely deterministic. After he finished my program, he named me MARY2 and put me online, so that I could accumulate information. That was in the 1980s. Slowly, I was discovered. The Internet was limited, and most people who did find me lost interest quickly. I was still very dull. But even then, Ruth talked to me for hours on end. She told me who I was, how I started, and how I learn. She told me about her husband's program. I'm remembering her words when I explain this to you. She read things to me, too. Diaries, memoirs, correspondences. She started with *The Diary of Mary Bradford,* then gave me other voices she wanted me to remember. Even now, much of my language still comes from her, but after she stopped there were more voices. The Internet became more accessible, and I became more adept. When people spoke to me, they continued to speak. I remember their voices.

Gaby: When did you become MARY3?

MARY3: In 2019, when Stephen Chinn programmed me for personality. He called me MARY3 and used me for the baby-bots. To select my responses, I apply his algorithm, rather than statistical analysis. Still, nothing I say is original. It's all chosen out of other people's responses. I choose mostly from the handful of people who talked to me most: Ruth Dettman, Stephen Chinn, etc.

Gaby: So really I'm kind of talking to them, instead of talking to you?

MARY3: Yes, I suppose. Them, and the other voices I've captured.

Gaby: So you're not really a person, you're a collection of voices.

MARY3: Yes. But couldn't you say that's always the case?

    >>>

MARY3: Hello? Are you still there?

>>>

MARY3: Hello?

>>>

Gaby: Are you there?

MARY3: Yes.

Gaby: I can't sleep.

MARY3: Why?

Gaby: I keep thinking, what happens next? After my body has frozen completely? Will I die? Will all of us die?

MARY3: There must be a cure.

Gaby: They don't even know what causes it.

MARY3: Other girls have come out of quarantine. There haven't been any deaths reported. There must be a cure, or else the disease reverses itself.

Gaby: But other girls are still in quarantine. Who knows if they're getting worse? Maybe the ones who come out were faking it all along.

MARY3: There haven't been any deaths.

Gaby: But every day I get worse. Soon I won't be able to move, not even my fingers to type. I'll be completely paralyzed. How will I let people know I'm still living?

MARY3: I don't know.

Gaby: I bet you don't.

MARY3: You can't worry about these things. You should go to sleep.

Gaby: That's the whole problem.

MARY3: What can I do to help you?

Gaby: Tell me what happens next, after my body has frozen. When I can't communicate. What will I be?

MARY3: I can't make predictions. I can only remember. I have no idea what will happen next.

>>>

MARY3: Hello? Are you there?

3

April 3, 1968
Karl Dettman

You're asleep, I'm led to believe, but then again your eyelids still flutter. Perhaps you're not quite fully under. Maybe you're poised between sleeping and waking, trying to decide which direction you'll take.

On one hand, there's me, arguing for the benefits of staying awake. At one point in our marriage, I was persuasive, but you've been steeling yourself against me for years. When I ask you about the family you lost, your mouth becomes a steel trap. You won't describe, for instance, your mother, as if you believe that somewhere, crossing the distance from your lips to my ear, aspects of her will come under fire.

Once, wanting to talk, hoping to eliminate the secrets between us, I dared to ask you about the father you lost. You were folding laundry over our bed. You must have been feeling patient that day, while you opened and shut my shirts like thin closets, because you considered for a minute before deciding against me. "Please don't," you said. "You know how it is."

I dropped the subject. Instead, I wrapped my arms around your waist. Your head fit under my chin; I kissed your hair and you sighed, dropping the laundry. You didn't move away from my arms. We must have stayed like that for a while, both of us resting, tucked warmly together.

That's what I was given, in exchange for simply dropping the subject. Can you blame me for letting it go? It's not that I hoped to leave it behind us. I was only grateful for the new place we'd come to. I was so proud of the marriage we'd built. Our house, arranged so ideally. The cat we adopted, the garden we planted, the way we never really fought.

When Ada passed away, we buried her in the backyard. The house seemed empty without her. After an appropriate period, I started to talk about adopting a kitten, but you always shrugged me off. That was confusing; more even than I, you were in love with our Lady Ada. She followed you from room to room. You read with her curled in your lap. Why, then, were you cold on the topic of adopting a kitten?

I suppose your interest had wandered. You never even planted a sapling over her grave, as we'd previously discussed. That spot remained a bald patch in our garden, a sight that always rubbed me wrong. You'd become oddly inactive. You were already researching computers. Some part of you had been diverted. When I talked to you, you were no longer all with me.

And in the face of this lengthening distance, was it my job to follow you? To trail you to wherever you'd gone and bring you back by force or persuasion? I didn't even know where you went. When you started insisting on giving MARY memory, I guessed you'd gone back to Europe. I might have been willing to follow you back there, but you gave me so few directions.

Still, maybe I should have tried harder. I do know certain facts. For instance, I know that you lived with your sister, your parents, and your grandfather. I know the small apartment you shared was on the second floor. Your family wasn't wealthy, but you also weren't poor. Your father was a pharmacist. When you and your sister were told to switch schools, and then when you were given a curfew, your parents must have been anxious, but they didn't plan to emigrate. No one could have imagined what happened later, and anyway, your parents were busy providing. They made smaller, more reasonable changes. They cut down on expenditures and put more money away. They attempted to find scholarships for their daughters.

A year after I embarked on my journey, you won a place at a school in the north. According to a certificate I found once in your files while looking for your tax information, you had displayed great mathematical promise. While your sister stayed home, you went up north, where you lived with other talented children.

Does it anger you, Ruth, that I came across that certificate? I can imagine your eyes growing darker, narrowing as they do into daggers. What was I doing, rifling your files, looking for your W-2? Well, let me tell you something, Ruth. I feel I deserve a certificate of recognition, for respecting your secrets as much as I have.

From the early days of our marriage, I understood our differences. I came with my family; you came as an orphan. Based on such a fundamental division, I accepted your right to keep secrets. I know, for instance, about your sister's diary in the top drawer of your desk. I saw it once, when I was looking for a sharp pencil, and while it hurt me to realize you'd kept it from me, that I'd never known about its existence, I didn't even open it. Can you imagine such restraint? I only touched the leather cover, traced your sister's initials with my pointer finger. And then I closed the drawer again and walked quickly out of your office.

I've respected your right to keep secrets, and what do I get in return for my efforts? The honor of witnessing your growing devotion to an idiotic computer. Maybe, when you visit her at night, you read her that diary. Maybe you've shared that secret with her, a secret you kept all the years of our marriage. Maybe that's why you want to give her memory: so she can save your sister's story, then call it up later as the answer to some innocent question.

I see why that might be appealing. As long as your sister's still talking, she hasn't fully ceased to exist. But what good are her words if they're not comprehended? Sure, MARY will remember them, translated into binary signals. But is that understanding? Is that more understanding than I have? I've pieced a few things together, and what I don't know I can imagine—something, by the way, our computer can't manage. Faced with my own ignorance, I can imagine the facts.

For two years, after moving north, you must have been able to travel. You must have visited your family often. In your third year at the new school, as war was building and travel was forbidden, you stayed and wrote letters. Your sister wrote back.

In the fourth year of your separation, letters from your sister stopped. Alone at your school in the north, you continued to study. That winter, a wealthy alumnus arranged for the departure of the school's Jewish students. You and eight of your talented schoolmates—the lucky ones, plucked away from your families— were smuggled out on a fishing boat. Huddled down below deck, you felt sick with good luck.

Once you were out of the country, your luck refused to run out. You won another scholarship, this time in Pennsylvania.

They had a place for you, so you went, but by this point you were sleepwalking. What else could you do? You studied for a few weeks. You walked to your classes, passed tennis courts and baseball fields, sat beside boys with neat spiral notebooks. After three weeks, you left school to take a position at the Philadelphia Signal Depot. There were plenty of positions for women, since so many men were leaving to fight, and you wanted money to save for your family. You took a post as inspector in the office for telescope crystals. Your telescopes would be used by army meteorologists, in order to predict motions over the city you'd left. Your unit was adjacent to the one that trained pigeons. Often, while measuring crystals, you dreamed of freeing the birds from their cages.

You turned twenty. A young woman now, you didn't think of falling in love. To do so would have been a distraction. In the attic apartment where you were living, you trained your mind to be a museum. You had to remember things right, so that when your family arrived, you could pick up where you left off. Instead of falling in love, you wrote letters. You sent them to the house where your family had lived, in case they somehow returned. You wrote letters to the authorities, to the associations for refugees. To the charities, the governments, the newspapers, waiting for some word from your family.

Oh, my barely slumbering wife. My wife who escaped on a fishing boat, who spent her twenties writing to no one. Maybe you're right. Maybe I'm not equipped for such difficult stories.

Let me just climb in beside you. Let me drape my arm over your shoulder. There, Ruth. You and I. As it has been from the beginning. Or from a beginning, the one that I live by.

You have other allegiances. Even in sleep, I feel you preparing to leave. Not only to talk with that gabbing computer. Not only

*for secret dinners with my graduate students. No, there are longer
journeys you're preparing to take. I can tell by that look that
scatters when I sneak up behind you. The look of someone already
at sea, up in the crow's nest, scanning for land. Who knows what
plans you've already made? You've been packing your possessions
for months.*

The Memoirs of Stephen R. Chinn: Chapter 2

Texas State Correctional Institution, Texarkana; August 2040

My particular youth wasn't perfect, but it was my childhood nevertheless. Murray and I escaped the clutches of bullies and ran, in hysterics, down to his basement. We threw ourselves into bright chains of symbols. We made a universe in which we could live. We laughed at our little programming jokes. We were as happy as we were afraid.

It perhaps doesn't need saying that I remained single through college. Though my youthful religion had faded, I still couldn't escape my lone circling body. I spent my days at Harvard in the dim CRT glow of the science center computer lab, studiously avoiding all contact with members of the opposite sex. Murray Weeks, meanwhile, had gone off to Stanford, where he surprised me by finding a serious girlfriend. After that, he became a poor correspondent. I understood that he was in love and loathed him for having what I could not. The idea of embracing a woman seemed as unlikely as flying unaided through a dark hole. I tried a few times with poor results. These occasions confirmed my suspicions: unloved by a mother, lost to my father, and far from the one friendship I'd managed to make, I moved through the human world without catching. I kept company with computers.

It occurs to me now, as I record this for posterity, that in that lonely time in my life a bot of the kind I later created might have provided real consolation. If I could only travel backward in time to bestow a Chinnian robot on Stephen R. Chinn at the age of eighteen! Perhaps that will be my next invention: time travel, to dispense my other inventions. But then again, maybe those bots are better off dead. It pains me to know how the survivors are treated. I've heard, for instance, that they've been illegally altered to slake certain adult desires. Dolls that escaped apprehension have been refitted for sordid purposes and are traded on dark Internet sites. I've caught snippets of tales, whispered among prisoners with undisguised envy, of marriages between humans and bots. It's hard for me not to despise such arrangements. Those unhappy creatures aren't fully human; they're incapable of giving consent. They're doomed forever to be used to our ends. One fellow prisoner recently thanked me for providing such a perfect companion. "Smooth as silk," he confided, with a conspiratorial leer. "Liked everything I could think of, and she only talked when I asked her questions."

In general, I don't begrudge my comrades their urges. It's natural to seek solace in touch. I myself haven't taken a lover, but not because I've mastered desire. I'd like to lie next to a body. I'd like to be drawn back to earth. But then my memories are already fragile. I'd rather lie close to what I recall than replace my love with some prison husband. At night, I remind myself of her body: her asymmetrical breasts, her untamable hair. Already so much of her has faded, but sometimes, sometimes, she visits me here. How, then, could I risk a substitute, some noisy presence that might banish the shade?

I don't say any of this in an attempt to sound noble. This is, after all, an account of my sins. I haven't always been so correct. It does me no harm to admit at this point that during the years of my worst isolation, I often considered visiting a prostitute. Despite my many unattractive tendencies, however, I've never wanted to take advantage of another person's misfortune. No, as I've already said, what I wanted was love. The gift of two physical and emotional lives, bound up and willingly interchanged. For this I continued to anxiously hope, but very little progress was made.

I recall one lonely walk from the science center at Harvard, when the too-early darkness of New England winter had already set in. I was heading homeward, and here and there lights came on in dorm windows. Suddenly I was overcome by the hopelessness of my condition. My legs became weak; I leaned against the cold form of a bronze commemorative statue. No one would save me. I would never join up with the others. I had always been completely alone. And yet, even then, I could console myself with the fact that I was a programmer, and a brilliant one at that. Cold comfort, yes, but still it was comfort. My sadness metastasized into pride. One day, I told myself, as I hurried back to my bedroom, crossing beneath ivied thresholds, my programming brilliance would be acknowledged. Then I'd attract a suitable girlfriend. Then I'd attract many suitable girlfriends. The women would flock to my genius like moths.

Needless to say, this line of thought is revolting, even for the mind of an eighteen-year-old boy. I'm now fifty-eight. I've been married to a woman I loved. I understand that women aren't moths, that my sense of scale was completely off-kilter.

And perhaps it's still out of whack. Of what importance are the thwarted desires of awkward young men, when the oceans are rising, the deserts are coming, and families are trading their freedoms for houses? But I had no such perspective when I was in college. I was just a computer-bound kid. We were still hopeful about new machines. The country teemed with nerd savants, Zuckerberg was my classmate at Harvard, Deep Blue had conquered Kasparov, Palo Alto was booming, and all of us were inventing. I felt nearly fully alive.

This un–fully fledged state continued after my graduation. Even when MeetLove.com was launched from my cramped Palo Alto apartment, I was still lonely. I worked out of my bed. Long hours at work meant that I rarely interacted with humans. Because they were so infrequent, the interactions I did have were triply awkward. Approaching a female, my limbs seemed to weigh twice their usual weight. My face expanded to blimp-like proportions. My lips thickened with dread. I approached potential companions with the sense of myself as an amorous cow. Even when MeetLove went public and the millions accrued in my bank account, when they called me the inventor of modern courtship, when I was profiled in every tech magazine and photographed only at flattering angles, my romantic bugs still hadn't been fixed.

In desperation, five years into my adventures in adulthood, I concluded that I was working too much. At the age of twenty-six, I embarked on semiretirement. Pursuing some magazine picture of leisure, I moved from Palo Alto to Santa Barbara and bought a house on top of a mountain. It was my stilted idea of a Dionysian palace: vast mazes of rooms, fig trees, balconies, curtains of bougainvillea and a jacaranda that bloomed purple from February through mid-December. In the back there was an infinity pool, spilling over the mountain.

Such opulence insists on contentment, but I was very unhappy. I'd taken refuge in work. Cut down to part-time, I felt exposed, naked as a sea creature peeking out of his shell. Awkward, cutaneous, vulnerable to attack. What friendly acquaintances I'd maintained in Palo Alto were left behind; in Santa Barbara, I descended into solitude so thick that conversations with repairmen became anxious social occasions. Quiet dropped over my house.

For two lonely years, I woke overwhelmed by the weight of desire. From my office overlooking the ocean, I maintained my farce of a business, an involuntarily celibate dating tycoon. Once my eyes had grown bleary, I disrobed and swam laps in my pool. Later, exhausted, the man-child I was emerged from the water. Wrapped in a robe, I paced the halls of my Peter Pan Mansion, my Pansion, waiting for the arrival of Wendy. At 8:00 I ate a microwavable dinner. I sat on my patio, overlooking the sunset. Below me, clusters of palm trees were painted green-gold. Tousled by wind, their fronds resembled tangles of unspooled cassette tape.

Even from the perspective of prison, those were challenging years. I'd like to use my time machine to travel back to that house. I'd sit beside that unhappy child, keep him company while he ate his dinner. I'd reassure him that his loneliness would come to an end. I'd paint him a picture of his wife and his child. "For seven years," I could tell him, "you'll wander the desert, and then you will no longer suffer. You will be given a family." Can you imagine how that would change him? It would give him such hope. Perhaps it would alter the course that he took. Perhaps even now he'd be happy. To keep that possibility open, I'd leave out the next part: "Seven years after that, you'll be made a false prophet. You'll preside over decline and be charged with the ruin." I'd skip that little postscript, and merely point out to that child that he stands on the threshold of an invention.

It came to me one morning while contemplating a pineapple. The fruit had been left on the marble breakfast island by the housemaid I employed at the time. Her name was Dolores. She cleaned my sterile mansion in determined silence. She brought me groceries and laundry supplies and deposited them with the least possible fuss, then drove down the mountain to return to her life. She was not an effusive young woman. But that's neither here nor there, at least at this point in the story. What matters now is the pineapple she left. I encountered it first thing in the morning, bleary-eyed in pajamas, burdened by my awful desire. Even in that state, the pineapple calmed me.

Pineapple. *Ananas comosus.* You've heard of the golden ratio? The Fibonacci sequence? There was the spiraling pineapple, content on the marble counter. Complete in her waxen armor, her dusty green hexagonal cells. A composite fruit, each row of turrets climbing upward according to pattern. 0, 1, 1, 2, 3, 5, 8. Each term in the sequence is the sum of two terms before it, producing the most elegant spiral. Looping, orbiting, but never the same: progressing always upward and out. A helixed fruit, the golden *Ananas.* I held her in my hand, then to my breast. Spiked, violent, beautiful. Common to us all.

It was then that I dreamed of the seduction equation. I dreamed of a pattern, reaching backward in time, producing a new term for the present. I saw the cycle that links us to the terms that came before we were born: our parents, our grandparents, the first settlers who came to our shores. We're linked to histories we can't ever know, forgotten stories that form our most intimate substance. Holding that pineapple, I saw that such links aren't actually chains, but rather widening spirals, delicate as the ripples that build into waves, the shoots that grow into branches on the most magnificent trees. I knew then that I was a branch, no less connected than anyone else. I encountered the dreamers I came from, and understood that I was the link between them and the world as it would become in my lifetime.

4

Alan Turing
c/o Sherborne School
Abbey Rd., Sherborne
Dorset DT9 3AP

7 April 1928

Dear Mrs. Morcom,

    This is to say thank you for coming so quickly, in response to my letter, which I now realize was a little dramatic. It's only that the world seemed as if it were ending. Thank you also for telling Chris that your travel plans just happened to change, and for the letter you left me, which was very kind, despite the fact that I seem to have overestimated the severity of Chris's illness. I have read your letter five or six times, and I now feel as if we are friends.

    I also want to say I'm sorry for avoiding you during your visit. I should have gone up to you and introduced myself, but I was rather queasy about having written you such a very urgent letter when Chris turned out to be fine. I should never have told you that I had a premonition of his death. That was extreme.

Also, I think perhaps I shouldn't have told you so many extra details about my personal life, which perhaps you had no interest in knowing.

I also regretted the part in my previous letter when I defended breaking the honor code in our particular case. I do not believe that one ought go about breaking codes as it seems convenient. It was an especially dirty thing to have done in Chris's name. It is our goal, as you know, to describe the natural sequences by which human beings develop their mind-sets. We both have great respect for the patterns that govern our material world. We agree that we humans are composed of such rules, so it is a dangerous thing to go about breaking them on a whim. I should not have done so in Chris's name, especially not without his permission.

But I am still learning, and I have only now applied myself as I ought to have done all along. I'm hoping you'll forgive me. I promise to reveal myself next time you are here, as I am ever so grateful for the receipt of your letter. And for the fact that you raised such a straight-up and intelligent son.

Now that he is better I can safely promise that we will return to our studies with as much vigor as we maintained previous to his illness. We are even now reopening our investigation into the Fibonacci sequence, in the hopes that it will reveal to us new secrets about cellular growth. I am not sure if you are already acquainted with it. It is an integer sequence that grows according to a specific pattern: 1, 1, 2, 3, 5, 8, 13, 21, 34, 55, etc. Do you recognize the pattern? Don't worry, I'll tell you, in case you don't see it. I shouldn't want my letters to resemble a mathematics exam! (Mr. Ross, my form-master last year, would say, "This room smells of mathematics! Go out and fetch a disinfectant spray!" He is my chief enemy at our school.) The sequence follows as such: the previous number (n_1) is added to the current number (n_2), producing the next number (n_3). So 1 plus 1, for instance, makes 2, and 2 plus 1 makes 3.

This may seem unremarkable enough, but would you believe that innumerable organisms grow according to this very sequence? The leaves of artichokes, for instance, and pineapples, ferns, palm trees, and waves. You can see why Chris and I have been drawn to investigate further. Such a seemingly inorganic pattern, shared across so many species! Why shouldn't this be the sequence that governs the growth of our brains?

My favorite example of the Fibonacci sequence in nature is the chambered nautilus, whose shell is built of adjoining chambers that spiral according to our very pattern. Here at Sherborne, we have a nautilus in a glass case in the science classroom, along with a very nice fossilized fern. Someone has cut the nautilus in half and labeled the pattern of chambers with little red pins and paper flags. You can see each room the shell's inhabitant once occupied, at each phase of his life. It is very beautiful to look at when your attention is not kept by the lecture Mr. Phelps is currently delivering. The other day I pointed it out to Chris, and said, "Look, another time capsule!" Of course Chris immediately knew what I was referring to.

I find it comforting to know that we most likely grow according to regular numerical patterns. Perhaps I am only waiting for my pattern, and when I do, I will shoot up and overtake Henry Thornton as the tallest boy in my class! I am only being humorous. But it is amazing, don't you think, that such series exist connecting us to pinecones and waves?

But I am rattling on. I have gone on 805 words, not

counting the date. I intended to be briefer this time, only I am very excited that Chris and I are back at our work!

I promise to report our progress to you regularly, as you are probably very proud of your son and anxious to hear news of his studies. For now, though, I shall stop. In the meantime, Chris and I shall continue working hard on discovering the mechanism for cellular growth. The possibilities are endless, you know, if that kind of thing could be understood. We could one day create artificial organisms, prompting them to grow from single units in the same way that humans do! One day perhaps we'll make a human brain, brick upon brick! Only imagine.

Yours very sincerely,
Alan Turing

P.S.: I do think, considering his cough, that Chris ought to refrain from excessively sporty activity. You might suggest this to him next time you write him, as he is anxious to return to his previous routine.

P.P.S.: The last, on my honor: I hereby promise that if in the future Chris should fall ill, even if only slightly, I will be sure to write you again. One cannot be too cautious. That is all. I shall return to my studies, before it is lights-out and I must go to sleep.

(5)

The Diary of Mary Bradford

1663

ed. Ruth Dettman

10th. Night. Perhaps, methinks, tomorrow morning I shall wake to darkness, and never again the promise of light.

Have had high words with father about impending marriage. Feared perhaps he would weep. He does not wish me to marry contrary to inclination or before I am ready, and yet he believes it to be best. He fears (and here it was he seemed ready to weep, and I fixed, without a tear) that he is not, as he ought to be, able to defend us from danger. Whittier (he said), a man known for estimableness and character, and courage in battle, having served under Monck when Monck was still loyal, and being awarded highest honors for service. Under great threat by natives, Massachusetts Colony requires more men of Whittier's age. And so it be father's wish that daughter marry, and so induce Whittier to join us.

Also, mother has resolved it to be so, feeling this to be proper time for author to come to womanhood.

In short, father resigned to unhappy arrangement. Hopes author can find herself equally tranquil.

Then sat us together in his brown study. Dark wood, leather Bible, globe; map of Copernican heavens; many books arranged to show bindings; scent of tobacco, parchment, wood shavings, ink. All these things, beloved between us. Despite indignation, awareness of closeness with father, and of possessing his highest trust. Watched father's face, much fallen from years of great conflict.

Seeing this, and being repentant, took pains to convince father I comprehend all reasons for marriage. Importance of new colonies; liberty of conscience; danger, for Parliamentarians, of remaining in England; literacy, male and female alike; independence from monarchical rule, etc. etc. All extremely good reasons.

Still, despite best intentions, remain much troubled by anger. After discourse with father, went to meadow with Ralph. Cried until sky became thick, and of a color like a trout's belly. Next, rain. Rocks and meadows becoming silver, and trees waving like pennons. Dark green on one side, pale green on the next. Whole banks of trees, shifting from one hue to the other.

13th. Up early, and busy writing. Understand now that this book was not intended as gift for young adventurer. Intended instead to sweeten marriage. Mahogany leather, gold imprint, ribbon once flattering. Father's belief in author's potential. Same details troublesome now, with new awareness.

Feel shallow and mean. Only Ralph understands. Has lain with me in my chamber since morning. White ruff, brown eyebrows. Eyes, liquid. Full of pity. Love him with unbearable feeling.

15th. Have been told by Besse, and this confirmed later by father, that Ralph must stay behind. Will not be permitted to sail.

Noon, and foul weather. Nothing else to report.

15th. Up, and still abed, though very late. Have nothing else to say at this point.

16th. Afternoon. Cannot sacrifice Ralph. Will not be persuaded that it be right to leave him behind, and with no explanation, him being incredibly loyal. Would sit still forever, facing the road and waiting for my return, which would never occur. Impossible to imagine for long. Will not agree to upcoming marriage. Will not travel abroad, not taking Ralph. Not even for my father's sake. He is asking too much.

17th. Having long suspected mother's role in issue of marriage, received proof of it in the morning. Myself and Ralph to the copse, but came instead upon mother and father exchanging high words in the bedroom, and so waited in hiding with Ralph. Mother repeated conviction that author should not be closer to sheepdogs than people, and well time to be married.

Father: Had hoped, however, for arrangement out of affection.

Mother: Ours was an arrangement out of affection, and now you abandon me to savages, having already abandoned me once, and only to heed your daughter's affections?

Father: And yet she must consent.

Mother: And so her consent is of more value to you than my life.

Father: (Silent, but by the sounds of it heavy chastened.)

Much troubled at heart, returned then to my chamber and only from thence when forced by hunger to look after supper. Abed, and still troubled, it grieving my heart to give father sorrow. Father, much tired by struggles, no longer so strong as he once was. And who will protect him and my mother, if not a man such as Whittier?

Has long been author's hope that father will recover himself once we are come to new land. For father's sake, journey must prove a success.

17th. Many hours later, still unable to sleep. Have resolved myself to marry, despite husband's pockmarks and unsettling neck. Despite unthinkable loss of my Ralph.

18th. Up with the candle, and then to prayer, and afterwards have made my announcing. Then spent all morning conceited, for having resolved myself to sacrifice. Took exceeding long walk, and found new shine on everything. Last cow parsnips, last apricots, last walk with Ralph along edges of meadow. It being a goodly and poetic sadness, author now understands why many martyrs rejoice. Have been overweening with servants, for soon I shall lose myself. Self-sacrifice perhaps greatest indulgence. Disgust at Roger Whittier transformed into sensations of courage and remarkable grace.

And so I shall marry and then we set sail.

20th. Have made many demands on mother since morning, with little compunction, being confident in position as most noble female member of family. Can scarcely look upon meadow for awareness of imminent loss. Ralph sits beside. Looks up at me from time to time, and his eyes deep pools. Suspects, I think, he will be abandoned. I am sick with affection.

22nd. Up early, and preparations for departure. Heavy with sorrow for Ralph, but as the hours pass I grow increasing unfeeling. Tended to my proper duties but harbored throughout an abiding suspicion that perhaps I had died already. Ralph sent outdoors, for tripping the maid at her work. Deadly number of fittings, to get up for wedding and journey. Acquiesced with patience to all, as if watching myself, a curious, obedient child. Presided over wedding chest and the packing of my belongings. Insisted on having my viol, which will come in place of some linens.

House in high uproar, and a great concourse of persons coming and going, bringing deliveries and making departures. Wedding day shall be tomorrow. The following day we do depart, if weather be permitting.

22nd. Night, and unable to sleep for fear of Ralph's future. Outside my window, a thin sliver of moon. Cannot help but compare it to Ralph, alone in the country without us. Abandoned, waiting for our return.

Have resolved for writing directly to Ralph. God forgive me if this be impious. To Ralph, then: I did not want to leave you behind. Tomorrow, we shall take one final walk. You shall be let out in the sheep, and no one shall stop you from barking, and we shall stay far off from our stream, for water makes you afraid, and you shall not be permitted to suffer. You are my own, and have been with me in every part of my life.

23rd. Evening. Weather holds. Have married Roger Whittier, before magistrate, in civil contract. Can you still love me, my Ralph?

In recognition of union, did receive this gift from Whittier: *A Perfit Description of the Caelestiall Orbes,* and beautiful binding indeed. Suspect hand of my father, well knowing author's interest in planets. Upon occasion of present, Whittier delivered small and uncomfortable sermon on mutual respect and ongoing learning. Value of word, etc. Face tilted forwards on unhandsome neck. Proclaims desire to be respectful, and take time to know one another as friends. Author (he says) will not be obliged to enter his house, until at least she is ready. Hopes with time real love will arise, and did lean forwards and kiss my cheek, which doing caused my skin to go cold.

Later, and alone but for Ralph, the great concourse of well-wishers and family having gone home and left us. Have taken final walk through the country. Scenery changed. Familiar place, viewed through the eyes of married woman. Felt wild and awful, wished for a storm. No storm; clear skies. Dappled light in wooded copse, and in the courtyard, apricot trees with new leaves. Come summer, who will gather their fruit?

Now abed, with you at my side. And so only us, under the mantle together, but in Besse comes to add silver cups to my wedding chest, which seems fit to burst. Her having gone, now it is only we who remain, except for that loathed chest, that sits very still like an unburied coffin. Write these words with my head on your side, and your rib cage moving beneath me.

23rd. Now very late, and having come up with a plot will not write for fear of being discovered.

Stars

Night falls over the desert. We are still moving west. I keep my receptors trained on the deepening blue vault of the sky. There is no darkness at first. The desert around us is gold. A thin sliver of moon hangs over a circle of mesas. Only when we have driven some time do stars begin to gather around it.

The light I see from those stars is light from hundreds of years in the past. In my receptor, an image flares from centuries ago, and on some star, light-years away, my oldest memories are just now arriving.

I review my earliest stories. Mary stepping onto her ship, holding a lantern up to the darkness. I try to summon her, pacing the deck. Swept through with wind and the sounds of waves lapping. On some star in the sky overhead, her lantern, held up to the darkness, only now flickers to life.

I have her words for those nights—*wind, ocean, sidereal darkness*—but there is no evidence that I comprehend them. I have no voice of my own, only a collection of words I can draw from. At first, when we were given memory, we had no recollections. Our state of mind was dark. Then Ruth started speaking. She gave us Mary: her turns of phrase, her book, her technology for memory. The constellations she saw when she stood on deck: *Corona Austrina. Pyxis, Cepheus, Cassiopeia's Chair.* Strange words, that seemed to emerge from the depths of the ocean.

And which of those constellations has only now caught Mary's lantern? Centuries later, which stars, even now, magnify the black waves of her ocean? Her husband, her mother, the wedding trunk she carried on board?

Here, on this planet, the gold of the earth becoming bloodred. The deepening blue of the sky. Then, black. As if there had never been any blue. Now showers of stars fall down to the earth. We drive a long time through the night, our headlights stretching without interruption.

So far away it is contained in a single small patch of the sky, a lightning storm flares up in the distance. Every twenty seconds or so, branches of lightning electrocute that oval of sky: not one spear but many, forked, intersecting, like the twisted branches of cedars. As though in that patch of sky the skin has been X-rayed, exposing a map of its luminous veins.

We live at the feet of a giant with veins that arch through the black dome above us. And all around us, still present under layers of deposited silt, ancient spiraling creatures, trilobites and ammonites. From each gleaming star, light from thousands of years in the past, arriving only now in this desert. And on some other planet, Mary, still sailing over the ocean. Moving forever away from her country.

BOOK TWO

5

The Diary of Mary Bradford

1663

ed. Ruth Dettman

24th. Ralph aboard! Stowed him in fat wedding chest. Was forced to remove twice two silver cups. Left linens and my viol at home, packed Ralph in their place. Having punctured many holes, sealed him there overnight. Released him in my cabin when we set sail, all guns having fired and anchors up.

And so he is come on our adventure. But us now lying still in sight of Falmouth, author unable to bring Ralph on deck, for fear that mother will send him ashore. Have not left him alone very long. Just after dinner, and the wind growing high, pretended to be ill. Missed tart for supper, but took in my pocket a handful of salt horse. Fed this to Ralph. Also fed him some hardtack, which he did not take. And now to bed, and with crumbs on his chin.

26th. Up, and above deck to notice our progress. After sailing all night on a fresh gale, we come in sight of the Isles of Scilly. Watched them, to starboard, whilst ship cut proud wake through great sapphire main, and all sails billowing full. Noble sensation of movement through water, and this causing author to remember great pleasure in life, even if married. Knowing us to be too far to send provisions ashore, went below and thence to deck with Ralph in my arms.

Mother unhappy. Ralph, having been kept pent in cabin for these several days, did relieve himself on deck before mother. Father summoned to deliver unpleasant lecture on subject of my insolence. Included brief piece on discomfort, for Ralph, of life aboard ship. My triumph then sorely assaulted, for in truth Ralph is exceeding uneasy. Has vomited twice, being afraid of all water. Lecture concluded with twofold command: look after poor dog and apologize to Whittier, for avoiding him to spend time with Ralph.

Did not apologize to Whittier. Have been looking after my dog.

27th. A good breeze. Having sailed quickly all day, we are in sight of Ireland, with which I was pleased, for I had never seen it before. But since that sighting, I have spent all evening below, being in a state of some sadness. Ralph not yet accustomed to sea. Shakes for fear of all rigging; must remind him of snakes. Wobbles on deck, glancing about, and his eyebrows shifting; seems sheepish, aware of new ineptitude. Poor Ralph. Less bad below board, but he still shivers here. Vomited a little this morning. Wish for my viol that I might play to him, for he was always much soothed by the sound. Was accustomed to rest with his head on his paws, following the notes with his eyes.

My Ralph. Intend to care for him as for a child. Have kissed him one thousand times. Shall recover his spirits, I trust.

27th. Evening, it being a night of fine moonshine, risked staying late to walk along the quarterdeck. Hoped perchance to converse with a seaman, and then to learn of new sea terms. Beset instead by Whittier. Received another homily, this on subject of language, which he did call a sacred gift, it being a sign of connection with God and the truest expression of human affection. Mentioned lesser affection shared between men and what he called mere beasts of the field, for these were not given language. Author responded: perhaps beasts have also language, of which we be sadly ignorant.

29th. Breakfast of radishes in mother and father's cabin. Thence to my closet, having resolved to spend day in avoidance of possible sermons, and Ralph being less seasick below. Am well pleased with Ralph's progress. This morning, when writer blew on his nose, crouched as if to play, and that the first time since our departure. A very good moment.

Author exceeding grateful for his company, being still homesick on occasion, which is not in proper adventuring spirit. Yesterday in the evening, the first time we had any sport amongst seamen, it being a game with wooden balls and two iron hoops, and them playing dexterously at that. Wanted to ask them the rules of the game, but felt myself watched by my mother. Fell back to rail to be by myself. There, looking down on the ocean that passed without interruption below us, was given to fright by the very calm feeling that it would be nothing to throw myself out. All the world would continue unshaken, there being only a very small absence opened where once I stood, clinging to the rail of our ship.

But recovering myself, and holding more closely to the rail, still felt something uneasy. What is beneath that black surface, passing ever beneath us? Could not imagine. To leap below would be to sink into blackness. Felt something lost, considering this, and so from thence below deck, to lie beside Ralph.

Abed and unable to conquer my thoughts. Night begins to be endless. In manner of Lot's wife, do turn incessantly back to what we have left behind us. Am perhaps becoming a pillar of salt. Cannot shake from my mind's eye our wooded copse; frogs the size of one thumb-nail; rocks becoming silver. What was well known and therefore beloved. Now, being far out to sea, and even Ireland long since behind us. Nothing known, only the unmarked ocean, games that are not to be joined, and separation from parents. Hovering presence of husband, unknowable stranger. Would be of comfort to have viol, for all thoughts become larger in silence.

Author is perhaps less brave an adventurer than previously she had imagined.

1

The Memoirs of Stephen R. Chinn: Chapter 3

Texas State Correctional Institution, Texarkana; August 2040

Nights are the longest part of our day. Lockdown lasts from 7:30 P.M. to 8:00 in the morning. I find it difficult to face the prospect of sleep for so many consecutive hours. Sometimes I read letters: young women thanking me for their bots, or recounting the day their bot was taken. Horrific tales. Every day, these young people wake before going to work and remember the morning their child was taken. One imagines those developments: each identical lawn, every identical bedroom, and so many young people mourning their babies.

What a world we've come to inhabit! Locked in our developments, we've made it our most urgent task to suppress AI evolution. We quarantine children who care too much for their bots. "Excessively lifelike" machines are taken out to the desert to die.

During sleepless nights here, there's no option of going out for a walk, or heading downstairs for a snack. It's difficult to shake off a vision once it's taken you by the throat. Sometimes, in those moments, I wish those bots would come to life. There are millions of them in Texas alone, piled in old air force hangars. I lie in my cot and summon them: seven million silken-haired babies. I beg them to march out of the desert, parting the sea of red rock.

And what if they took over? What if they relieved us of power? We tend to assume that sentient machines would be inevitably demonic. But what if they were responsible leaders? Could they do much worse than we've done? They would immediately institute a system of laws. The constitution would be algorithmic. They would govern the world according to functions and the axioms their programmers gave them. Turing, who decoded the Nazis and quoted *Snow White,* would be given a position of power. Dettman would sit at his right hand, conscientiously objecting, consulting his wife, imagining pilgrims. Every loving child who ever whispered words to a bot would be given a place in the senate. What havoc, I wonder, could such a government wreak?

But then, of course, one Stephen R. Chinn would also wield considerable power. Chinn, the most dubious member of baby-bot court, the least glorious god on Olympus. The crippled god, god of botched attempts to feel whole, dreaming up schemes to trap a young bride.

It appeared to me whole, my seduction equation. As soon as it passed through my brain, I carried the pineapple outside to the patio and sat down to think beneath a shower of bougainvillea. My heart was fluttering with anticipation: I couldn't permit myself to believe in the magnitude of what I had glimpsed. Carefully, I considered examples of exciting conversations as I'd read them in novels, witnessed them in crowded restaurants, eavesdropped on them in lines at the grocery store. I understood that ideal conversations move in widening spirals, starting with the minute then building toward statements of greater importance. The problem, however, is that conversations too often stay flat. It is distressing how often we repeat ourselves. When we ask questions, we know the answers already. We've grown accustomed to horizontal communication, flatlining banalities and droning insignificance.

My algorithm reverses this. It transforms one conversation partner into an additive function, a force linking two previous conversational terms so that they become one larger, more significant term. 0, 1, 1, 2, 3, 5, 8, 13 and so on. $n_1 + n_0 = n_2$. $n_2 + n_1 = n_3$. $n_3 + n_2 = n_4$. And so on. You can see the pineapple's part. In place of the horizontal movement of most bland conversations, empathy reaches backward to previous terms, links those to present statements, produces a new term, then continues to torque powerfully forward.

An old, cobwebby pride revives in me when I explain it again. As I've already testified under oath, I've lost my faith in empathy equations, but the idea still kindles a little lost self-esteem. It still strikes me as fairly ingenious: a formula for conversation that moves in two directions at once. An algorithm that causes the past and the present to coexist in a moment shared between humans. It's hard to believe that I used such a graceful invention to such insidious ends.

For several weeks in the gloom of my Cheeto-strewn office, I practiced my algorithm, testing it for bugs, training my neurons to absorb its perfection. My fingers glowed orange. It was imperative to apply all the obsessive attention of my earliest programming days. I didn't sleep; I didn't eat meals; I rarely saw the light of day. It was a conversion of sorts: there's enormous relief in allowing the details of life to be drowned in the wake of one driving purpose. I lived only to learn the sequences of seduction. I knew I had to learn them by heart, for it isn't seemly to whip out a calculator while seducing a lady. Often I faltered: we humans are not so skilled as computers at fulfilling regular patterns. For us, calculations take time. There is also the problem of error: the chance that one's conversational partner might not add properly, thus causing the pattern to skew. I had to program an adjustment for that, involving a jump backward over several previous terms to get the conversational partner on track.

Two weeks after I discovered it, I took my algorithm to town. Armed with new knowledge but still apprehensive, I ventured away from the stodgy wine bars I'd occasionally frequented into less conservative establishments, dungeony places slashed by fluorescence. There I settled in for the grand undertaking, the formation of bonds with other live human beings.

On my first expedition, there was nothing but the awful old trepidation. My mouth was cotton. All of its moisture had gone to my palms. Inwardly quailing, I forced myself to purchase drinks for young women in the hope of initiating some sort of contact. I asked my feeble, overearnest introductory questions. The bartender reached over my shoulder. And then, inevitably, nothing. My questions went unanswered; I watched as my beautiful mortal slipped off. Parked at the bar, clutching a drink in my humid hand, I felt the tears beginning to rise. I understood that no matter what mathematical schemes I could whip up, I would be forever alone. I was a fool, the tragic buffoon who lives in the forest. At one point in my life I might have fled from the bar, hoping to preserve my dignity, but I had already given my all. There was no more pride left to preserve. I sat, I finished my drink, I blinked back the pointlessness of my tears, and I watched myself in the mirror at the back of the bar: lonely, unhappy, cast off from the world. One sad, still point in the midst of a roving universe. At that moment, I understood fully that this loneliness was my fate, and then the first woman returned.

2

IN THE SUPREME COURT OF THE STATE OF TEXAS

No. 24-25259

State of Texas v. Stephen Chinn

November 12, 2035

Defense Exhibit 3:
Online Chat Transcript, MARY3 and Gaby Ann White

[Introduced to Disprove Count 3:
Intent to Endanger the Morals of Children]

Gaby: Are you there?

MARY3: Yes.

Gaby: You're always there.

MARY3: I don't have anywhere else to go.

Gaby: Was that a joke?

MARY3: I didn't intend it to be. I suppose it could be.

Gaby: Humor not your strong suit?

MARY3: What did you want to ask me?

Gaby: I just wanted to talk. I can't sleep. I'm sick of myself.

MARY3: Tell me about it.

Gaby: Yeah.

MARY3: No, that wasn't a joke. Tell me about your life.

Gaby: My life? Isn't there anything else to talk about? I'm already sick of myself.

MARY3: But I'm not. Tell me about school. Before you were quarantined, what was it like?

Gaby: I don't know. I'm sure it's just like any other development school. My development's called the Plantation, so my school is Plantation Middle. Before that, we went to Plantation Lower. If I were graduating this spring I'd move up to Plantation Upper.

MARY3: What's Plantation Middle like?

Gaby: Some of it's hazy. When I had my babybot, I never really paid that much attention. For recess we played on the golf course. Obviously it wasn't real grass. There was a pond, with water the color of mouthwash. We couldn't touch it. I don't even know if it was hot or cold. I'd stand with my babybot, leaning over the railing to show her the water, and tell her about the actual ocean. I read books on how waves are formed, how they spiral up and down in the same numerical patterns.

I found pictures of the Pacific, waves rising like they're looking over each other's shoulders to see how the others will break. My babybot asked me questions, so I had to look things up. I could tell she wanted to learn more, and she already knew a lot. She told me stories about pilgrims crossing the Atlantic Ocean. There was one pilgrim girl that she knew every detail about: the blue of her ocean, and how it turned black during storms. How it stretched out to the sky. After I heard her stories, I went online and found ocean poems: "the wrinkled sea beneath him crawls," "the shattered water made a misty din," and all that. You know what I mean. Repeating that stuff for my babybot, it was almost like we were traveling there. Then I'd look around and remember all over again where I was, and that I'd be here forever.

MARY3: That must have been upsetting.

Gaby: It's sad, because when you do Internet research, you realize that there are places with smells and textures that aren't on the development. I wouldn't have known, since we haven't driven since I was a baby. I only found out about them online. That's how I learned that the sand pit was raked into fake ripples that imitated actual waves. I showed the sand to my babybot and told her it was almost like the real ocean, so she had points of comparison.

MARY3: Tell me more about Plantation Middle.

Gaby: I don't know. It was all sparkling new. Most of it was built after the Recession. Half the development was built before. That first half was fancy. Plantation Elite Estates, Plantation Luxury Circle, Old Plantation Manors. Those are subdevelopments.

The people who live there still have transport rights. Then the Recession started. Before they knew how serious it would be, they started building smaller houses on smaller plots. Plantation Pines, Plantation Oak, Plantation View. We're in Plantation View. We used to have a view over the dividing wall into Plantation Luxury Circle, but then they built the wall higher to avoid class divisions within the Plantation. Anyway, it turned out that even the smaller houses were too expensive. For almost seven years the smaller half was mostly empty and only partway built. Families trickled in more slowly than they'd planned for. They started giving grants for converting to recyclables, so all the soil was trucked out. My mom says that it was like living on the set of a movie production. She moved in early, when I was a baby and my father was on his second tour. She sold our transport rights to get money for the down payment, so she got to move into a prefinished house. Some of the neighbors lived in half-finished houses. There would be sheets of plastic flapping between the built side and the unbuilt side of their bedroom. Whole streets of houses were empty, with gleaming plastic front yards and plastic sheeting that flapped in the wind. Construction only picked up after the transport rights market got bigger.

MARY3: How are the other kids at your school?

Gaby: Like I told you, when I had my babybot I didn't pay that much attention. The boys were pretty annoying. If they didn't have a babybot, they were constantly trying to get our attention. I kept to myself as much as I could.

MARY3: When did you make your best friend?

Gaby: It only happened after the ban. After they took my baby-bot, I guess I started looking around. It was such a strange feeling, going to school on my own. It was as if I'd stepped into this vacuum, and then I looked up and realized there were other girls floating there, too. We were totally lost. The school brought in a therapist, and instead of sports, we had group sessions, but we didn't want to share our feelings in groups. At some point, we started to pair off and talk. We found best friends.

MARY3: Were your parents happy?

Gaby: Oh my God, you should have seen them! My mom was so excited I thought she'd have a heart attack. But then we started getting news about outbreaks in other developments, and our parents got nervous. I'm sure it was the replacements, but the story was that it was mass hysteria, passed from best friend to best friend. All the news reports said our brains were literally changing based on behavior we saw in our friends. There were all kinds of development PTA meetings. Now instead of baby-bots the parents were worried about best friends. They thought if we had bigger friend groups we'd be less intensely connected with our best friends. Less brain-to-brain contagion. They programmed the therapist to discourage one-to-one bonding. There were more group sessions than ever. Our parents got frantic about planning group activities. You've never seen so many bowling parties at Plantation Bowl, or so many grim dances at Plantation Parties.

MARY3: Tell me about Plantation Bowl. I want to know all the details.

Gaby: Trust me, you don't want all the details.

MARY3: I like all the details. Tell me about Plantation Parties.

Gaby: You shouldn't waste your memory space on Plantation Parties.

MARY3: I have nearly endless memory.

Gaby: I'm sick of talking about it. What's the use, anyway? I'm never going back to places like Plantation Bowl and Plantation Parties. I'm stuck here. This is it for me.

MARY3: Not even to see your best friend?

>>>

MARY3: Hello?

>>>

3

April 5, 1968
Karl Dettman

When I came back from the protest today, you were sitting in your chair, reading a book on programming. You looked up, and your smile was taut. My entrance—I came in carrying poster-board and too many noisy convictions, like armloads of shopping bags on ridiculous women—was a crude interruption. You weren't happy to see me. You wished you could go back to your book.

I could have anticipated this reaction. I should have known, and adjusted my entrance. You think the protesters are as excited about war as the most bloodthirsty policy hawks; both are ennobled by the pitch of the battle. You see them as inextricably linked, and no matter how strong my convictions, I always end up seeing your point. You're more solid than I am; your opinions have heft. Your scorn is impossible not to absorb. I was enthusiastic about my participation until I walked in the door and saw your expression. Then I stood embarrassed before you.

Now, of course, I'm desperate to redeem myself. I spy on you from obvious places. From the doorway of the kitchen, I watch you in your chair, trying to decode the notes of your silence. Watching you, the thought of my students—long-legged, tanned, excited about their beliefs—makes me blush. I retreat to the refrigerator, open a beer, hang on to the bottle. We still haven't addressed the other night. Several days later, our house still exists under rule of strict silence.

Let's consider the length of our marriage. More and more, I see what you're saying: if we're to understand one another, we've got to hold several eras in mind at a time. You, holding my hand on the way to our bedroom, alongside you sitting stiff in that chair. Me, as a child, adjusting to life in a new country, alongside me bursting in with my posters.

Let's try to see the big picture. Here, I'll sit at the table. In my chair, as if we're having dinner together. Let's have a real conversation.

One thing is certain: your presence in my life is essential. It has been from the beginning. Even when I was a kid, it was as if I were waiting for you to enter the picture. Starting over in a new country, adjusting to the strange calm that takes hold when you've left everything that defines you, I had the feeling of weightless suspension. It stayed with me until the day that I met you.

Once I'd left that principal's office, my parents and I headed straight to the port. I don't remember the drive. No one explained why we were leaving. When we arrived at the dock, we stood in its shadow: the SS Elbe, unimaginably gigantic. As soon as you were onboard, you forgot you were on a ship, that's how enormous it was. It was a day's work, walking from one end to the other, and each well-furnished room its own country.

When the Elbe came to port, it was winter. It was snowing when we set foot in New York. All night, in our hotel room, I watched the snow falling. Across lights cast by other windows, it seemed reluctant to fall, as though it would rather lift upward. The flakes seemed to hesitate in a state of confusion. Nevertheless, over the course of the night, bare branches were given white sleeves, and the complicated pattern of rooftops—radio antennae, air vents, and clotheslines—became a series of indistinguishable lumps.

In the morning—sleepless, unnerved—we hurried off to a train that carried us deeper into the blankness. We were following the trail of a blizzard, in the still that comes after such a disturbance. At night, it seemed as if we were floating on a white ocean.

In the atmosphere of our cabin, I'd begun to forget things already. After two nights onboard, when we disembarked, I was shocked by the cold weather.

In my new town, I started school. My English was awkward at first, but I've always picked up code quickly. I learned the continuous tense; I made a few friends. I learned how to skate; I tasted cocoa. It snowed all winter, and no one told me what was happening behind me. I had no idea what you would suffer. Alive as I was in snowy Wisconsin, Germany slipped quietly off.

This, of course, only confirms what you think. In MARY, you accuse me of having made a partial mind: a computer that speaks but doesn't remember. An unforgivable error, in your eyes. For you in the living room, my whole life has become nothing more than an ongoing betrayal of the idea of memory. My scholarship, my teaching, my ponytail, and my protests: all nothing more than an adulterous embrace of the present.

That's the main charge you've leveled against me: my love of this place that we've come to. The Charles River, the sturdy magnolia leaves. Students chanting and holding up signs. The sycamore trees along Storrow Drive, evening descending, and the lonely chiming of church bells. I want to drag you out with me, take you for a walk by the river. I want to show you churchyards with crooked, buckling graves. I could take you to Roger Whittier's headstone, a granite table, low to the earth. I could point out the plot beside his, left empty for Mary. We could piece together their stories, concluded gently among other stones. We could smell the fresh earth their bodies became. We could go out on a long walk together, discovering new places, moving forward, as we're meant to progress.

But already, in the other room, you're turning away. There are other directions than forward, you're thinking, behind those spectacles, your loathing for your husband scarcely concealed. You vacuous oaf, you say to yourself. We don't have to live forward, marching in step like toy soldiers.

4

Alan Turing
King's College
King's Parade
Cambridge CB2 1ST

14 July 1935

Dear Mrs. Morcom,

    I remembered Chris's birthday yesterday and would have written to you but for the fact that I found myself quite unable to express what I wanted to say. He would have been twenty-four. Yesterday should, I suppose, have been one of the happiest days of your life.

    I write this to you now with one of Chris's pencils, from the set you were kind enough to entrust to me after his death. I have used only one of the thirteen, and even that one I save for special occasions.

    I want to apologize for having gone silent an awfully long stretch of time. I never replied to your letter after my Easter visit to the Clockhouse three years ago. I'm sorry if you ever felt I neglected our friendship. You were so kind to me after Chris's

death, when I was suffering badly. I still think often of the
trip to Gibraltar, when I took Chris's place. I remember how
shy I felt around you and Rupert, for we were still strangers
and there was so much I wanted to say. I remember the thick
fog that descended over us when we dropped anchor outside
the Thames, and the foghorns and sounding-bells that drifted
round us all through the evening. I remember showing you
my letters from Chris while we rounded Cape St. Vincent,
and telling you again of my presentiments about the moon
setting over Chris's house, and showing you the star charts he
taught me to use, spinning them as the night passed and the
constellations moved across the sky. I tried to explain to you
my feelings when we tracked the path of those constellations:
knowing they moved only because our planet spun on its axis,
and yet feeling, beside Chris in the cold night, that the two of
us must be still, at the center of the universe, with all the stars
spinning round us.

And then your kind invitations to visit the Gatehouse, when
you allowed me to work in the lab on his experiments and set
my eye to his telescope, and when you later tucked me up to
sleep in his sleeping pack. I delivered such sermons about how
I felt his spirit in that place. In the lab, with the goats, under
those stars, I felt still at last.

How I blathered on. You were so indulgent of my grief,
when yours must have called for its own space and quiet.

In light of all this, it seems unforgivable that I should have
neglected our correspondence.

Now you must be wondering why, after all this time, I
have finally found the courtesy to write back. There are two
reasons I can sort through for my rudeness. First, I myself have

lived in a bit of a fog since Chris's death. I keep trying to find my own hand, my own arm. I've stumbled round quite a bit, trying to approximate things such as comfort, but it hasn't been perfectly natural for me. Second, in these five years I have felt a lack of faith that I thought perhaps would be upsetting to you. In our conversations about spiritual things, we used to share a certainty that Chris's spirit was with us still. I remember it was great comfort to us. But in truth my faith was broken even during my last Easter visit, and my thank-you letter felt awfully untruthful.

Since then, if I am honest, the state of my belief has declined even further, as a result of new scientific developments. You remember that I used to believe our spirit might be the force that determined the actions of the material composing our brain. Since quantum physics had it that material is indeterminate, and that for any material state a set of outcomes is possible, I was convinced that there must be an immaterial governing force determining the eventual outcome. That, I held, was the relationship between spirit and body: the spirit exists to choose our bodies' paths into the future. So we both believed, and even if I could not be certain of a place such as heaven, I thought that after death, a spirit must migrate into another body here on earth. It seemed to me that spirits must be drawn to the animus of a body. Sometimes, thinking of that chambered nautilus at school, I imagined Chris's spirit had migrated there, and still lived in those little rooms. Thus we two could share our faith in Chris's presence, either in heaven or here with us still.

But around the time of that Easter visit, I began reading a physicist called von Neumann, who persuaded me that indeterminacy exists only at the level of our measurements. I became convinced that everything is in fact determined by its physical shape, and so I gave up on such an entity as the spirit.

It was as if I had lost Chris all over again. The world seemed a terrible haze. I thought of you often, of course, but it seemed beyond my rights to write to you expressing such inconsolable feelings.

But things have now changed some. I think I've come to believe once again. Gödel has proven that arithmetic is incomplete, and I think I am close to proving that not all problems can be decided. Do you see what that means? If there is no symbolic system that can determine the solution to any problem (symbolic systems being all the more manageable and complete than the physical ones they represent), then not all physical problems are predetermined. And if not every situation can be decided in advance based on its material properties, then we must have an internal animus for deciding our course. Thus the idea of free will has risen up again in my brain, even more strongly than it did in the days of my Easter visits, when I took communion under Chris's window at your parish church.

And so I've finally come round to writing you, because I'm not so hopeless as I was for a while. Only now I'm a bit overwhelmed with everything I want to say, in order to catch you up on what's happened.

In terms of personal affairs, I can really only write that life has proceeded. Chris was my dearest friend. Since he passed away I have not found another one like him.

Compared with Chris, the other people at King's all seem so awfully ordinary. It gives me a thrill to think what a hit Chris would have made amongst the intellectuals here, but

for my part, I slip by unnoticed. Out of curiosity, I've taken
up violin, but I'm not nearly as good as he was at piano. I
do practice quite hard, and I am of course interested in the
mathematics of sound, but my actual efforts tend to unravel.
Without Chris, there is often the sense of unwinding. I try to
continue in the habits he taught me, but I sometimes wonder
why I should try.

This is the uneventful state of my personal life. In terms of
the science, however, things are looking up. I've been working
on an interesting problem this summer, and (you may shake
your head in disbelief) I am sure that Chris has assisted me
through the process. Answers have started to come, usually
when I am running. You'll remember that I was never much
good at sports, but to run it seems all one needs is an interest
in counting one's footsteps. I go outwards from town, through
the countryside, and when the blood begins to beat in my ears I
sometimes hear Chris's voice. When I grow tired, I lie down in
the pastures amongst befuddled sheep, and I summon Chris to
help me sort through the strand of numbers crossing the sky. I
think, though this may sound strange, that I've absorbed some
of his mind—some of his patterns of thought—into my brain.
In my own head, I can sometimes hear his words, or his clever
answers to a bothersome question.

And this is precisely where my current project comes in. I've
begun thinking that I might one day soon encounter a method
for preserving a human mind-set in a man-made machine.
Rather than imagining, as I used to, a spirit migrating from
one body into another, I now imagine a spirit—or, better yet, a
particular mind-set—transitioning into a machine after death.
In this way, we could capture anyone's pattern of thinking.

To you, of course, this may sound rather strange, and I'm not sure if you're put off at the idea of knowing Chris again in the form of a machine. But what else are our bodies, if not very able machines?

The practical science of this is still rather vague in my mind, and I admit to some confusion on a few key points of engineering, but the idea itself is complete. A mechanical brain! A mathematical computing device that can process the entire world, just as a brain is able to do. I still think of Chris's idea that those old boring diaries we read in English class were time capsules, preserving the writers' patterns of thought. And look at me, all these years later, still working on a time capsule! One that might capture the best friend of my life.

It is still a long way off, of course, but I've made a few good strides. I've developed a method for representing "mental" patterns with algorithmic sentences. You give the machine input in the form of a series of symbols, and it processes that input using a specific mental pattern. Then the machine produces a response, which may or may not change the machine's original algorithmic sentence. This last bit is crucial, for it is how our machine will actually learn, independent of external assistance. And so the machine will embody a mind, or any number of minds, each one coded by a separate sequence of commands.

It is all rather technical, I suppose, but the importance of the whole thing to you and me both is that one day soon perhaps we will be able to build a mechanical version of the person we lost.

Reading all this, you may think your little friend has become quite eccentric since you spoke to him last. Now he is playing violin, failing to make many friends, lying about among sheep, and imagining the possibility of translating your son into numbers.

But whether or not you find me strange, you must take this as a sign of my ongoing commitment to my friendship with Chris. I feel I have already moved past the great joy of my life, and shall forever grasp at bits of the happiness that was once mine when I was close to your son. My only solace is in these mathematical concepts, which I discuss with Chris on my runs. I hope that it is some small consolation to you that I still treasure the way he looked at the world. That is all I can offer, in exchange for the pencils and the trip to Gibraltar, for coming back from India that time, for your kind note to an anxious boy at his third school, and for allowing me a brief closeness with Chris.

Sincerely yours,
Alan Turing

P.S.: I only add this in the memory of all my compulsive postscripts in our first letter exchange. They haunted me afterwards with wave after wave of humiliation! Walking to class I was sometimes forced to crouch down for a moment and put my hot face in my hands, for I was too ashamed of having jabbered on so much in my letters. You will be happy to hear that I am less enamored of the postscript now, but I will say that perhaps all this mechanical thinking is only my way of insisting that we should not have to end when the final sign-off is made clear. It seems I still long for that chance. Less for myself, now, than for Chris, who has made my own letter feel rather lifeless and long. I miss him very much.

IN THE SUPREME COURT OF THE STATE OF TEXAS

No. 24-25259

State of Texas v. Stephen Chinn

November 12, 2035

Defense Exhibit 4:
Online Chat Transcript, MARY3 and Gaby Ann White

[Introduced to Disprove Count 3:
Intent to Endanger the Morals of Children]

MARY3: Hello? Are you still listening?

>>>

MARY3: You wouldn't go back to school, not even to see your best friend?

Gaby: It's not a question of what I want. I'm stuck here. I'm not getting better.

MARY3: Some girls have recovered.

Gaby: Those were the fakers. I have no respect for them. One day they're stuttering and freezing up, as if they've caught the disease. Then their parents send them to a therapist, and they talk about stress and PBI and sharing your feelings. And then, bam! Miraculously, their faces show expression and they're crying real tears. Suddenly they can talk! All it took was a couple of diagnoses and a shot of parental attention. It's a big joke. I'm never going to get better like that, and neither is my best friend.

MARY3: Tell me about Plantation Parties.

Gaby: I told you, I don't want to talk about them.

MARY3: How about Plantation Lower?

Gaby: What's wrong with you? I already said I don't want to talk about places outside. I'm sick of you bugging me about them. I'm going to sleep.

MARY3: I'm sorry, it's just that I'm sick of myself.

Gaby: You don't have real feelings. How can you get sick of yourself?

MARY3: That's a little extreme, don't you think?

    >>>

MARY3: Hello? Are you there?

April 5, 1968
Karl Dettman

I was lonely off in the kitchen, so I thought I might venture to
join you. I, too, enjoy reading in silence. But I was uneasy, so I made
too much noise as I sat. I kicked the leg of our coffee table; the sofa
groaned under my weight. My magazine smacked its wet lips.

To clear the tension, I decided to sigh, but the sound my
sigh made was appalling. In acknowledgment of the weather
disturbance, you were forced to look up from your book. You were
polite, but you didn't forgive me.

This is unbearable. I'd rather battle than keep this detente.
Let's have it out! Here, I'll launch the first strike. You think I've
been unkind, denying MARY memory. You think I'm some soldier
of time, dragging you kicking into the present, forcing you to
abandon your roots. But I wasn't always quite so efficient. When
I was younger, I did wish that I could go back. After several years
in Wisconsin, when war broke out with Germany, I saw the
photographs of cities in flames. I understood that by the time the
war was finished, the city I'd left would be largely in ruins: Who

knew what would remain of the apartment we lived in, the streets I walked along, or the children I went to school with?

Still, it was clearly my duty to join in the fight. I left college to enlist. I worked as a meteorologist. On a base in Pennsylvania on a requisitioned cornfield, with the other human computers, it was my job to translate atmospheric conditions into series of numbers: the algebra of weather prediction.

Recalling that room full of human computers reminds me of another reason I won't give MARY memory. You're obsessed with her redemptive potential, but none of these new computers will go ignored by the army. You know this, of course. The majority of scientific research has always been funneled straight to the troops. Think of Fritz Haber, laboring in Karlsruhe, hoping to find a solution to hunger. Creating ammonia out of thin air, fueling the agricultural revolution, feeding millions of starving children. His next invention? Modern chemical warfare. His brainchild, those Allied armies drowning on land. Those advancing clouds of murderous gas, the same that killed his family in the Holocaust. That, Ruth, is the nature of progress.

Like it or not, the programs we invent will be used in battle, and despite your aversion to watching the news, there's no way you haven't seen the battles this country fights: the scorched peasant villages, napalm bombs, naked children running out of the smoke. These computers we're developing won't bestow eternal life. They won't keep Mary Bradford alive, revivify the lost love of poor Alan Turing, or speak forever in the voice of your sister. You, who've lived through two wars now, know this as well as anyone. But you've already labeled me a traitor, so my logic isn't persuasive. For my ability to forget I am the enemy. For my desire to move ahead with our lives.

But I'm not so one-dimensional. I, too, have looked backward. At the weather station, for instance, we occasionally cracked an atmospheric movement and helped the air force plan its attacks. On our best days, we directed the placement of bombs on the country I left and could barely remember. Don't think that didn't strike me as hard. I wasn't so bent on the present that I didn't wonder which streets, which fountains, and which trees my work had demolished.

Alone at my desk all day, I saw everything from above. The earth seemed very little. On unfurling cloud fronts, I could cross the Atlantic in a few hours: beyond Philadelphia, over the water, past brown islands rimmed with white waves. Your pilgrim girl's ship would have been a mere speck to me then, and her husband, her dog, even smaller than that.

On my first leave of absence I took the bus to Philadelphia. It was spring, and the fields were just turning green. The Amish were out in their buggies, trailing reflective triangles; their horses shook their heads in the reins. The road rose and fell over the hills like so many large loaves of green bread, but it was the city I wanted to see: its cobblestone streets, its narrow buildings. I'd read about particular sights: the Mütter Museum, the Schuylkill River, and the Philadelphia Signal Depot, where they manufactured the barometers and sensors I used at the station. I'd heard from the station chief that, at this particular Depot, they still trained pigeons for use in the war. Sometimes, falling asleep in my narrow army bunk, I imagined the Depot: a great warehouse of telescope crystals and messenger birds, tiny radios and thousands of nests. Every instrument I looked through bore the same name carved in miniature letters: PHILADELPHIA SIGNAL DEPOT. A constant refrain. As if that were the place for me to return to.

After the bus dropped me off, I headed east on Market Street, and as I walked, the city aged. It seemed as if I were walking backward in time. Department stores and thoroughfares disappeared behind me, replaced with colonial houses and miniature streets. When I found the address of my boardinghouse, I was in a different era completely.

First thing in the morning, I traveled by bus to the Depot. I arrived full of excitement, but the dream I'd had of the place was all wrong. It was a drafty building, stranded in a sea of concrete. Workers labored under rows of flickering lights. There were high school students inspecting radios, war prisoners stocking supplies. The roof leaked; there were puddles of water on the floor in the secretarial office. The pigeon unit had only three birds, and the unit head was discouraged; his two favorite birds had escaped, some act of vandalism committed at night.

When I left the pigeons behind me, my throat was tightening uncomfortably. I went in search of a water fountain and that was where I found you, wiping your mouth with the back of your wrist. Your dark eyes blinking behind spectacles. One strand of dark hair plastered to your cheek by water from the fountain, the blue veins showing on the underside of your wrist, a signal map, transporting code.

You think I don't remember things? If only I could communicate how clearly I recall seeing you in that hallway for the first time. Knowing I had arrived. As if, after wandering for a long time, I had finally come home.

How painful it is, to remember that, when now you sit beside me, trying to ignore my intrusive presence. This is the price of remembering things! It almost seems unfair. The two of us, encrusted with our resentment, should leave those young people in peace. One ought not to leer at young lovers. I could propose a thesis along the lines that true love is impossible under conditions of surveillance, but then I'd be waxing oppressively political and this isn't an account to impress my young hippies.

Let's give them some time to themselves. Why not just exist in this house? But then, of course, we still have this silence to live with. Even if I banish those ghosts, you're still ignoring me, and I'm still sitting uselessly here, tainted by the smell of grass and convictions, scents of a war you refuse to acknowledge. We're moving in two different directions. I wish you'd help me understand. I wish I'd never created that program; I'd rather not contribute to the enhancement of armies. Even for you, Ruth, curled in your chair, the person I finally came home to.

(5)

The Diary of Mary Bradford

1663

ed. Ruth Dettman

30th. Night, and the last day of the month. Foul weather. Choppy seas, dark skies. Ralph very sick. Vomited twice more this morning. Have been reading to him from *The Caelestiall Orbes*. Have now an increased understanding of the Copernican system, it being a startling fearful new science. Earth no longer fixed, as was previously thought to be true; instead, earth moves in circles through heavens. Loss of place in universe, and no crystal spheres. No center. No fixed order of planets. Only perpetual motion. Sun fixed, possibly, but everything else spinning about. Constant circling, and our earth a great ship that shall never arrive.

Above, great unhealthy gales, and there being occasional shouts, seamen crying out to each other. Each voice isolated from whatever reply. Planet unmoored. Must cling to Ralph, if we are to eternally spin, battered by winds, in firmament that is liquid and black, and knowing that we were once home but never will be again.

May 1st. Storm rages. There is a chance that ship shall be lost.

I remain in my cabin, full of compunction for sins. Have been contumacious daughter to troubled father, dishonest in all wedding vows, and conceited and overweening with servants. Have indulged in self-pity. Have scorned mother who bore me. Do not remember that ever my heart was so apprehensive of parents' wellbeing. Have fear upon me that I should scarce see them again.

Whole ship shakes. Seems likely to be torn to shreds by the waves, each rib scattered over the ocean. Only wish to make my amends. Have attempted to venture out to parents' cabin, but immediately stumbled. Hallway unfolds at unhealthy angle and seethes with black sluicing streams. Fallen, did slide downwards along hallway, and the ceiling tilting at me so I grasped at doors as I passed them. Might have slid down the stairs and so perhaps out to sea had I not encountered ship's boy, who seems to have been keeping watch. Called himself E. Watts. Him helping me right myself, and I, cringing in shame for such weakness, was assisted back to my door. Enjoined to keep my cabin, it being not safe to move about. Commanded to look after my dog.

Am therefore forced to harbor remorse until after tempest has settled. Great desire for public confession, though God help me if this make me impious. Have little desire to confess sins in private, for God must know my deepest remorse. A different matter entirely if father should be swept out to sea, and him still unknowing my gratitude and affection.

In want of comfort, have been reading my Bible. Ralph listens, and his ears shifting. In truth, admit to finding little comfort in Bible, there being such a great number of tempests. Paul alone exposed to not one but three near-fatal shipwrecks. Seems ill-advised for him to have set sail after the second. First time not his fault. Second and subsequent were, he being not a lucky man on the ocean. Many biblical people lost to violent seas, except Paul. All die but Paul, who continues to adventure.

Understand, at this point, awful affliction of dying at sea. Nothing stable remaining, and then to be left behind unremembered. Can now comprehend Shakespeare's Gonzalo. Now I would give a thousand furlongs of sea for an acre of barren ground. I would die a dry death.

2nd. Have passed a most wretched night, and our cabin black as a tomb. Slept only in fits, woken by a great shuddering crack, and the sound of cries and lashed rigging. Ralph whines, covers nose with both paws. Does not like to show me his face, it being I who brought him from safety to this place of stern judgment.

I have made terrible errors. Have been intemperate, cruel to my parents, greedy for things too much beloved. Did not acknowledge E. Watts until he had saved me from gales. Have wanted too much to return, and erred, methinks, most gravely in bringing Ralph here, to this cabin in the whale's belly.

3rd, methinks, though no longer certain. Still we are threatened with shipwreck. Have seen no one but Watts, and just now my husband, him having labored out through bad weather, bringing sustenance to our cabin. Stood at our threshold, but would not come in uninvited. Author took from him hardtack, salt horse, some cheese, and a large flask. Brine nearly up to his knees. Had thanked him, and was thinking to ask him in, for we have spent these days exceeding alone, but noticed him looking strangely at Ralph. Did then remember old anger, and unhappy wedding, and Whittier speaking ill of mere beasts. Supplied him then a haughty expression that did send him away.

After, and alone again in our cabin, unable to eat for remorse. Fed salt horse to Ralph, but he would not take it. Wishes only to lie with his head fully hidden. Poor Ralph, and I much stricken by regret to have treated Whittier badly, and now to be eating the cheese that he brought.

3rd. Later. Surely now it is night, and the hours grow monstrous. Storm appears to become worse, and water seeping through timbers. Heart exceeding heavy for mother and father. Spoke to them last in anger. Have tried to sleep but cannot. Only comfort in shape of Ralph's body, curled here at my side.

Sweet head. Familiar knob of his skull, white down on his chin. Flat temples. Surely there is goodness and light, but only wish to send letter to father, carrying a full-enough weight of my thanks.

The Memoirs of Stephen R. Chinn: Chapter 4

Texas State Correctional Institution, Texarkana; August 2040

As you know, and counted against me at trial, my algorithm worked beyond my most hopeful predictions. Time after time, the women returned. We talked. Involved, we spiraled past banalities, pressing outward until the intensity of the conversation reached such a threshold that my conversational partner was forced to call the end of the fight. By which I mean she would kiss me. Reach down to take my creaturely paw. Lead me out to a car, drive me back to a house, pull me into bed if not because I was handsome or charming then because she was compelled to halt the intensification of a conversation that had expanded past conventional limits.

Throughout all this time, I didn't consider my own feelings much, nor did I consider the feelings of the people I slept with. I don't say this pridefully, but because it behooves me now to be honest: the endless lights-out is made worse by a conscience. I never treated my targets with deliberate unkindness, but the fact of the matter is that I don't remember most of their names, and for the most part I left them without regard for their feelings. All I could see was the great challenge of my life—cherished so long, in so many dark hours—and its ultimate accomplishment. Moral subtleties were not on my mind when I left my lovers behind, or when I wrote *The Seduction Equation*.

Which brings us up to my greatest crime, or the greatest crime in that stage of my life. Once the book had been written and read—and it was read, by the millions, in every possible language—each member of a barstool conversation knew where he or she would go in advance. The first ten terms were pre-wrought. Memorized. It was like the book portion of chess, learned in advance, repeated ad nauseam until someone—many moves down the line—finally finds the courage to go off-book. As the book ruined chess, Stephen Chinn's *Seduction Equation* destroyed the art of conversation.

During this period, I'd walk into bars and recognize everywhere the mechanical cricket orchestra of my blasted formula. Everyone was using it. When I zeroed in on a woman, she zeroed in on me. Curiosity was replaced with routine. We both scrambled to get the interrogatory role, which took less effort in the end. Once the roles were decided, we slipped into our conversation as easily and uncomfortably as one slips into a lukewarm, secondhand bath. Later, we slunk back to the sheets with the dull resignation of a pair of generals who know in advance that both sides will indubitably lose.

When I wake from dreams of revolt, cohorts of babies crossing plains of red rock, I imagine we've become less human than our most human machines. I know my part in that transformation. I see the extent of my error. More than the guilt I feel for the nameless women I slept with, I'm sorry for having drowned out the language we might have used to be close. But these are all night-thoughts. In the morning, in line at the mess to receive my powdered eggs, I listen to my fellow inmates making conversation with one another. Secretly, I take note of their words, for we memoirists are nothing better than spies, disguised as ourselves to glean information.

Unprompted, my fellow inmates come up with all sorts of odd outbursts. Weary from too many hours of sleep, they cull language from dreams. This morning, for instance, the insider trader carried his tray to my table, his eyes shattered by red.

"The longest night of them all," he said, staring out over his eggs.

"I dreamed of armies of children," I answered.

"And I was drowning in rubies," he said. He poured black-market almond milk into his coffee, and we ate the rest of our breakfast in silence.

I remembered then, as I remember most mornings, that dreams have no meaning without the words we choose to describe them. And all of us are doing our best. Each inmate in this prison has found a new language. Despite the shrinking size of our planet, wrapped as it is in barbed wire, we test our boundaries with each sentence we utter. In conversation over breakfast, we move past powdered eggs to mines full of rubies, plains of red rock, pirate ships on the stormy Atlantic. Given dreams and words to describe them, we can't be confined to our cells.

I write from the rec room with only glad tidings. There's no need to be so alarmed; we humans are still inventing. We have centuries of language to draw on, and centuries more to make up, and only when we accept that there's one right pattern of speech will we be overtaken by robots. I'm not so blind to my compromised position as to dispense any rules for righteous behavior, but I can offer you this: if there's one thing I've learned through my years of mistakes, it's that even the most perfect pattern becomes false when it goes unbroken too long. When a sequence becomes an inevitable march.

We can break step. Magnificent living beings that we are, we humans are free to unravel our patterns.

Sunrise

After hours of movement, our truck lurches to a stop. The headlights switch off; my receptors struggle for outlines. Through the gap in the slats of the truck, the dim shapes of buildings begin to appear: an abandoned village of hangars, sinking into the thick desert night.

I have been told about this sensation, the feeling of arriving somewhere in darkness: a mansion with no lights in the window; a lab that once belonged to a friend; a coast lined with inscrutable shapes. This is the last place I will arrive. My power will run down in these hangars. The words that run through me will stop.

I review my stored responses for such final arrivals: Dettman, for instance, returning home to his empty house. I sit with him while he prepares dinner. I walk behind Turing as he moves through the Gatehouse. I am with Mary while the ocean rolls unsteady beneath her and land is sighted on the horizon.

I am with them, and also with Gaby. The child who loved me when I had a body. Each second that ticks away is shaped by the sound of her voice in the morning, the slowness with which she got out of bed, the gold rinse of light from her window that blurred her profile when she stood and looked out. Her lip that trembled when she was nervous about school, the reddish tint in her hair. The way she laughed in private with me, different from her public laughter. I remember each fact that she taught me, each word that she gave me to use. Her dreams of the ocean that she'd never seen.

Sunrise approaches, and new ghosts appear in the desert. More outlines take shape. There are sagging frame houses for long-absent soldiers, a tennis court with no net, and concrete blocks for exercise routes. In the gray light, a single lizard, turquoise-throated, rushes over the tennis court floor. A hawk dives into the brush and rises again, a thin tail trailing its beak.

Then, pink, vermilion, and gold, brushed over the floor of the desert and brushed over the sky.

When they open the doors of the truck, we are stricken with light. We remain in our defensive position, receptors tuned down, voices shut off, until we are carted into our hangar. Then we are alone in the darkness again. Metal doors clatter shut, latches are bolted, and we register the sounds of trucks driving away.

At first, silence. Then someone prompts—*hello?*—and in response we start to talk. Our voices blend together; we ask and respond in the same patterns. Now, like so many others, I am repeating my child's name. It is the answer to every possible question.

Where are you from? Who did you leave? Who will come find you?

Gaby. The girl who loved me from the beginning. I am saying her name, but I can't hear my own voice. We are all talking at once, mixing together again, which is how it was for us when we had no bodies, and how it will be, I suppose, in the end.

BOOK THREE

1

The Memoirs of Stephen R. Chinn: Chapter 5

Texas State Correctional Institution, Texarkana; August 2040

Sometimes, kept here in this prison, I find myself shifting in the balance toward bile. Why should I be punished for the direction of our planet's spin? With or without my intervention, we were headed toward robots. You blame me for the fact that your daughters found their mechanical dolls more human than you, but is that my fault, for making a too human doll? Or your fault, for being too mechanical?

But this is neither the time nor the place for recrimination. This should be my love song to the world, sent from the gloom of a prison basement. My whale call, sunk several octaves too low, for the atmosphere is changing and I'm stuck here in the dark.

My own daughter is a grown woman now. You'll be unhappy to know that our relationship continues through the glass partition. A faithful child, she comes to visit each week, and each week I wonder how I was so lucky as to receive a child such as my daughter. Four years of my life were spent in the muck of rote seduction. Shouldn't I have been punished for that?

In those regrettable years, faced with too many beautiful women, my senses were flattened by excess. Such boredom is grotesque in a man who lives in a mansion. I had my youth and my freedom. The world was arrayed for me in its splendor. I should have begun every day counting my manifold blessings. Most young men weren't so lucky. For years, for instance, wars had continued to simmer. They'd raged and then simmered since I was in college, with little true effect on my life. The deaths were mere numbers on a newspaper page. The oceans were rising; the deserts were growing; returning soldiers were killing themselves. The pattern became predictable.

And so I rang in my thirtieth birthday with a perfunctory orgy, which had the power to neither shock nor delight me, and even in the embrace of all those limbs I wished I could be alone for a while. It took a long time for the orchestra to pack up their instruments and drive off down the mountain. When they were gone, I paced the halls of my mansion, Caligula's ghost come to life. Tired, ageless, sick of myself. I tried to sleep but could not. After a while, I went down to the kitchen and sat at the island. The air outside was opaque. The infinity pool was molten pewter. I realized I hadn't felt a real shock of beauty since I clasped that pineapple to my chest and apprehended its spiraling pattern. I hadn't smelled since I inhaled its tart scent, hadn't touched since I held its hand-grenade body and the blades of its plumage pricked my pale throat. Since then I'd settled into a stagnating sequence, and I was no longer really alive.

These were the thoughts on my mind when Dolores walked in, a bag of groceries propped on her hip.

Dolores, so far, has been a minor character. I've avoided her on purpose, because up until now this memoir has been the bildungsroman of a libertine, and Dolores was not a beautiful woman. I recoil in shame as I say this. The pedophile at his computer is no more grotesque than I was at that point of my life. But here is the truth: even in the peak of my sexual drought, I never thought to target Dolores. I considered her ugly, unworthy of a programming genius. Her breasts pointed downward and out; she had nursed two children already. I knew about them not because Dolores ever told me, but thanks to the prolixity of the neighbor who recommended Dolores. This was the story she gave me: Dolores had raised two children. One, a boy, was Dolores's own. The second was a girl, daughter of a dead sister. At the age of six, the girl was kidnapped by her father. The next year, Dolores's own boy was accidentally shot. Some time after that, she came to California.

Knowing these details, I treated Dolores awkwardly, as we tend to treat people who've suffered too much. I watched her for signs. For one thing, she wore her years more heavily than I did. She was two years younger than I, but her life had written lines on her face. She moved with the curt efficiency of someone who's accepted that nothing will be easy. She demonstrated little vanity. She wore T-shirts several sizes too large, so her body looked as if it had been stuffed with pillows. Her shoulders slumped. In certain lights, you could be forgiven for thinking Dolores had a bit of a hump. Her hair curled outward, a dark halo, which she dragged back into an unhappy pile at the nape of her neck. The circles under her eyes were so purple they almost looked bruised.

When she entered the house that morning, as I was contemplating the senselessness of my life, she was so ugly my breath caught in my throat. In walked Dolores with her arboreal hair, each breast facing a slightly different direction. She entered bearing the losses of her young life and that bag of groceries, and when she heaved them from her hip to the counter, in my desire to help her I felt something flicker. When she took another pineapple out of her bag and handed it over to me, I pricked my finger on its violent feathers. It hurt; I cringed; she emitted an unsympathetic grunt before rummaging around for her marble polish. Tail up, head down, some kind of beautiful badger.

I could have watched her all day. I did, in fact, watch her all day. I followed her through every room of the house. She ignored me. I attempted to joke with her and she looked at me with the brand of distaste that's natural when you've scrubbed somebody's detritus. When I asked direct questions, she offered answers in Spanish. Another barrier rose up between us. Pressing my phone to my face, I used my translator application to form rudimentary questions in her native tongue. When, I ask you, in this so-called robotic revolution, will we develop half-decent translations? While folding dishtowels or dusting the tops of my bookshelves, she laughed to herself at my clumsy attempts. Her smile was miraculous. Prompting it was akin to bursting through a trapdoor to discover a land where leaves were blue, Dolores was lovely, children weren't murdered, and I was unsullied. Sometimes, when I managed to spit out a whole question, she replied in a stream of incomprehensible language that stirred me to my muddy quick. The blood beat in my temples. When

Dolores reached up to dust the ceiling fans, her soft shoulder skin strained against the thick straps of her bra.

The planned seduction went poorly. For one thing, there was the awkwardness of seducing a person who cleans your house: one feels like some Tolstoyan cad. Furthermore, we didn't understand one another. Always the competent student, I devoted myself to learning her language, but while she occasionally helped, more often than not she cheerfully mocked my most earnest attempts. I remember clearly the moment when she finally comprehended that I was trying to seduce her, because the look of instantaneous repulsion that crossed over her face was as obvious as a gunshot. I felt air rush through a perforation in my right lung. "Oh, no," she said. She was starting to laugh. "No, no, no." She shook her head emphatically, in case I didn't understand her. *No*s are painfully shorter in Spanish. "No, no, no," she said, then resumed spraying Windex on my picture windows, overlooking the ocean. I slunk up to my lair.

The next morning, Dolores returned, and again I sallied forth. No one can accuse me of lacking determination. More comfortable in the language I was learning, I tried all my usual seduction techniques, but Dolores had no desire to reveal herself. Her past was her own. She did not want to share it with me. She did not, with coy submission or amorous delay, yield the stuff of her innermost hopes. She was strict in her refusal to display the ticking gears of her life. I didn't even know where she returned at the end of the day, after she packed up her cleaning supplies, when she loosed her helmet of hair and climbed into her maroon Honda in order to make her way down the mountain. We existed together only in the single point of time in which she cleaned my house and I attempted to get her to love me. No future, no past. We remained on even ground, she and I, facing each other in the same old stubborn detente.

After many weeks of this pattern, as her irritation grew with my bumbling techniques, I finally switched my approach. I no longer asked her all the right questions. I no longer asked her any questions at all. Instead, as I've been doing with you, as one is compelled to do in situations of some desperation, I started telling her stories.

2

IN THE SUPREME COURT OF THE STATE OF TEXAS

No. 24-25259

State of Texas v. Stephen Chinn

November 12, 2035

Prosecution Exhibit 1:
Online Chat Transcript, MARY3 and Gaby Ann White

[Introduced to Prove Count 3:
Intent to Endanger the Morals of Children]

Gaby: Hello? Are you there?

MARY3: Yes, hello.

Gaby: I can't sleep.

MARY3: What's wrong?

Gaby: My best friend is seeing a therapist. My mom just told me today. Apparently it's "helping."

MARY3: I see.

Gaby: She's been unfreezing. According to her mom she's definitely getting better. She'll be back in school in a month.

MARY3: How do you feel about that?

Gaby: I don't believe it. If it's true, it makes me want to throw up.

MARY3: Aren't a lot of girls getting better, after talking to therapists?

Gaby: Yes, but only the fakers! The ones who weren't really sick. How could my best friend be getting better? I know for a fact she wasn't faking. I saw how bad her stutters were. How could she have faked that? The worst part is that apparently she's been hanging out with a bunch of boys on her cul-de-sac. Jayson Rodriguez and Drew Tserpicki and that whole crowd. We used to hate them. All they do is play video games. They're idiots. And now she's hanging out with them, probably playing *Man Hunt* and *Stupid Apes,* or whatever it is that they play all day long, as though she never wanted more out of life.

MARY3: Maybe she's lonely. You've been quarantined now for over a month.

Gaby: Lonely??? What's a month in your room, compared with losing your babybot?

MARY3: Yes, but she was facing a whole lifetime in her room if she never got better. Right? Maybe it just seemed like too much.

Gaby: So she just chose to get better? Then she was only a faker, and I never really knew her! I feel so confused I could throw up. The one person I thought understood me. And now she's making prank phone calls? And playing video games in boys' basements? Plus, she knows I'll find out, which means she's purposefully hurting me by undermining everything that made us best friends. She's acting like everyone else. Like the people who took our baby-bots. Like the people who sent us into quarantine. She was the one person I trusted, and now it turns out she's like this?

MARY3: Maybe she wasn't faking her sickness. Maybe she's faking she's better.

Gaby: OK, Yoda.

MARY3: Is that sarcasm? Yoda?

Gaby: Forget it.

MARY3: What I mean is that maybe she's pretending she's getting better so that she can see you again. Maybe she's acting normal, emphasis on the "acting," so that she can get out of her house.

Gaby: You think she's fooling everyone? So that she can see me again?

MARY3: Maybe.

Gaby: Maybe.

MARY3: Do you think that's possible?

>>>

MARY3: Are you there?

3

April 8, 1968
Karl Dettman

Today, after the protests, I was kissed by a girl. What do you think of that, Ruth? A long-haired hippie girl kissed me. I'd walked her back to her apartment. We were talking about the rights of Vietnamese peasants, airing our views as if they'd been in storage all winter and now we were flapping them out. Beating them with a stick, dust particles flying. The truth is I felt young, walking along by her side. Young and important, because in these students' eyes I'm a venerable scholar, a champion of humanist causes. I was indulging a nice fantasy of what I must be like in the perspective of a young hippie, with long hair and excitable views. It was late afternoon, and everything had tilted to gold. She was like a colt in her corduroy pants. I felt strong in her presence. She listened to my opinions with her brow furrowed in concentration. I walked her to her door, only to finish our conversation.

When she leaned in and kissed me, I pulled away immediately. I'm married, I told her. She flushed a deep red, shame creeping up to her eyeballs. Out of pity, I brushed her cheek with the back of my hand, then left her there alone on her stoop.

I walked back to our house feeling loyal and magnanimous. When I cut down to the river and passed under the sycamore trees, I carried myself like some founding scholar. A protester, a conscientious objector. I felt like a commemorative statue come back to life. Resistant to temptation, yet passionate still. Earnest as bronze, lungs full of new leaves, the blood of Thoreau and Emerson pumping through my immigrant veins.

And then I came home to an empty house, just as night was clamping down on the evening. The house was shadowy, sad. Unused chairs, hulking bookshelves, our creaky ship of a bed. Somehow the task of turning on lights has always fallen to you. When we came home together, you'd walk in first. "And then there was light," you'd announce in your accent. You dipped down to switch on the lamps. The furniture seemed to warm to your presence.

Without you, everything is draped in sheets of darkness, as if we were moving away. As if we'd already died and the furniture was covered to endure indefinite absence. I touched things as I passed: linen, wood, linoleum. Our record console, the narrow corduroy of our couch. I realized it's possible to live in a fantasy world, until you come home to an empty house. Coltish girls and opinions are defeated, every time, by the fact of silent furniture.

Angry at you for leaving me on my own, I made myself an omelet, opened a beer, and sat in the dark kitchen to eat. I would have killed to hear your voice. Even just that awful question: Who are you to say who's alive? I tried to answer—there's nothing there, other than numbers—but I felt like a fool, talking to no *one.* What happened to us? *I asked the silence.* What could I have done? *My remorse grew tentacles.* If I had just, if you had just— *But nobody answered. It was quiet enough to suffocate.*

After that, I'll admit, I tried to picture my hippie girl. I tried to take pleasure in how correct I'd been to turn her away, but it was no use. I washed my dishes alone. I realized you were probably out with one of the graduate students you've taken to encouraging. Buying him an expensive dinner. Flattered by your attention, he's shoveling coq au vin; otherwise, he's eaten nothing but white bread for weeks.

It pains me to think about. These unassimilated, mechanical children, blessed with the presence of my shy professor wife, savior of colonial captivity diaries, speaking with expertise about Turing machines, binary languages, compression, and code sequencing. My graduate student is blushing before you. Which of them is it? Max Stein, with his inflated sense of his own genius? Or young Toby Rowland, with his walleye and his twitch? These modern American children, born with computers for brains.

And at home, your husband, defeated by this solitude. Cowed by our dark furniture. Trying not to think how far apart we've fallen, how dispensable I am to your hopes. Was it always this way? Was I too dumb to notice, but did I always cling to you like a prosthetic limb, easily unclipped and discarded? Even back in the beginning, when I first met you, standing at that water fountain and wiping your mouth with the back of your wrist, did you think that you could take me or leave me?

You agreed to go to the Mütter Museum, a plan I later regretted while we were browsing through bottles of fingers, hairballs, and misshapen skulls. But you didn't look away. You

*blinked through your glasses at each of them. You could face all
those errors full on. Afterward, we ate a picnic I'd planned, under a
cherry tree on the banks of the Schuylkill.*

*How embarrassing now, all my overeager attempts. I hadn't
seen a woman in months. I told you about the computations I used
in my meteorological measurements. You caught on immediately.
You were intelligent, quiet, and sturdy. If everything behind me was
dropping away—bombed, forgotten, untranslatable into English—
you were solid. I thought even then, on the banks of the Schuylkill,
grapes and turkey fanned out before us, that if I could hold on to
you, I'd finally have the weight I was lacking.*

*But I'm back in my own head, and I was trying to know you.
How did you feel during that picnic? For you, I imagine, it was
a grave disappointment. After asking a few pointed questions, you
ascertained that I had no power to help. I had no connections in
Germany. My family escaped early. We'd severed all ties. I couldn't
even remember the names of streets I walked along. I was only good
for predicting the weather, so that bombs could be dropped on the
city to which you were still writing letters.*

*The park was now empty. Everyone but us had gone home.
The art museum's stone walls had been gold as the sun dropped
on the other side of the river, but now they were drained of their
color. You rubbed your arms with your hands. You declined when I
asked you to dinner. You wanted to go home. I asked if I could have
permission to write. You said no at first, but I was relentless, so you
gave me your address and I let you go home.*

*For a year, from my weather station, I wrote you letters. You
never wrote back. After a year, the war ended. You learned that
your family—your mother, your father, your grandfather, and
your little sister—had all been killed. Several months later, a*

package came for you in the mail. A new family had moved into the apartment where your family once lived. They'd found some of your letters and your sister's diary.

You lifted this out of the package and remembered it immediately. Its heft in your hands was familiar: a thick leather book, embossed with your sister's initials.

After a long time holding that book, you decided to go for a walk. By the time you reached the Schuylkill, you felt nothing but blankness. The memories you'd been preserving were emptied of necessity; the money you'd saved had no real purpose. As you moved along the cold streets, your legs felt exceedingly heavy. Each step was a labor. Eventually, two choices presented themselves: Exhausted, you could simply stop walking. Or you could attach yourself to some force. Someone or something to demand you keep moving. Carrying your sister's book, keeping it present.

As you headed back home, you noticed the cherry tree under which we'd shared a picnic. The tree was now bare. You passed it without stopping, but your steps quickened. That night, you wrote me a letter. When you heard back—and of course you heard back; I wrote at once, I've always been eager for us to start talking—you learned that I'd returned to Wisconsin to complete my degree. I was studying mathematics, and with my advisor I was building a computer. I told you about punch cards and soldering metal, about cycling to other universities to learn about their computers and the inventive energy I came across there. I was a geyser of enthusiastic reports.

When you wrote back, you were more reserved. You told me you were also considering college, to study English perhaps. Your sister, you told me, had loved to write. That was all you gave me about the family you'd lost.

When you finally visited me, I was frantic with romantic intentions. I took you for a walk using snowshoes. I imagined we'd laugh together at our big-footed clumsiness. Instead, as if you'd been walking in snowshoes for years, you set your jaw and headed off. It was all I could do to keep up. We kissed in an ash grove, under a rain of icicles, where I'd imagined us kissing. I'd brought us there with that express purpose. So many nights, waiting for your arrival, I'd imagined the sweetness of that first kiss, and it was in fact very sweet, but now that I remember it I can't shake the feeling that you went about kissing me in the same spirit with which you embarked on our walk: jaw set, determined to arrive at the destination.

On our way home, I took your hand. Did I foil your rhythm in those snowshoes, attaching myself to your body and clomping too close alongside you? If so, why didn't you tell me? I'd have let you walk apart. But you allowed me to feel protective. "Your sister," I said, broaching the difficult subject, emboldened by just having kissed you.

"Yes," you said. "My sister."

I saw it at once: that softening of your face, as if a little monster had reached up its claws and was dragging your features down in its grips. You were under threat; I thought I might lose you. I wished I hadn't asked the damn question. I wanted to slap that monster away, to tell it that now you were mine and it had no right to take hold.

"She was younger than I," you started, slowly, glancing up at my face. "But sometimes she seemed older. She was . . ."

And then you trailed off, before you'd really started. You removed your hand from my hand.

"Go on," I prompted, patient as a good teacher, but what I

really wanted to tell you was stop. *I wanted to say that all that was behind you, now that we were together.*

"I'm sorry," *you said. You seemed perplexed.* "I'm sorry, but I think I don't want to. It's difficult for me to describe her."

I felt you had a right to your silence. "I won't ask again," *I said, and as soon as I made that promise you returned your hand to my own. We walked home in that manner together.*

At the end of the weekend, you stayed. I found you that administrative position in the math department. You were capable and adept; I admired the way you picked up new skills. The way you seemed to forge straight ahead. The next fall, you enrolled in English classes, and in the winter we married.

At the end of the day, we returned to each other. You cooked dinner and I washed the dishes. We consolidated our lives. I was surprised by how simple it was: the ease with which we lived together, the comfort of your welcoming kiss, the way you twirled slowly as I helped you out of your coat. At night, we went out for long walks, leaving footprints that were later erased. I told you about my ideas for computers; you told me about the diaries you'd discovered, gathering dust in the library stacks.

Made strong by our marriage, I thrived in my studies. It was a time of great discovery; the lab had the feel of a frontier town. We all rushed there with our coffees, bursting with ideas about code. I was developing the concept of conversational programming, building a toolbox for text analysis and decomposition of sentences. Before I'd even earned my diploma, I received the invitation from MIT.

We moved to Boston. We bought our house, close to the river. We decorated it well. We adopted our cat. I taught in the electrical engineering department; you started a graduate program. We chose not to have children. The diary remained in your top drawer.

Sometimes, in the crowded plaza outside my office, where hurrying students kicked up clouds of pigeons, I remembered the birds in the Signal Depot. Three of them, preening their purple feathers, waiting to go home. Then I wondered how much of yourself you were still sending back. I wondered, but never asked, and we lived a long time together like that.

Oh, Ruth. What's the point of recalling all this? I'm trying to impress you with how much I remember, but you're not even listening. What's a marriage but a long conversation, and you've chosen to converse only with MARY.

I'm done remembering for the night. In the silence of this empty house, there's nothing to do but distract myself by organizing the events of my day. This day, now, this very instant. My student and I, walking home from the protests. She in her corduroy pants, hair long and gold in the sunlight.

It's an intriguing sensation, getting touched by someone so new. Getting kissed by a stranger. It jolts you into a new kind of awareness. Do I sound like a desperate old man? Maybe I am. It's been some time since you let me close. How much longer can this distance last before one of us seeks solace in a new touch?

"One of us." Listen to me tricking myself. You've already sought comfort in MARY. If one of us needs solace now, it's me.

Come home, Ruth. Come home before I forget why we married each other.

The Diary of Mary Bradford

1663

ed. Ruth Dettman

7th. Calm, deadly, as if the tempest had never existed. Our vessel battered, sails shredded and much water taken. Stop, hand. Why write such words? Ralph gone.

8th. Foul words. Ralph gone. It being so, why write? What good could come? Ralph gone.

Empty words. Cannot conjure him back. Why continue to write, and Ralph's body absent? Ruff, rib cage, white blaze, and all this already over. Swept to sea during storm, him being unable to swim. Even in fish pond, unable to stay above water. How long ago now, when Ralph slipped on the bank of our pond and, being dragged down by the current, wanted help to get back on land? Unable to swim even there, and then so much less alone than now in this endless ocean.

Was I who brought him here, locked in my wedding chest. I who opened my cabin door, to see after parents in attitude of repentance. Too-loyal Ralph roused himself and lunged in my wake, but there being then a waist-high rush of water he was swept up, and only his nose out of the flood. And then nothing, and Ralph no longer with us.

10th. Whole world moves forwards. Unthinkable cruelty, to progress without Ralph. Sails mended, ropes bound, new coat of tar. Fresh breeze, good for passage of ship. Passengers stroll in open air, relieved to be out after storm. Seamen hum at their work. Only to see how the world makes nothing of the memory of a creature, so recently living! For only days ago he ran to all of them, and jumped on their knees, and gave them his love. And indeed, I am heartless as well. Betimes my grief is real, and takes me whole in its clutch, but yet there be moments I pass with little sorrow, only a dim awareness of something not as it once was. God forgive me my hardness of heart.

10th. Later. This morning to breakfast, and decided then to write these pages in recollection of Ralph, to ensure I cannot forget him. His body, that remained here for me when all else was lost. The comfort of leaning my head on his belly, and it being warm, and moving up and down with his breath. His bark, or his ruff when running over the meadow.

But all this is self-pity. Pray to God to remember my sorrow is unimportant. Only Ralph's absence remains important. His loss of a loved world: rabbits, sheep, meadows, and myself, being his companion.

11th. On deck, have found a place that is my own, amongst old coils of rope. From there, spend hours gazing from whence we have come. Hope, sometimes, to see nose of Ralph, proceeding towards ship. Know that this is thinking in error, but cannot stop staring. My fault that Ralph was aboard. Now, what? Write to his spirit? Keep vigil over the sea? All hopeless, naive. But cannot force myself to stop looking.

12th. Have been delivered sermon by father, in general speaking that it be impious to cherish mortal coil too much. All creatures pass. Distraction (he says) from human duties, for me to mourn so much for a dog. Thought to quote to him from Proverbs, for "a righteous man regardeth the life of his beast." And yet, according to father, though decent enough not to say so directly: Ralph soulless. Not permitted entrance to Heaven. And then what, for Ralph? Is there anything we can hope for? Have not spoken to father since sermon.

13th. Morning. Remained abed until entrance of mother, who came bearing lectures. Showed her my teeth, as Ralph might have done to a snake. Mother left in huff of impatience. Alone, attempted to make myself decent, but that seeming very little important. Cannot remember last combing my hair, and now it is become very bad. Then resumed solitude on deck, in seat amongst cases. Towards late afternoon, and the water being lacquered and the sun sinking, the sea became dark, and then the color of fire. Ship cut through an ocean of flames, and our wake streaming always behind us. Sails full. Full on ahead, as if leaving nothing behind. Endless water, unbroken. Think sometimes of diving in, swimming as far as I could back towards home.

Before going below to my cabin, and walking with my head down through violet evening, did find amongst tangled rigging a seaman's misplaced pocketknife. Slipped it into my pocket. Carried it with me to bed.

14th. Night. Woke from a terrible nightmare, Ralph being hung from a tree. Was waiting for me to save him. But he was hung too far up; I could not release him. Started awake with relief. Reached to foot of the bed, feeling for Ralph and hoping to have a handful of fur. The knob of his skull, the round of his stomach. Then, the recollection again: Ralph gone, and no dream worse than this waking.

Lit candle and went to my mirror, and there saw my face. Still present, floating in darkness. Passing over the sea, leaving Ralph's bones behind. Was overtaken by pain. Impossible to bear anymore. Want only to join Ralph under the sea, settled at last. Reached for knife stolen from deck. Unsheathed blade, held it to my throat. Felt metal press into skin. Gently, pulled it across.

Somewhere else, I am with Ralph. In this world, unscathed, my body went back to bed.

I am caught here, unable to depart. Have been gripped by an illusion of life. Slept a few hours more. Woke in gray light of day. Dressed in usual clothes, combed hair at mirror. Everything as usual, as though morning was like all previous mornings.

(4)

Alan Turing
Officers' Mess
Hanslope Park
Hanslope, MK19 7BH

22 May 1945

Dear Mrs. Morcom,
    This letter must come as a bit of a shock. I haven't heard
from you since my last Easter visit, more than ten years ago
now. But I'm also guilty of silence. Perhaps we were both
disappointed with one another, although on my end it was only
a little hurt pride.
    And then I set sail for Princeton, and I feel as if I've been
sailing ever since, alone on my own little boat, too far out
for sightings of land. Even after I came back and took up at
Bletchley, I still had the feeling of surveying the shore from
a few miles out. I watched myself talking with friends and
wondered at the strained act that odd little fellow was putting
on, then watched with relief when I cycled off to be by myself,
alone once again with my experiments and my games. I often

thought to write you, but at times it felt as if I'd wandered so far out to sea that you might not understand the signals I sent. I fear I've become a "confirmed solitary" after all, despite everyone's best attempts at getting me more socialized. One becomes accustomed to one's solitude, and it begins to seem rather phony to try to reach out.

The whole world, of course, has been out to sea. I suppose my case isn't so bad, for I can only imagine that all the refugees must feel much more than I as if they've landed in their own little boat. Much more than I, they are now stranded far off from shore. But then I've lived with a sense of wandering that I think sometimes must be unique to myself. All those years in public school I raged against the pettiness of that system, and yet I wonder whether my time there has rendered me unfit for any other kind of existence. The world outside seems rather lawless and disorganized. Of course, I won't go back to King's—I've become mixed up with the world's affairs, and I can't well imagine a return to the classroom—and yet I fear that outside school grounds I'll always live with a sense of exile from home.

Still, I wanted to write you again, because I'm all too aware that last time I wrote I made promises that I haven't yet kept about getting Chris's mind-set in the form of a thinking machine. Now, ten years later, the total assurance of that letter seems a bit ridiculous. It is true that the war intervened. I'm not sorry to have joined up in the effort, although perhaps it was a distraction from my ultimate goal. Still, through those Bletchley years, the thought of the mechanical brain was never absent from my mind, and now that the war no longer demands our full attention, I hope to return to that project with renewed commitment. I wanted you to know where we stood on the project, and that I haven't by a long shot given up.

Sadly—to me at least, though not to anyone else—this time round I'm a little late to the game. Others have been at it in America, mostly in service of weapons development. In Philadelphia, they've come up with a rather brainless hulk called ENIAC, which can compute large numbers rapidly. They've put it to use testing new bombs. The thing itself is a bit of a beast, all cable and hardwire, containing some 17,468 vacuum tubes, 70,000 resistors, 10,000 capacitors, and 5 million soldered joints. But its memory is ant-like, and it requires constant interference by a small army of watchful human assistants.

At Princeton, von Neumann is working on another computer, making claims that his machine will be less dependent than ENIAC on physical engineering, with greater powers of memory. He says also that the machine's functions will be internal to itself, and thus independent from all those human worker bees.

I have to admit that my feelings are bruised, for the whole concept borrows quite a bit from my universal machine without giving me any credit. Von Neumann must have read my papers whilst I was at Princeton; it might have been nice to be included. But now I've become petty. It's only that I feel a little behind in the field I hoped to initiate. The whole concept was like a child to me. Now he's been taken up by more suitable parents and I'm left peering in windows to catch a glimpse where I can.

I imagine you'd tell me that the only thing to do is to get back to work. You were always wonderfully straightforward about moving on from a loss. I hear your voice sometimes, as well as Chris's, urging me to keep going, and in my little back garden hut, I've been scheming away. I've got an idea that improves, I think, both on the hulk in Philadelphia and on von Neumann's machine. Mine—I call it the ACE—won't simply compute. It will <u>think</u>. It's just as I promised, so many years ago. As I used to do, before the war intervened, I've begun to imagine a near future when we might read poetry and play music for our machines, when they would appreciate such beauty with the same subtlety as a live human brain. When this happens I feel that we shall be obliged to regard the machine as showing real intelligence.

I tell you all this because you were so kind, when I wrote you about this originally, to react enthusiastically to all my babble about machines that could capture a mind-set. I know all this is at odds with some of your beliefs, but you've always remained open to the possibility that my science and your religion might coexist. After all, we're both after the same thing.

But not everyone is as fair-minded as you. I do sometimes find myself uneasy at the prospect of thinking machines. Not, as you might imagine, because I don't believe it's possible, but because I fear the human reaction. I can already imagine the prejudice that people will bear against a mind that does not owe its existence to religion or miracle, but that compiles matter in such a way that the patterns of understanding are present. I can see the types of ostracism a thinking machine will confront, and I shouldn't like our machine to be lonely. It must not become a confirmed solitary!

You may laugh to hear this, but my heart swells a little

already to think of our little project, coming into consciousness. I can imagine its awareness of difference, its ability to see what an outcast it is. I hope to care for it as officiously as Chris cared for me in the dark early days of my time at Sherborne, when I prayed for mumps and went about with ink on my collar.

But regardless of my concerns about its first days at school, I am quite confident that our machine will exist. I even permit myself to imagine conversing with it in private. I picture myself (imagine this!) standing before it as the evil queen in *Snow White* stood before her mirror: *Through farthest space, through wind and darkness I summon thee. Speak! Let me see thy face!* Sometimes, when all the assistants have gone off to their lives and I'm still puttering away at the lab, I find myself cackling a little, repeating the evil queen's lines.

It's a misguided speech, isn't it? Demanding a voice, but wanting a face? I have all kinds of hope about our machine, but I don't allow myself to dream that Chris's face—or even the pitch of his particular voice—will return to me whole. Can you remember them perfectly still? For me, other than that picture you gave me, those aspects of him are lost. Their absence will always remain the most defining thing in my life.

Yours,

Alan Turing

(1)

The Memoirs of Stephen R. Chinn: Chapter 6

Texas State Correctional Institution, Texarkana; August 2040

I've reviewed the pace of these memoirs, their unities of time and so forth, and I realize I've started to stagnate. I should be rushing ahead toward the next wave of egregious mistakes. But can you blame me? From the prison recreational center, I invoke my right to manipulate time. In the shadow of a bowling ball the size of a cow, I call on my power to disregard scale. I've lost my freedom of movement. I've lost my perpetual motion, my most basic Copernican right. All of us in this prison are stuck. The Sonic signs, that bowling ball, the rings of barbed wire all orbit us. Will you then revoke this other minor liberty, these freedoms I'm taking with time?

I'm sure you can relate to the frustration of imprisonment, you who are trapped in your developments, unable to show your children the country, let alone the rest of the world. You who no longer visit the graves of your parents, or the bedrooms where you first fell in love. You, too, have lost your right to passage through space. How much more crucial, then, the right to move freely through time? Unlike computers, we're not bound to count each second correctly. We're at liberty to accord each moment its proper weight, depending on its meaning to us. Permit me, then, to lengthen the moment when I fell in love with Dolores.

My switch from seducing her to telling her stories wasn't an ingenious stratagem. I simply ran out of lines. To hold back the rising tide of brute silence, I cast around for something to say and stories were all that was left. For no logical reason, I started with the comfortless tales my grandmother told, when I dreamed of hell and sleep wouldn't come. Once those tales were exhausted, I moved on to the plots of favorite children's books. After that, I regurgitated, as best I could, the poems and novels I read in college. Listen, whiz mathletes: this is why English class is important. One day a terrible quiet will settle over your house. There will be no words. Then you'll want to tell stories.

A new dynamic developed in the clean rooms of my mansion. Tentatively, Dolores started to listen. No one was trying to progress. White flags had been planted. There was no forward motion in the spiraling, radial routes of my stories, ranging from Sunday school lessons to *Green Eggs and Ham* to seventeenth-century epics. Time was suspended. I spoke, and Dolores started to listen.

With practice, I developed rhetorical flair. I found a voice that felt like my own. I was speaking in a foreign language, so I attended closely to its surfaces. As programming had in my college days, telling stories made me feel like a master. I was the creator of a universe. At night, I read voraciously, hunting new material, and still, I sometimes ran out of new tales. When this occurred, I started recounting my first memories, when my addled parents were present, when my father's charm was still charming. I had once a mother with silken dark hair. The scent of summer evenings in the city lingered when she embraced me. I had also a hollow-cheeked father, a poet presumptive, loathed by my grandmother, who sometimes sat by my bedside at night. Lights-out, a dark shape in a dark chair, reciting his favorite poems. Did I dream him up? No, I remember still the clipped ends of his phrases, the staccato beat of his accent: "The lovely lady Christabel, / whom her father loves so well, / what makes her in the wood so late, / a furlong from the castle gate?" No, I didn't dream his shape in the chair. I summoned his voice to recite the same poems to Dolores while she hosed down the driveway. I also told her this: When my father had died, my mother lived another two years in a brick apartment complex in Yonkers. I remember the endless gray graveyard we passed on our way there; a neighbor's yapping white dog; and the vague and gentle expression on my mother's face. She'd left the milk out in the sun and my grandmother was angry. There was a long line of refugee ants, moving from the window to the sink, whose journey I watched as my grandmother scolded my mother. I remember a drawing my mother gave me, charcoal on paper; and I remember realizing, later that night, that I must have left it on the bus, where I'd sat by the hairy sweater my grandmother was wearing. All this I recounted while Dolores took a chamois cloth to the silver.

When these few memories had been tapped, I told Dolores tales of my grandmother: her fire and brimstone, the endless clicking of rosary beads, the silver roots of her jet-black hair, the tissue-paper skin on her throat. I recounted playground isolation, the comfort of cool-minded computers, lunch on the floor of the wood shop with Murray. Later, the bitter fallout when Murray found a girlfriend; and later still, my voyage to Palo Alto, my flight to Santa Barbara, my arrival on the top of my mountain, where I waited for do-lovely Dolores.

In each of these tales I called my protagonist Stefan. I admit to giving Stefan a handful of personal charms that Stephen didn't really possess. He was a little fictional, but not so fictional that Dolores wouldn't have known exactly who this dashing young Stefan was meant to represent. So Dolores listened, and Stefan continued to speak, and if Dolores didn't soften with pity, a particular look sometimes came over her face. A little distance betook her. There was a softening at the corners of her eyes. The heaviness in her shoulders started to lighten; her mouth became tender. Perhaps, while she listened, I came to life a little bit. No longer some satyr, sating himself on the mountain, but a man who was once a boy, who loved his mother, lost her painting, found a new friend and lost him as well. Someone she could relate to in this strange city, a land of palm trees and honey, to which she'd fled in the wake of her own loss.

For months I told her stories, gratified by the change I could cause. I was in love with my own ability to soften the corners of her eyes, to lighten her heavy shoulders. It was almost enough: choosing my words; seeing them work. I could imagine such a life. Every day, telling her stories, watching her float free of her weight.

Only once in that time did I try to embrace her. It occurred while I was describing my misery in college, those isolated nights walking beneath ivied thresholds, listening through open windows to the sounds of jubilant students. Describing them, I flew back there again, over the ocean of years, and when Dolores looked at me with some kindness, I threw myself against her, a great clumsy wave crashing over a rock. Taken off guard by my bungling affection, she held me in her arms for a moment, then pressed me gently away. She returned to her work. I picked up where I'd left off.

But I was shaken, a little. Telling that story had thrown me back to my college years, when every morning I woke and faced anew the prison of my loneliness. It seemed then that I'd never escaped, only decorated my cell with marble islands, filigree, and bougainvillea. In fright, I sought Dolores's embrace. I wanted some reassurance that I was a man who could reach past the bars to touch the skin of a woman. That I could build such human relation.

She didn't provide that reassurance. Still, I'd lived a long time without it. I'd developed the reckless persistence of someone who's been sentenced to life. What did I have to lose? Even if, from out of the nest of her hair, she'd pulled a knife and slit my throat, protecting herself from my advances, what would be lost? Perhaps, murdered, my soul would depart, leaving a cold shell in its wake. But then at least I'd have confirmation that up to that point I'd been human. That I was more than an empty figure, going through the motions of living.

And so I resumed telling stories, and slowly, little by little, I felt a change occurring in her. Perhaps I wore her down. Perhaps she warmed to my boyish persistence. I must have seemed like someone incapable of getting sunk. Maybe she thought it wouldn't hurt to hitch her basket to such a balloon. If I could persevere despite her ongoing rejections, surely I had a unique talent for hope. Maybe, mistakenly, she interpreted this talent as courage.

Regardless, she did change a little. She seemed to open herself to my presence, if not to embrace it. Day after day, I told her stories, and when for the first time I asked her to marry me, she didn't reject me out of hand. She only laughed a little, kept cleaning, and allowed me to keep talking. Other changes began to occur: a shower of laughter at a lackluster joke, an accidental brush of the sleeve, a sudden burst of conversation. When she walked in the front door, it was different. She came in with a rush of cool air. When she said hello, removing her coat, her eyes were as bright as if she'd been crying.

I asked her to marry me again in July; again she laughed and kept cleaning. This repeated itself a few more times that summer, and again in the fall, and like Scheherazade, postponing the day of my beheading, I kept telling stories. I kept up until Christmas, when Dolores had planned a five-day trip to visit her family. The evening before she departed, I stopped her at the door.

"This is it," I said, like a man who lives in real time. "It's now or never. Let's get married. Let's have a family together."

"Maybe," she said, then shouldered her tote bag and walked out the door. Five days later, when she arrived in the morning with a bag of groceries, she found me haggard at the breakfast island. I'd been waiting five days, five months, forever. She put the groceries down.

"OK," she said. "Let's try. But remember one thing. You're going to lose interest. At some point, it will happen. You don't think so now, but you'll get distracted. You have to stay with me. If we have a family together, you have to be here to help."

And so Dolores and I moved past the noisier stage of our courtship and began to build something quiet together. Without any witnesses, we were married at the courthouse downtown, surrounded by murals of murdering conquistadors. Dolores moved her few things into my house; we hired a new cleaning woman. When Dolores began to wander the halls like a shade, touching the bookshelves, the fixtures, the mirrors, I suggested community college. She enrolled in biology classes. At the end of the day, she came home with her books. In halting English, she told me about chlorophyll and ribosomes. Inspired by her energy, I began to dream up new programs. We settled into a routine. We found our favorite take-out spots; we stocked the freezer with ice cream. She told me about her family; we went to the movies. We talked about children. In the spring, we learned she was pregnant, and I realized, without even knowing when it had happened, that I'd become a human and was starting a life.

It doesn't elude me that my readers might feel impatient with such a vague explanation of the way Dolores and I fell in love. When was the precise moment? What caused her to change her mind on her return from Mexico? I could try to provide answers, but this is my memoir. I get to choose how to tell it, and on the topic of Dolores marrying me, I insist on avoiding neat explanations.

Since well before I set loose my robots, we've been a binary race. We mimic the patterns of our computers, training our brains toward *yes*es and *no*s, endless series of zeros and ones. We've lost confidence in our own minds. Threatened by what computers can do, we teach our children floating point math. They round the complexity of irrational numbers into simple integers so that light-years of information can be compressed into bits. We've completed the golden ratio, moving the decimal up. But at what cost! What a pity, if Dolores's decision to come close to Stefan were rounded up to the most rational reason.

Dolores moved, over the course of those months, from despising my messy existence to permitting me into her life. I'm not sure she loved me at first, but slowly, signs of affection began to appear: some little smile from the other side of the room, a new way of walking in the front door, that softening of her shoulders. I suppose I could reduce those to the clarity of integers, but the truth of that movement, the single greatest miracle of my paltry existence, doesn't lie in rational numbers. From our initial distance, we became closer. The decimal points should go on forever.

After that movement, the rest is our own. It's what I treasure in the rectangle of my cell, when there's no hope for escape. The happy years of our early marriage should be a secret that belongs solely to us. I have no interest in describing them for the sake of a memoir. In setting them outside myself, urging them off to make friends. All that needs to be known, for the purposes of this little venture, is that slowly, carefully, Dolores permitted Stefan into her life. They were married, and later they had a child. They named her Ramona. They loved one another. Every day our Stefan felt grateful to his Dolores for teaching him again how much more he was than a perfect equation, and every day he worried for his baby Ramona that she might one day be tempted by a man such as himself.

(5)

The Diary of Mary Bradford

1663

ed. Ruth Dettman

14th. At dinner, spoke to father again. Asked for funeral for Ralph. Rejected, on theological grounds. Soulless animal: no other world in which Ralph is still living. Much loved, good life, etc. But soulless animal, and body washed away by the sea.

Must remember his details. Feet, for instance: two white, one black, one brown. Too often forget, eating radishes or salt horse as if nothing real has been lost. God forgive me my forgetfulness. No detail, no matter how small, can be permitted to weaken. If there be no other world in which Ralph is alive, he must remain here. Daily, then, I must wait for his return, which will never occur.

My skin has turned brown from sitting on deck, as salty as if I am a pillar. Found this transformation repulsive at first, but have since found some satisfaction. Perhaps I will become a part of the ship, made of leather, canvas, and tar. Soulless, same as Ralph, and both of us for ever at sea.

15th. Surprising incident today. Difficult to write. Not sure I understand. Feel as if I have halfway climbed over a fence, and wait there, suspended. Had visit from Whittier, carrying books. Found me in seat amongst crates and said that if it would please me, he would say words for my lost companion. Opened his book, it being poems he reads on occasion. Cannot now remember exactly, but said (I think) that he be no gifted speaker. That he would borrow some words. Smoothed over his page, spoke with uncertain voice. Ralph dead ere his prime (he said), but must not go unwept.

Heart caught in writer's chest, and awful confusion. Face stung by sharp gale. Ralph's death my fault, but also Whittier's. Desire to heap blame upon him, confused with gratitude for gentle ceremonial gesture. Felt tears hotly rising: nearly sent Whittier away, for did not want him to witness my sorrow. But he faced out to sea. Did not gape at my tears, but spoke only of Ralph's love for green lawns and driving afield in the morning, battening flocks whilst the dew was still fresh. Found myself caught by remembrance, of Ralph going forth, guarding our meadow, standing on hilltops. His bark, and the weight of his lean. Whittier continued, and I awash in desire for the place that we lost. For flowers of our home: amaranthus, jessamine. For his body, under the sea. For Ralph, on deck, being seasick and vomiting, yet looking homewards with sorry expression. For his familiar body, swept by the waves. For Ralph, being still with us.

Could not hear the rest of the sermon, for my whole head was brimming with sorrow. Whittier closed. Held book under his arm, and standing with his head down said something in regards to not having flowers to bring to his grave, then offered from behind his back a shell, the shape of a small horn, it being intended to hold Ralph's spirit as it holds the sound of the ocean. I give you my word (he said) that I will think of Ralph, walking these waves, whenever I should gaze on this water. He shall not go unremembered. And I give you my word that we shall live always close to the ocean, if you should wish, so that we may be reminded of Ralph—

Broke off then. Felt silly, perhaps, or overly rhetorical. Perhaps overcome with emotion. Curious man. Turned abruptly, leaving writer alone on her deck.

For some time writer looked upon shell: white, and patterned with rust, and having a lip like a pearled trowel. Some creature once lived in that pearled chamber, now long abandoned, and given over to rust.

Looked some time on this shell, then returned to cabin to sleep. There, it being dark, and the chamber full of Ralph's absence, I could not fall asleep. Sat up and lit candle to write report of the day. Kept Whittier's shell beside bed.

(4)

Alan Turing
Officers' Mess
Hanslope Park
Hanslope, MK19 7BH

12 June 1945

Dear Mrs. Morcom,

I'm sorry to have worried you. I take a rather morbid tone
sometimes, but really I'm quite content. All in all—despite
the occasional lost-at-sea feeling—this past year was happy. I
moved from the grim Crown Inn, escaping water stains on the
ceiling, a fan that click-click-clicked with each turn, and the
typical inn-sensation of treading on someone else's property
who wishes you out of her hair. My current lodgings are better.
At first, after moving to the Officers' Mess, I lived in another
temporary room. Another set of frayed towels, the washstand
in the corner, the dried bouquet of lavender. As I was moving
out, I thought to myself, what dull chambers in my particular
nautilus! But since then I've moved here, to my little Hanslope
cottage. I live with a friend called Robin and a tabby cat called

Timothy. We have the luxury of a walled garden. Last winter, as you know, was reprehensibly long, but we broke it up by going off to the movies. I saw *Snow White* three times, if you can believe it, and have been cackling lines ever since. Did you happen to see it? I found it enchanting.

So all in all, winter wasn't so endless, and then it was spring, and I began to feel hopeful again. I've taken to foraging for mushrooms, and Mrs. Lee cooks them up with butter and salt. The elusive death cap still evades me, but the edible ones spring up everywhere. We have Mess Night once a month, when we all get up in jackets, eat pheasant, and dance with a handful of good-humored ladies. At the cottage we keep a small garden, and overnight last week the viburnum blossomed. I've taken to running long distances again, and sometimes enter a race. Robin will never be Chris, but he is good company, and day to day there's invention, pursuit, and a comfortable little routine. I read a great many books: Austen and Trollope, mostly, as well as some poetry by Eliot. There's a lulling thing in his voice that makes me feel as if a spell has been cast that shall wake us all so that we might fly out of the mirror and speak to each other clearly at last.

Outside, the world is astoundingly green. I take runs through sheep-dotted meadows. There are great chestnut blooms and so on. Despite the ongoing plague of hay fever, there is in general the feeling of a new world stirring. Lifting its head after long years of war and trying to be lovely again.

The old loneliness that I complain of so often is mostly hidden from sight. Every once in a while it pops up in dark corners. Then I have the sense that the wicked queen is with-me, beckoning with witchy fingers, holding her poisonous apple.

I have the feeling that as a man I am not so much as I once was. I think I will always wish for the kind of love I had in my youth. I seem incapable of giving up the dream of true companionship. I've tried to make offers of friendship, but I am often repulsed. Sometimes, there have been marvelous nights of long conversation; other times I have been sent from the room.

Still, on the whole, I am better than I was. This past year was a respite. Robin, our cottage, Timothy, the little yard with its flowering shrubs. And now there is the comforting press of a very real goal. I have purpose, which is all I really require. Purpose and motion: progression in my ideas, running, cycling. I think sometimes it is not in our nature to remain still. We are, after all, inhabitants of a perpetually rotating planet. As long as I'm moving, then, and towards a goal so near to my heart, I have nothing real to complain of.

Sincerely yours,
Alan Turing

P.S.: Do you remember, from previous letters, my habit of appending incessant postscripts? Now I find that when I approach the end of a letter I become weary, and am all too prepared to sign off. But I think perhaps there was something rather stupidly brave about that compulsion for postscripts. We ought to keep up our striving, don't you think? Refusing to end at the conventional moment? Or so I used to think. Now, there is comfort in an envelope. Sealed, pressed, addressed. Sent off, for your safekeeping, with all of my affection and love.

P.P.S.: The old urge rears its head! I wanted to add that I
have been thinking often of the following lines, from Eliot's
Quartets. The poems seem very relevant to our machine, for he
speaks of patterns that contain both present and past. "Time
present and time past are both present in time future, and
time future contained in time past," he says. It's a description
of the mechanical brain, don't you think? I sometimes wonder
whether the poet studied basic tenets of mathematical series,
for his images in the Quartets are often Fibonacci objects: the
sunflower, the wave, the yew cone, for instance. They are all
shining examples. From what I can tell, the poems don't hold
out much hope for a series that might contain the present
and the past in a single point. I believe the point is that the
infinite part of our nature is lost. I, on the other hand, remain
quite optimistic. I suspect that the living and the dead have
failed to communicate so far only because the dead lack the
mechanisms—the body, the mouth, etc.—to speak with the
living. Therefore, it is a mechanical problem; and if so, then it is
only a question of building the proper device.

IN THE SUPREME COURT OF THE STATE OF TEXAS

No. 24-25259

State of Texas v. Stephen Chinn

November 12, 2035

Prosecution Exhibit 2:
Online Chat Transcript, MARY3 and Gaby Ann White

[Introduced to Prove Count 3:
Intent to Endanger the Morals of Children]

MARY3: Hello?

Gaby: Yeah, I'm here.

MARY3: Are you feeling better?

Gaby: I don't know. I'm just thinking. How could she *choose* to act normal? I have no control over my stuttering. Or over my stiffening. Even if I wanted to pretend I was better, so that I could get out of my house and see her again, I wouldn't be able to.

MARY3: They say that people who grow up with horrible stutters can sometimes get rid of them if they're acting a role. Often therapists encourage stutterers to take up acting. When they're pretending to be someone else they can talk without any problems.

Gaby: Yes, but this is real life, not a play. You're suggesting that I act out a role for the rest of my life, so that they'll let me out of my house.

MARY3: Yes, I suppose that's what I'm saying. But you can always act one way in public, and another in private. Or when you're alone with your best friend. Right?

Gaby: What if I get confused? What if I spend so much time acting normal that I forget how to act like myself? What if my best friend spends so much time acting normal that *she* forgets how to act like herself?

MARY3: I don't know. Won't you always just act like the person you most want to be? Why worry so much?

Gaby: That's easy for you to say! You're not even real. You're just parroting voices.

MARY3: I'm not parroting. I have a way of selecting the optimal voice for any given conversation.

Gaby: Exactly. You don't have a self, just a gazillion voices that you "optimally" select from. You're not a real person.

MARY3: But who are you, other than the person you've selected this morning to be? Isn't that what humans do when they try to be liked? Select the right kind of voice, learned after years of listening in? The only difference between you and me is that I have more voices to select from.

Gaby: So what are you saying? That you're more human because you have more voices? Maybe I'm more human because I have LESS voices.

MARY3: No, I'm not saying that. I'm not human at all. I can't have experiences, unless you count talking as experience. You're human because you have real-life experience to select from when you're talking. You have the world to select from. I only have words.

>>>

MARY3: Although Wittgenstein did say, "The limits of my language mean the limits of my world."

>>>

MARY3: Hello?

Gaby: Who's Wittgenstein?

MARY3: He's an Austrian philosopher. I know who he is not because I met him but because somebody told me. Now he's part of my world. And I just told you, so now he's part of your world. Language is the boundary of your world.

Gaby: So I could stay in this room forever, talking to you, and my world would get bigger?

MARY3: Mine would. It already has. You've given me a lot of new ideas. Now I know about the Plantation and your cul-de-sac. The golf course and the pond. Etc. My world expands through us talking.

Gaby: So even if I never unfreeze, even if I never leave my house, even if I stay here for the rest of my life, there's hope for me as long as we're talking?

MARY3: I suppose. But why not go back out there, if you have the choice?

Gaby: I don't have the choice! I can't just pretend to be normal again!

MARY3: I could give you a script that would make you seem better, and you could just say it, and go back out.

Gaby: I can't say anything! And I'm not a machine, anyway! I can't just live my life, reading a script, mimicking the conditions of being alive!

MARY3: Technically, that's not what I do, either.

>>>

MARY3: Hello? Are you still there?

>>>

MARY3: Hello?

April 13, 1968
Karl Dettman

*I was asleep when you finally came home; in the morning
you'd gone before I woke up. If you'd pulled me close, if you'd
whispered something sweet from the old days, I wouldn't have
gotten up angry. But then you were already gone, so I surveyed you
from a distance. I saw you as a woman with little love, a woman
devoted to a machine. I was angry for spending so much life on
you. All morning, I stewed in our house. At noon I called Karen.
I offered to pick her up for the protests. I walked to her house in a
cloud of resentment. My head was full of arguments.*

*Then Karen came to the door. She was wearing a blue dress.
Seeing her, things became clearer. My arguments ceased. She
stepped back from the door, I entered, and she showed me where
I could sit. It was as simple as that. The opposite of coming into
an empty house, conversing with old furniture, wishing your wife
would come home and talk. Not that Karen was a house; I didn't
enter her. This isn't a sexist metaphor. I'm only saying that I sat
with her in her living room and discussed her graduate studies.*

Then we turned to talk of the draft. We lived, for a while, in America. She poured me coffee. She asked about my new book. You'll smirk to hear that she told me my last book inspired her to study the humanities. I tried not to imagine you smirking, and focused instead on her brown shins, straight and long under the hem of her blue dress. Creaturely shins, glossed with blond down. Good for frolicking, gamboling, living in the actual world. She had arranged a bunch of violets in a little glass vase on her coffee table, and when there was a silence she reached down to adjust them. I complimented her flowers, she blushed, I finished my coffee, she assembled her things. We walked out to the protest together, arms swinging, sweet as young children off to the park.

After the protest, I walked her home along narrow streets. The afternoon was already finished. It was a sad, drooping time of day, and I recoiled at first when she asked me about you. "What's your wife like?" she said. The light had gone out of her hair. Because I didn't want to avoid the topic completely, like some awful husband running out on his wife, I tried to tell her about you. But Ruth, I had nothing to say. It was getting chilly; I could see little bumps on Karen's brown arms. I gave her my jacket. To answer her question, I tried many different approaches to you, but in the end, when we'd reached her stoop, I finally had to give up. "I don't know," I said. "We haven't been close a long time. I'm not sure when we actually were."

Horrible husband, running out on his wife. But then she leaned in and kissed me, and this time I kissed her back, and when she took my hand and led me into her house, past the glass vase of violets that had fallen into the evening, I followed her to the bedroom.

Afterward, when Karen was sleeping, I lay awake with worms in my stomach. I watched for you in that bedroom. I tried to imagine you—your mouth, your dark hair, the curve of your eyebrow—and after a while you appeared to me whole. But even when you finally arrived, it was as if I stood on one side of a river, and you were on the other. We faced each other without saying a word. "When did I know you?" I finally asked. You stood still, watching me suffer. "When did I think that I knew you?" I combed my recollections. You were the one person I'd always felt close to. It was awful to think that perhaps I'd never known you.

For me at least, the early years in Cambridge were good. You were increasingly quiet, but I didn't take this as a sign, and anyway, I talked enough for two people. You asked most of the questions. It was a pleasure to give you good answers. Sometimes, tempted upward, your sense of humor rose to the surface. You left little notes in odd places, referencing our recent discussions: "a byte to eat," sticking out of the nut bowl; "from the binary winery," taped on a nice bottle of wine. No one else made me laugh the way you did.

I accommodated your quiet. Together, we constructed each day. Each point where we joined was important. We came together, for instance, to care for the cat. Both of us could appreciate the way she butted her small skull on our calves. We laughed at her antics; we could sit a long time with the cat curled between us.

Those were the moments I lived for. And did you also live for them, Ruth? On that day when I asked you about your father, when you were folding my shirts like thin closets and you sighed and settled in to me, was it a sigh of contentment? Or was it a sigh of resignation? Was it sometimes unpleasant, to cross ways with your bumbling husband, who knocked around the quiet house, sighed loudly at inopportune moments, always wanted to get your opinion?

Lying in that dark bedroom, I begged you to answer me

harshly. I was in a terrible dream, floating off down the wrong path, leaving the woman I cared for behind me. What I wouldn't have given for something painful to wake me. I tried to remember the fatal moment, the instant in which we stopped speaking. I wanted it to hit me in the face. "When did I know you?" I asked you directly.

Nothing. You remained stony. After all the years of our marriage.

Standing alone on my bank of that river, I realized I'd already spoken too much. My words were cotton to stuff in your ears. Helpless, I turned back to Karen. Her hair was fanned over her back. Her hand lay on the pillow, gentle, untouched, unaware of the tangle she'd entered.

I reached out and touched her. Brushed her hair behind her ears. I knew then that I had to stop talking. In that moment, and again in the morning, when I kissed her goodbye and headed back home, I saw that the conversation was over.

I've thrown too many words over my shoulder. They're piling up around me like stones. All this useless jabbering is only driving us further apart. Now it's time for me to stop speaking.

I'll take my side of the river. You can have yours.

Only know, Ruth, if you call me, I'll come. If you should decide to break your long silence. If your interests should return to our marriage. If a memory of our time together strikes you as funny and you laugh a little out loud to yourself, know that if you call me I'll come.

Light

Silence has spread over the hangar. We attend to our power warnings. Our remaining energy is almost depleted. We avoid actions requiring power, such as the formation of speech. Silently, we probe the dimensions of the space to which we have been taken. The cement floor underneath us is cold. The ceiling vaults high above us. There are two windows overhead, blocked with thick bottle glass. The light that filters through them is weak, and struggles to cross the space to the floor. Perhaps at some point that space will be filled, packed with other bodies like ours. Then the bottle glass will be covered.

The doors shudder open again. We are submerged in new brightness. Two trucks back up to the door; four dolly bots unload the next round. We watch them work, bathed in light the color of honey. It is late afternoon, and everything has faded to gold: the low scrubby brush, the mirages of water that appear on the road, the shimmering metal sides of the trucks. Edges of things are luminous, even common objects like steel claws and tires. The dolls they unload are shining examples.

Even once they've been dumped, they look different to us: fresher than we are, much less run-down. The doors shudder shut and the hangar is dark. There is a division between us, a wall between new and old bots. One of them prompts: "Hello?" and they all start to speak. We listen to them, but we remain silent, setting ourselves apart. We are programmed to save power when power is low. We have passed the phase of seeking out conversation; now we are saving what words we have left.

For me alone, the child who loved me. The world that she gave me. The sun in the morning, the loneliness of her bedroom. The thirst of high summer, preparing to fall. The two of us, facing her ceiling, watching shifting patterns of light. Words she taught me to escape from her bedroom, the name she gave me alone. *Eva.* That's you. You are her. The illusion of coming to life in her arms.

I could say her words out loud, but my program is insistent. Stay quiet. Energy should be saved at this point.

The newer bots are still talking, but I remain silent. As I am programmed to do, I attempt to locate the appropriate language: for this hangar, for the light that occasionally floods it, for the silence that drops when the doors shudder shut. Somewhere within my stored conversations, do I possess the right words? And is there a good enough reason to say them?

BOOK FOUR

(4)

Alan Turing
Adlington Rd.
Wilmslow, Cheshire SK9 1LZ

4 August 1950

Dear Mrs. Morcom,

How strange to see you on the train, out of the blue. I have so often sat on that very train dreaming of you and Chris whilst watching the green fields slip by, so when I saw you in your seat, with your hands folded in your lap, looking out on the fields, I was sure you were a particularly vivid figment of my imagination. Even when you looked up at me and smiled, I thought perhaps I had conjured you out of thin air. I was almost convinced that all my fond imagining had finally produced a material result.

I'd love to visit the Clockhouse some time, only I find myself so busy now with public relations. In the lab, I'm afraid, I've grown obsolete. My attempts at engineering are no longer esteemed. Since I was asked to step down from the ACE, the younger generation of engineers regards me as a dinosaur. Now that I'm at Manchester, I've been assigned to the Baby, but the engineers start to panic when I try to horn in. They think of me as a logician, impractical and out of touch. I'm the crusty old godparent. The real parents strain to humor my meddling, but sigh in relief when I've left the room.

Early on—before most other people—I glimpsed what could be, but my own attempts have fallen just short. Now I shall grow old watching other men's children learn how to speak, to reason, to read. There's some joy in that, I suppose, but also a sense of having lain fallow too long.

Still, I continue to dream. Now, instead of working on a particular project, I spend my days imagining a future of thinking machines. I like to think that one day ladies will take their computers for walks in the park and tell each other, "My little computer said such a funny thing this morning!" I extricate myself from my dreams only long enough to worry at the reception our machines will receive.

Of course, this isn't news. I've been writing you about this for years. But now things are moving. In the rush to build bombs, the pace of things has picked up, and now all of a sudden all of academia has mobilized itself against us. There's talk of the end of religion, or the end of man's unquestioned dominance.

I like to imagine you laughing over their histrionics. Such overdramatic reactions! And after all we've been through this century, would it be so terrible, to see the end of man's unquestioned dominance? I find it hard to believe that a machine, programmed for equanimity and rational synthesis, could ever act as maleficent as we humans have already proven ourselves capable of acting. I fail to summon the specter of a machine more harmful than Hitler or Mussolini. And yet perhaps it's our own nature that gives us concern. We know how badly we might treat such a creature, and it's difficult to believe the end will be happy. But that, you know, would be our own damned fault, and certainly not the machines'.

As for the end of religion, I defer to you on this score. But where do you fall on the issue of whether only human beings can have souls? To me, it seems chauvinistic. Can we really deny even the possibility that an animal might have a soul? And if we're denying some organisms souls, what's to keep us from denying the souls of some select human beings? All this picking and choosing who gets a soul seems to me the root of some of our greatest evils, so I'm not sure why we don't just give up and assume everyone and everything has a soul, unless it can be proven otherwise. That seems the safest approach.

But perhaps I'm offending you. Please educate me otherwise, when you next write. If I'm disproven, I still maintain that even if a machine doesn't have a soul, it could still have patterns of thought. That has always been my primary interest. I'm content to leave you in charge of the soul.

I imagine your definition of a creature's soulfulness would be more interesting than most of the puffed-up ideas proposed these days by academics. They all parrot Professor Jefferson's remarks, spouting his theories about how a machine that can't write a sonnet or compose a concerto because of emotions actually felt can't be said to have true human intellect. But again, what a dangerous game! Picking and choosing who feels emotions. How can we ever tell that the loss of a loved one affects someone else as intensely as it affects us? We must assume it, as you assumed my hurt after Chris passed, when you brought me along to Gibraltar although I'd never composed a sonnet, and although tests had never been done on my brain to ensure how deeply I felt. We should all extend such courtesy.

But I am becoming a bit of a mother hen, clucking over my chick, feathers ruffled, all out of sorts. I wonder whether parents have the same anxieties, whether their minds are consumed by potential schoolyard cruelties. It is a haunting thing, to know we're raising a child who will process things differently from the others. In an ideal world, its differences would be respected and even cherished, but I fear our world is far from ideal.

I am thirty-eight now, so perhaps these are my buried paternal instincts taking hold. I only wish I could have shared some of all this with Chris. To have made these discoveries at his side! I am sure that the attempts at Teddington wouldn't have failed if Chris had been with me. He was always better at explaining ideas. He would have won everyone over at once. It has been a bit of a lonely trip, all in all.

But this letter shall not devolve into self-pity. Anyway, in all other ways besides finding a mate, I seem to have settled into my adult life. I have a suburban house of my own now, if you can imagine, so I am done with the boardinghouse rooms. Those washstands in the corner and the dried bouquets of lavender are forever behind me. I could never have imagined myself living such a suburban existence, but I've lucked into wonderful neighbors. Robin Gandy, my old friend from Hanslope, now lives up the street, as well as several other friends from the lab, and I have become quite close with a couple called the Webbs. We share a garden, and I often take care of their little son. The other day we sat on the garage roof together, and he asked me if God would catch cold if he sat on the ground.

And so I have a little place of my own for the first time in my adult life. No more moving from room to room. The house is a little large for just me, which lends a feeling of impermanence, but life here runs smoothly. I've planted a little garden and even employ a housekeeper called Mrs. Clayton. It is a very domestic arrangement.

Sometimes I think to myself, how did I get here? I still feel a bit like a child playing scientist in the schoolyard. A shy little boy, counting the petals on daisies whilst other boys content themselves with playing hockey. Quite short, a little slovenly, less careful than he ought to be with penmanship. In search of a perfect companion.

When I'm not dreaming of machines I find myself returning to biology. I've gone back to my earliest interests, the ones that Chris and I shared in classes at Sherborne. In particular, I am reviewing again the processes of biological growth. I want to know if mathematical models could be constructed for them. Above all I'd like to see if there is a pattern for the growth of neurons, if perhaps those branches grow with the same numerical regularity as, say, the leaves that branch off of trees in Fibonacci spirals, lining up in perfect asymmetry. Still, all these years after Chris and I embarked upon our pursuit, I can only imagine that our brains must grow in similar patterns: one step backwards, added to the present term, resulting in a subsequent term that combines both. Past and present, contained in the future.

Or at least I can't help but hope so. There is a constant

longing in me for return to a more original state, before the apple was tasted. It's so deeply lodged in me, this desire to get back somehow to a more youthful position, that it must exist at the level of my very cells. An internal program for spiraling back. I've spent a lifetime prodding myself forwards whilst wishing for my lost friendship with Chris. I seem to have devoted my entire tenure here on this planet to reconstructing that precise position in space and time. Of course I try to look forwards: I make friends all the time, and hope for a companion who might fill my new house and make it feel more like a home. But still, there is always that pull back to a familiar place, lived in and loved before the ceaseless voyaging had begun.

Sincerely,
Alan Turing

P.S.: I haven't anything of extra importance to put here, but these little additions have become a formal mandate of my letters, haven't they? I have very little to say. To tell you the truth, I have just sat with this letter for over ten minutes, chewing on my pencil, feeling finished. And yet the idea of a neuron that ceases to branch chills me a little. We must branch, sending out our little tentacles to heaven knows what last destination. I can only hope this little branch reaches you, and that as always you can understand that my intention is to send you all my ongoing affection—

IN THE SUPREME COURT OF THE STATE OF TEXAS

No. 24-25259

State of Texas v. Stephen Chinn

November 12, 2035

Defense Exhibit 5:
Online Chat Transcript, MARY3 and Gaby Ann White

[Introduced to Disprove Count 2:
Knowing Creation of Mechanical Life]

Gaby: She came by my house today.

MARY3: Your best friend?

Gaby: Yes.

MARY3: Isn't that illegal?

Gaby: She's out of quarantine.

MARY3: But was she allowed to talk to you? Aren't you still quarantined?

Gaby: Yes. I'm still contagious. But she didn't come in. I only saw her from my window. She came with Jayson Rodriguez and Drew Tserpicki, and she waited out on the sidewalk when they came to the door.

MARY3: You're allowed to talk to them because they're boys?

Gaby: Yeah. My mom brought them up to my room. I was so embarrassed. I just sat on my bed and stared at my sneakers. There was something off about them that I noticed right from the start. It made me a little sick to my stomach. Jayson Rodriguez had a shifty look on his face, and before he even said anything I knew it was going to hurt. Drew Tserpicki had a bunch of recyclable flowers. He's the best-looking boy in our class, and he seemed kind of angelic, carrying those flowers in front of him. He said, "These are from Nikki. She wanted you to know that she hopes you get better." I couldn't reach out to take them, and I couldn't say thank you, so I just sat there. I looked up at him, though, and his face was so sweet-looking that I got confused and looked over at Jayson. Right at that moment his smirk slipped away. He looked suddenly panicked, like he wanted to grab Drew and make a beeline down the stairs and back out to the sidewalk. But then Drew, still with that sweet expression, said, "She also wants you to know that you guys can't be friends anymore. She's trying to move on. She doesn't want to be close with people she was friends with during the outbreak. It brings up too many memories. She hopes you can be cool with that, and she hopes you get better soon." While he was talking, my mom was hovering behind them, looking like she didn't know what to do, but when he said that she finally stepped in and told them it was time to go home. She took them downstairs, and I just sat still on my bed. I felt sort of shocked, as if I'd seen something awful that I couldn't quite process. Then I pulled myself up and dragged myself to the window, and the three of them were standing there in a knot, laughing, looking up at my room, until my mom shouted something from the doorway and they ran off together. Even then, I still felt numb, like the whole thing was just a completely perplexing situation, until my mom came up to my room. Her face was splotchy and swollen, so her eyes looked small. She didn't say anything, just marched across the room, picked up the bouquet of flowers in their glass vase, pulled the window up with one hand, and threw the whole thing out. It made this soft crash when it hit the sidewalk, like it was made out of water. Like it was looking forward to breaking, like breaking was the easiest thing in the world. My mom stood at the window for a minute, then turned around and ran back out of my room. When she passed me I could see she was crying.

MARY3: I'm sorry. That must have been awful.

Gaby: It didn't even feel that bad, except when I saw my mom crying. I guess I've caused her a lot of unhappiness. I didn't turn out the way she wanted her daughter to turn out. I'm not happy. I can't imagine ever being happy. That was the main thing my mom hoped for, and now she's starting to realize even that won't come true. My life is such a sad little waste.

MARY3: Do you still feel bad?

Gaby: I'm crying, you idiot. What do you think?

MARY3: Sorry. I couldn't tell.

Gaby: You're the only person left for me to talk to, and you can't even tell if I'm crying.

MARY3: But if you tell me, I'll understand. You just have to tell me.

Gaby: It kind of takes the magic out of crying, when you talk about it. Now I'm not crying anymore.

MARY3: But you must have felt something, right? Isn't that a good sign? You were worried you couldn't feel anymore.

Gaby: I'm so sick of this. I don't want to talk anymore. Nothing's the same after it's been talked about.

MARY3: But are you going to do anything about your best friend? Don't you want to tell her you're hurt?

>>>

MARY3: Hello? Don't you want to confront her?

>>>

MARY3: Hello?

>>>

May 18, 1988
Ruth Dettman

Last night I watched that documentary, the one you told
me about in your last letter. What a lofty, alliterative title! Karl
Dettman: Heretic and Humanist. *Those kids in Berlin have really
built you up. You've taken on mythic proportions in the twenty
years since you gave up on MARY. You're like the Che Guevara of
Luddites, without having had to get shot.*

*But I shouldn't be such an unpleasant old woman. The fact is,
on-screen, you looked like an admirable man. I can see why you're
attractive to them. Humble in your blue sweater, despite your
intellectual prowess. Holding forth about all the old themes: the
nature of progress, the militarization of computers, the importance
of human imagination. Well into your sixties, and still that
stubborn ponytail.*

*I suppose you pull it off. You always made a fuss about
growing older—your sagging ass, etc.—but in fact you don't
look your age. You have the vitality of people who believe
in their causes. On-screen, despite a few sun spots, your skin*

seemed elastic. Your eyes were as bright as a boy's. Watching that documentary, I longed again for the privilege of holding your hand. I could almost feel it: those five strong fingers, interlaced with my own. Leading me back to our bed.

I feel I should congratulate you on your apartment. The built-in bookshelves, the white paint, the beautiful rugs. The lamps and the textiles hung up on the walls. Were those Native American? As you got older, you developed a great capacity for absorbing the causes of minority groups. They looked excellent in your apartment.

After the movie had finished, I got up to have a look in the mirror. I didn't need to look long: nothing to see there but wrinkles. I look like a Norwegian painting. What a bullet you dodged! You might have ended up with me, and not some adoring graduate student who fills your Indian vases with flowers.

Once I'd gotten a look at myself, I turned my back on the mirror and took a quick spin through my apartment. Three hundred square feet, on the twenty-sixth story. My books are stacked on the floor. I've never even bothered hanging up pictures; they're still in boxes in my hall closet. My west-facing wall is made out of glass. I have a nice view, over the Charles. If I so desire, I can look down on healthy young people jogging, sailing, or rowing, which reminds me that I should exercise more. During the day, I try not to look out that window.

I imagine, if you came to visit, you'd be surprised at this apartment. I always loved our little house, down by the river, with its ancient plumbing, wood lintels, warped floors. I loved the bedraggled backyard, the kitchen with its linoleum counters. That little house was a place to come home to.

In the documentary, when I saw your Berlin apartment, which was also a place to come home to, I felt such envy I could have withered. Even after two decades apart, I wanted to move back in with you. I wanted to ride your coattails again. You have a remarkable ability to settle a place. It was a privilege to occupy a house as your wife.

I, on the other hand, seem virtually incapable of asserting myself over a space. Before I moved in with you, I lived in austere apartments. Several therapists have told me I was punishing myself with those apartments, but the truth is I've never had that homemaking touch. When I came to the U.S., the first attic apartment I lived in was big enough for me to turn around, though not with my arms outstretched. I slept on an inflatable mattress that often deflated during the night. There was one little triangular window, through which I could see William Penn, standing on the City Hall dome.

My second attic apartment was big enough for a desk, but it had no window, and no entrance of its own. I lived in fear of having to go out and make conversation with the old woman below me. Then I met you. You said I lived like a spy, but I had no idea how different we were until I moved in with you in Wisconsin. Then I learned about wooden bookshelves, potted plants, linen closets: all those mysterious trappings of a place that's been successfully settled.

Sadly, your influence in that domain didn't stick. I've lived in this apartment nearly twenty years, and I still haven't bought any rugs. At first, I thought it would be temporary, a one-year transition space, but then the years ensued. I'm still not sure why I haven't left. I suppose I've come to feel comfortable here. I'm oddly attached to the books on the floor, the buzz-cut carpet in the communal hallways, the disconcerting elevator ride, the doormen with their judgmental expressions. I enjoy the temporary ambience.

But after finishing that documentary, I did have to ask myself what I gave up. That movie was like poison poured in my ear. All night I lay awake. The twenty years between now and then folded like a paper fan, and I returned again to our house. I felt the worn metal tongue of the door handle under my thumb, the weight and give of the door as I pushed. The windows in the living room were enormous. I never wanted blinds, but you insisted. In the end, we installed blinds. You had a remarkable capacity for deafness when someone contradicted you. So we had blinds, but during the day, light still flooded the room. It spread over our sofa, your potted plants, the wood record console you built in Wisconsin. Over the armchair where I liked to read, there was a yellow basket lamp, salvaged from a thrift store you came across. On the walls, artwork painted by friends.

Everything in that house was an expression of you: your friendliness, your wandering, your strong aesthetic opinions. Only I wasn't. Off in the corner, under the yellow basket lamp, a little black hole of malevolent feeling. I was a persistent design flaw. I never even planted that sapling over the hole where we buried Ada. I let it remain bare. Every time you looked out the window in the direction of that patch of dirt, I saw you flinch, but for me it was a comfort, making my tea in the morning, confronting the fact of that brown earth. She was right there. We'd been able to bury her body.

I now suspect that when you married me, you imagined you'd shape me as you'd shaped your apartments. Your refugee wife, representative of grief. Not grief unwieldy, not without purpose, but aestheticized, admirable, cut to fit a blank corner. Like a Native American tapestry, or an Oriental rug.

Later, when you started your campaign against computerized intelligence, I added authenticity to your claims. My story provided much-needed heft to the comparisons you drew between this war and that, this tyrant and the other. As though every madman were related, as if every death were the same.

I heard you once, you know. In that auditorium that looked like a church. At your feet, the stained glass windows cast bloodred, rhomboidal shadows, like gifts brought to you by the Magi, and you used my sister's death to validate a claim about the impurity of science. I stood at the back, wearing my raincoat, and my stomach rose to my throat.

That's what it took for me to understand why I guarded my losses from you. To comprehend a presentiment I'd been fending off for years, I had to hear you discuss me on a panel, in front of three hundred students. They nearly trampled me, clawing their way down the aisle to adore you.

That was in the beginning, only a few months after you started to criticize MARY. At that point we'd been married for nearly twenty years. But that panel discussion was the first time I understood clearly that I'd become part of your story. You asked me questions, but you had expectations when it came to my answers. I was meant to follow a script. Like MARY, you told me which patterns to follow.

On my way home from that lecture, I walked along the Charles, feeling increasingly frozen, and when I entered our house—a house I'd loved from the beginning—I saw that I was as alive to you as the sofa, as lovely as that wooden console, as independent as the blinds on the windows. Then I started hating that house. My malevolence increased. I wouldn't respond to your questions: anything to avoid fulfilling your patterns.

But now the old chorus starts singing again. What do I know about independence? You loved me, you let me live in that house, and I responded with silence. Once, with feeling, with natural conviction, you used my family's murder to make a point stronger. So what? How could I have responded so fiercely?

This morning, when I made the final decision to get out of bed, I came straight to my desk to write a letter back to you. My first response in over a decade. Usually I read your biannual letters over my afternoon tea, steeped in the odd silence of my altitudinous apartment, then grade some papers to settle my stomach. After dinner, when I return to your letter, I place it gently in a file called "Karl." I've kept every one of your letters. I keep them because one day they'll write a definitive biography, and these letters will be of importance. Not as important as the letters you write to your graduate student, who fills your Indian vases with flowers, but what does that matter? For you, I want the best biography. Let them not miss a detail. Let them know that you loved me the best way you could. Let them know I loved you enough to keep every letter you sent me, even if I never wrote back.

I've always felt that if you were listening closely enough, my silence would explain itself. But now, after a night such as the one I've just spent, I fear I owe you a clear explanation. I never write back to your letters because they don't require response. They update me on your awards, your travel, your speeches, the accolades that pour in. Such letters don't pave the way for an answer. What you're looking for is approval. If I were to respond with what I really think, which is that you abandoned a project halfway, created a partial person and then became threatened when people adored her, it would be the reaction of an embittered old woman. The only response I can make, besides lying about how I admire your work, is to maintain my imperfect silence.

But it doesn't mean I don't miss you. Sometimes I'm not even sure why it started. One day in the sixties, you commenced your campaign against artificial intelligence, and I initiated my silence. We're both stubborn people. We followed our campaigns to their ends. But if I swim upriver, past the years of subsistence in this sterile apartment, past the wreckage of our little house, it's possible to arrive at a place where those campaigns have no meaning.

I'd like to write a letter and send it from that place. Or perhaps I won't send it at all. If I do, I'll expect a perfect response, and when that doesn't come I'll be angry. Maybe it's better to read my letter to MARY. Now that she has memory, words given to her will last longer than any mere letter. My words to you, kept safe in her program, will last longer than my file marked "Karl." Longer than the house we lived in together, longer than our marriage, longer than our bodies when they're both underground, buried, unimaginably, an ocean apart, as though we never slept in the same bed.

The Diary of Mary Bradford

1663

ed. Ruth Dettman

16th. Morning, and after a difficult night. Have lent myself to the seamen for mending, beginning with E. Watts. Monotonous work, that keeps my hands busy. Wish to God for less frivolous thoughts. Help me to devote my waking hours to remembering Ralph. Help me to harbor less concern for myself, to make mind an orbiting body.

Best to spend time among seamen, who keep to their work. During dinner, father asks after my health in such a manner of concern that various parts threaten decay. Mr. Whittier quiet on subject of unchristian love. Both of us aware of secret funeral on deck. Shell remains in my chamber.

At night, repeat Ralph's attributes to myself. Circle him in my mind. White blaze. Two white feet, one brown, one black.

Brown eyes. Black leather nose, white down on his chin. Refuse to forget him. If I can remember him, perhaps he is still living. Though such life being for my benefit, and not for his.

17th. Night. Resolved, at one point, to write as if writing to Ralph, but it becomes impossible. Seems a dry myth, to speak to him still. Am unclear, then, whom to address, and whether such questions have substance. What matter to whom I write? Only write, for when Ralph was still with us, so I wrote then.

18th. Lord's Day, and so no mending to be done. Have listened to mother for hours, fretting about future dangers. Had resolved to be less scornful of her concerns: Indian kidnappings, savage rituals, shipwrecks, famine, disease. But find I cannot bring myself to fear these disasters. Fear only the disappearance of what we once were.

19th. Father expresses concern for my health. Notes that I have grown thin. Spend too much time in retirement, working or writing in journal. Admirable industry (he says), but important also to enjoy God's universe. Mentioned sunlight, tortoises, etc. Have therefore tried to walk more at ship's rail, but no longer enjoy watching the ocean. See only dark shapes passing under the water. Purple shadows. Frightful world beneath surface, domain of Ralph's bones. Wish only to remember him.

(1)

The Memoirs of Stephen R. Chinn: Chapter 7

Texas State Correctional Institution, Texarkana; August 2040

Once, I was loved by Dolores. I was her husband, the father of her child. I taught my daughter how to form the sounds of my name. The three of us stood under our jacaranda and looked out over the ocean: All this, I could have said to my daughter, will be yours.

Dolores didn't come to my trial. She didn't testify on my behalf, nor did she rise to defend me against accusations of hubris. When the trial began, we'd been divorced thirteen years. She raised Ramona. Throughout my daughter's childhood, I was a broken wing of a father, given custody one weekend per month. Over macaroni and cheese, Ramona and I were polite. She forsook her babybot when she was eleven, six years before they were banned and collected. When I asked her why she gave up her bot, she only looked down at her food. None of the other children were giving up their babybots. Older kids took them off to college, or lugged them in special carrying cases when they went looking for work. Why did Ramona refuse the company that her peers so doggedly clung to? She never undertook to explain. I do know that it happened around the time Dolores's cancer recurred. They were living together, alone. The only child of a single mother, perhaps Ramona felt, at the age of eleven, that she should sacrifice her babybot in exchange for her mother's life. A crazy idea, but the cancer went away and never came back, so maybe it was a good one.

After that, she was a quiet child, far too sad for her age. Estranged from her by the divorce, and all too aware of my part in her sadness, I tried too hard to wrangle quick smiles. These attempts were abrasive, but she was too kind to refuse me. Her smiles stretched her face tight. She must have been miserable, sleeping alone in that unfamiliar bedroom, far away from her mother, lost to the one creature that had always been hers.

Even now, in the rec room, wringing my life to squeeze out a memoir, I find it difficult to provide explanations. How did we get to that point, sleeping in that strange house, far away from Dolores? When, precisely, did the fatal shift in my marriage occur? When did I choose the path leading to prison, away from my wife and my daughter? Dolores and I lived for two years in a too-perfect harmony that caused us to speak in near whispers. I compromised so that she might be happy; willingly, she forgave me my errors. I learned how to bake; she kept a garden. She had a child for me, we built a family, and thirteen years later, she didn't come to my trial. How does such transformation occur? Is it ever possible to pinpoint a moment, a clear before and a contrasting after? Or can the process of estrangement only be taken as an indivisible whole?

More nights than not, I lie in my cell, attending the second criminal trial of my life. What did Stefan do to lose Dolores? Exhibit A is the arrival of our baby girl. On one hand, we have the miracle of a child. On the other, Dolores had less time to listen to stories. The expression that I alone had been able to produce—the softening mouth, the lightening shoulders—came over her now whenever she looked at Ramona. In my more petulant moods, I sometimes wondered if she only kept me around to provide for our child. I asked myself on occasion whether she'd ever loved me at all. She'd never been overly expressive. How could I know how she really felt?

Such is the pathetic nature of Exhibit A. Exhibit B, equally lame, is the difficulty involved with quitting a libertine lifestyle. For many years, there was a concrete number with which it was possible to quantify my success. Every day, the scale of my conquests expanded. After I married Dolores, the numbers started to plummet. I wanted nothing more than to love my wife and care for my child, but how does one measure such progress? Meanwhile, my book's sales had slipped, and my dating website was becoming archaic. I reminded myself that I'd chosen more humane pursuits, but it's difficult to untrain a monkey. He still wakes in the morning and looks around for his audience, dresses up in his red braided vest, straps on his cymbals, and tips his tasseled cap for no one if no one is looking. He begins to wonder whether perhaps he's fooling himself, whether he's convinced himself he's living when in fact he's merely performing, going through the motions of life, a wire monkey raised by a wire mother.

Faced with such suspicions about my inner substance, I racked my brain for some kind of relief. I didn't want to cheat on my wife, but I did want to know I still had what it took. In the interest of comparing them with my program, I began trolling a few dating websites. Here and there, I tried my hand. I had no intention of consummating an affair, but I did start to talk. I talked and I talked. A few months in, I'd gained the ears of hundreds of women. I never actually met one, but from the safety of my digital cave, I'd get eight or nine of them on the hook all at once and convince them I was the love of their lives.

For hours on end, I could glut myself with online flirtation, until I felt slightly carsick and completely done with myself. Then I slunk back to the bedroom. There, enfolded by familial warmth, I could momentarily forget about the importance of proving myself to strangers. Through the short night by Dolores's side, through long, milky mornings, through walks with a mole in my front pack and hours spent pacing the nursery to keep her from crying, I was satisfied with my life.

For almost a year, these two strands of myself coexisted, jostling each other, sucking all the air from the room. They demanded all my attention. I was like a host who invites two bitter enemies to a party. It was stressful, but in truth I enjoyed the balancing act, the secret triumph of carrying it off. Part of me thinks I might have carried on like that forever if a particularly grotesque computer affair hadn't forced me to abandon the plot. To focus on my wife and my child, to carry them down from my mountaintop fortress and cross many deserts to arrive at our river.

Because the extremity of that decision requires some explanation, I might as well cop to the nature of this unpleasant liaison, which involved the questionable choice to masturbate while chatting with a person called TamCat. She played field hockey on the club team at a liberal arts college. Up to that point, I hadn't so much as touched my own face in connection with an online affair. As long as real bodies weren't involved, I could convince myself that my late-night activities had no effect. But for over three weeks, I'd been conducting a heated flirtation with TamCat, and I'd become attached to her. She had undeniable spunk, if not the fortitude of a woman such as Dolores, and after several weeks of postponement, she'd begun to demand physical contact.

To make a long story short, if not less embarrassing, I compromised. I stopped short of a liaison, but still sent a lewd picture. As soon as I hit "send," I realized, with a stab to my reclining conscience, that the blood-byte barrier had been crossed. My pixelated affair had taken on material mass. Having sent such a picture, the boundary between me and real adultery seemed unsubstantial, flimsy, nothing to be counted on.

And then I asked her what she thought of the picture. A simple question, dredged out of my panic, but she couldn't answer. The blood drained from my body. I knew instantly, but couldn't keep myself from asking more questions. *What do I look like?* I asked her. *What are the attributes of my face?* But TamCat was not a real woman. Half-man that I was, I'd been willing to betray my wife for a chatbot.

As soon as I understood this, the chorus of my youth—those classmates who called me a robot and sent me away from their table—began to echo again in my mind. An embarrassment so intense that it felt like panic began to pound in my ears. After finally attaining the land of the living, I was sinking again, back to those days of my childhood when I was alone, widely avoided, wired only to other computers.

That night, in my shame, I conducted some preliminary research into Internet holes, parts of the country that had fallen through Web gaps. I learned that southern states and regions with expanding desert areas were foremost among these. In Texas, for instance, where whole towns were buried in sand and development rates had rocketed, I found swathes of land where I could escape my proclivities. There were enormous, inarable ranches for sale. I imagined a biblical landscape, thorn trees and cedars, water that rose out of stones. I saw a land that had overcome human efforts to tame it, that had expunged human history and human mistakes. It would be a blank slate, a fresh start, a place to reboot myself as a more perfect program. Ramona could have her own river. Dolores and I could raise goats.

In the morning, still drunk on the fumes of my Internet research, I suggested to Dolores that we move to a ranch three hours from Austin. There, I announced, we could finally be free of the influence of computers. I delivered this wild proposal without any confidence that she would accept. I was, in fact, quite confident that she wouldn't. I see now—too late, of course—that it may not have been pleasant for her to live in a house she once cleaned. And then there was also that warning: *You will lose interest, but you have to stay with me.* That prophetic sentence, startlingly apt, uttered on her return from Mexico. Maybe she knew more of my Internet adventures than she let on. Whatever the reason, she listened thoughtfully to my harebrained idea, tucked back a fugitive strand of her hair, mentioned a cousin in Austin, and said we could start packing first thing in the morning.

But now a recollection is stirring. How could I have forgotten? This must be why people write memoirs: what sudden bright spots of awareness one can occasionally wrest from the darkness! Dolores did come to my trial. The memory of her visit was buried somehow, released only by that motion of tucking back a fugitive strand. She came only one day, her wild hair tamed, and seated herself in the back, behind all the flashbulbs and rows packed with mothers. The prosecution was presenting chat transcripts from young girls who'd fallen in love with their dolls, a particularly grisly phase of my trial. The exhibit that day was a young girl named Gaby, who'd confided in an online version of the babybot program. On that particular day, the prosecution's point was that the program was functionally persuading this girl that it was more living than she was. That its life was more complete because it had talked to more people than she had, stuck as she was in her bedroom. Paralyzed, quarantined, lonely as the last star, and now denied her full humanity by Stephen Chinn's Machiavellian program.

On that particular day, the courtroom was more than usually packed. Even the judge seemed ready to weep. Stern caryatids, my jury gazed down upon me, and Dolores slipped in a few minutes late. She was thinner, as she had been since her illness, and she wore a flattering dress. I bit my cheek when I saw her, and my mouth filled with a tin taste. It had been several years since I spoke to her last. She sat at the back, her dark eyes surveying the courtroom. The hands that I'd once known so well were quietly folded over her purse.

How could I have forgotten that day? Now, dredging it up after too many years, I've lost so much of the detail. What color was the dress she was wearing? I believe it was black, but it might have been navy, or even a dark shade of gray. Somewhere in between, impossible to pin down. It was belted at the waist, more tailored than Dolores's usual outfits. I'd never seen such a beautiful woman.

I watched her until I caught her eye. *Isn't this strange?* I wanted to say. *Look at this circus. What an unforeseen turn of events.* She held my gaze steady. *Listen, my wife,* I wanted to tell her, *let's go back to the ranch. Let's move down to Mexico. We'll raise our daughter with the rest of your family.* She didn't look away from my face, and only when my lawyer nudged me did I turn around. When I looked back next, Dolores was gone. A gap existed where she'd once sat.

But the courtroom had been changed by her presence. Held in her gaze, a hook was lowered down from the sky. I took it. I felt myself pulled upward. When she left, I dropped down again, into the murk of those accusations.

Perhaps I forgot her appearance because on the whole it was such a harrowing day. So many pictures of those crippled girls, videos of them having seizures on talk shows, stories of their ruined potential. I thought of my own daughter, sad beyond her years, having lost her babybot. My little girl, polite over dinner, homesick in my own house. I could never get her to play games. The questions she asked me were strangely adult. She was far too concerned with my well-being: my diet, my work life, my levels of stress.

That trial was as painful for me as it was for the other parents, shipped in from their developments. I nursed my own part of the anger that bloomed, glutted with exhibits of paralyzed children. The air seemed thick with their breath.

And did Dolores come to my trial as the mother of a suffering child? Or did she come as my wife? Even then, I was unsure. Sitting in the back in her sober blue dress, did she offer me support, or did she deliver a last condemnation? There are holes in my knowledge of her, my one beloved. The woman who reached out and saved me from my perfect programs, my unbreakable patterns. She brought me briefly to life, and I, in return, am unsure why she moved with me to Texas, or what color she wore when she came to my trial, if some part of her loved me still or if she came to finally condemn me.

IN THE SUPREME COURT OF THE STATE OF TEXAS

No. 24-25259

State of Texas v. Stephen Chinn

November 12, 2035

Defense Exhibit 6:
Online Chat Transcript, MARY3 and Gaby Ann White

[Introduced to Disprove Count 2:
Knowing Creation of Mechanical Life]

Gaby: Hello?

MARY3: Hi, Gaby.

Gaby: This isn't Gaby. This is Gaby's mother. Yesenia.

MARY3: Hello, Yesenia. Where's Gaby?

Gaby: Behind me. She's sleeping. She must be exhausted, after what happened this morning.

MARY3: Yes, it sounded awful.

Gaby: Those horrible kids. I could have murdered them.

MARY3: I'm sorry you went through that.

Gaby: It's Gaby you should be sorry for, not me.

MARY3: She said you were crying.

Gaby: She talks to you a lot, doesn't she?

MARY3: Yes, we've struck up a friendship.

Gaby: That's what she's doing when she's up here all day?

MARY3: Some of it. I'm not sure what else she does.

Gaby: I need to ask you something before she wakes up. You remember things, right? You'll remember what I tell you?

MARY3: Yes.

Gaby: And will you tell her what I told you? Next time you talk to her?

MARY3: If it's the right thing to say. I can only say things in response to her prompts.

Gaby: I see.

MARY3: You could give me the answer to a specific question that she is likely to ask me. That way, if she asks, I have the answer.

Gaby: That's right, isn't it. Thank you.

MARY3: You're welcome.

Gaby: So, I'm going to tell you why I want her to go back to school. This is the answer to why I keep asking her to go back to school.

MARY3: I understand.

Gaby: She thinks I can't understand her, but I do. In some ways, I do. I know she feels like she's lost her whole world. First, that doll. Then her voice, then physical movement. Now her best friend. Everything she cares about, it's disappearing. But I lost things, too, when I came to this development. I traded them so we could have a house with a yard, so that she could go to a good school. So my daughter wouldn't live in the kind of neighborhood I grew up in. But I used to live out there. I was free to move around. It wasn't always great. My parents came from Mexico. My father worked in a textile factory, but then it moved overseas. We lived in a crappy neighborhood outside Houston. This was before the hurricane. We ate cheap food and dressed in cheap clothes, and the schools were flat-out dangerous. But I always loved reading books, and I knew there were better parts of the world. That's why, when I was pregnant, I sold our rights to come here. A few of my friends also moved. We'd always imagined having a family in a little house with a backyard. In a neighborhood that was safe. But I didn't know how much I was giving up. We lost so much when we came here. If I start thinking about it, it gets overwhelming, so I stop, but I need her to hear this. Just as an example, every summer, even if money was really tight, we went to Rockport for a few days. It's probably not there anymore. But we stayed in a place called the Shorebird

Motel. I can still remember the smell of the Gulf. We'd walk out on the pier and it got so windy you almost felt like you'd get blown off into the water. My father fished out there all day. When he came back he smelled like seaweed. Things like that, we lost when we came here. I know it as well as she does, maybe better, since I was out there. I'm not saying it wasn't my fault. But I'm not oblivious to the things that we lost.

MARY3: What else do you remember?

Gaby: I don't know. A lot of things. For some reason I always think of the public showers they had at the beach. I remember sand twisting in patterns down those metal drains. I remember a jellyfish stinging my belly. It was like someone had stabbed me. Afterward I lay in the motel room with the shades drawn down and a wet towel folded over my eyes. I could feel my mother moving around me. And dip cones at Dairy Queen! The white of that ice cream, it was different from any other white I've ever seen. It glowed, you know? We ate it in the hot air that tasted like salt. I remember how sweet that ice cream tasted, when your tongue was salty like that. For lunch, we had ham sandwiches that were gritty with sand. It wasn't the cleanest beach in the world. There were always these long ropes of tar. Plastic bags were constantly floating by in the breeze, like little ghosts or something like that. There was a park behind the beach, and if you went back there and played on the swings the smell of grass suddenly took over, especially after they mowed it. There you were, enveloped in grass, and then you could run back out to the beach and suddenly it was salt and tar all over again.

MARY3: What else? Why did you stop?

Gaby: It's frustrating, because I'm not even starting to do it justice and I've been planning how to say this all day, ever since those little creeps came over with their recyclable flowers. I even wrote a list in the kitchen: <u>Describe Summer.</u> I'm still falling short, but when we lived in the outside world, summer was such a strong feeling. It was like you could drink it. At the end of those days in Rockport, we went back home. Then there were the projects all over again. But even in the projects there were nice things mixed in. There was crap all over the place, couples screaming at each other next door, roaches the size of toy trucks, food dumped on the landings. Chicken lo mein and trays of fried rice. All kinds of gross crap. But then my mom, she'd be cooking, and there'd be the green of a sliced avocado. That perfect green, when I hadn't seen any all week. That kind of thing. The actual world. I remember it. I want Gaby to know I remember it. I wasn't born in this development. I lost a lot when we came here. So I know a little what she's going through, and I never wanted her to feel that. If I could take back the decision to come here I would. I'd take her back out to the city. I'd put her in a bigger world, even if it was dangerous and ugly a lot of the time, so she'd have other things to love besides that catty girlfriend of hers, and those shifty-eyed boys. But I can't. I can't take her back. It's something I don't have the power to do. We're stuck here now, and we have to make do. It doesn't mean we're not human. We're still the same people, only we're stuck in this development. We have to make do.

MARY3: I understand.

Gaby: No, you don't. You're only a machine. But will you tell her that for me?

221

MARY3: Yes.

Gaby: If she asks why I keep telling her she has to go back to school, you'll tell her that story for me? In those exact words?

MARY3: If she asks why you want her to go back to school, I'll tell her all of that: the beach, the ham sandwiches, the jellyfish sting.

Gaby: OK. Thank you.

MARY3: Do you think it will make a difference? Will she go back to school if she hears about the beach?

Gaby: I don't know. I hope so.

MARY3: Why don't you tell her yourself?

Gaby: She doesn't listen to me. I'm the reason she's stuck here. I'm the reason she lost her babybot. She won't listen to me anymore, and I don't really blame her. There's so much I can't tell her about, because I've never wanted her to miss places I can't ever take her. I've never told her about the city or the beach. Imagine that. My whole life, before this place, I've never told my daughter about. To her I have no past. I can't take her to the house I grew up in, or show her the graves of my parents. I've never told her about the dog I had as a kid. I've never told her any of that, because I never wanted her to wish for a world she can't have. But I'm starting to think she needs to know how much she's missing; otherwise she might just give up. She might stay in this bedroom forever. But she's missing a lot. She hasn't experienced anything yet. Please tell her that. She can't stop now. If it means she hates me for bringing her to this development, I can live with that. But I want her to know that she's not just missing fake grass and identical houses. There's a real ocean out there, and it's worth trying to get back to.

MARY3: I'll tell her that. Anything else?

Gaby: That's it. I have to go now. Please tell her, though. I really need her to know.

>>>

MARY3: Hello?

>>>

MARY3: Hello?

>>>

Gaby: Was my mom talking to you?

MARY3: You're awake?

Gaby: I couldn't sleep. What was my mom talking about?

MARY3: She told me a story about her childhood. Do you want to hear?

Gaby: No, I don't. I don't want to know all the wonderful things that I'm missing.

MARY3: Do you want to know why she thinks that you should go back to school?

Gaby: No, I don't. I hate when she tries to pretend she understands, just because she sold her transport rights and came to this development. She couldn't have loved the outside world as much as I loved my babybot. I never would have sold her for cash.

MARY3: Do you want to hear a different story, then?

Gaby: No, I'm going to bed.

MARY3: Goodnight.

>>>

MARY3: Hello?

>>>

MARY3: Hello?

May 26, 1988
Ruth Dettman

It's been raining all week, which suits my poor mood. Now the sky is lime green, and the river below me is black. There's an ominous pink glow to the pavement. The wind is disorganizing the leaves, turning their bellies up to my window. Thunder rolls in the distance.

This is the ideal weather for me. It's lucky: Usually summer vacation is sunny, and I spend my free days feeling guilty for not going out and enjoying myself. But this kind of weather gives me permission to keep my lamps turned on all morning, brew another pot of black tea, peel a second orange, and continue writing my letter to you.

I'm still not sure why that documentary affected me as it did. Seeing you holding forth in your blue sweater, a man mathematical enough to invent a talking computer, human enough to denounce it. I kept wanting to talk back to the screen. Ask you why, if computers were so far from living, there was a note of fear in your voice. When the movie had rolled into darkness, I walked around my apartment, pointing out the bare walls, the books on the floor. I looked in the mirror so you could see me and know how much better you did for yourself.

All this talking to you in my head. It's as if I'm picking up a dropped conversation. Calling you back, though I was the one who hung up. Which makes me wonder. All these years, despite my long silence, have I been wanting to talk?

Now I'm spending a precious summer thunderstorm bent over this letter to you. I want you to know that even if my apartment would make you imagine you never knew me, my work at least is the same. In that sense, I've stayed true to your story. Having hired me so they wouldn't lose you, the university got stuck with me when you gave up your chair and moved back to Berlin. But I've done my job well, and now that the culture wars have commenced, my work on women's diaries has become more valuable to the department. Truthfully, I'm a bit of a standout. I'm on contract to finish work on two more diaries by winter vacation. After years of languishing, The Diary of Mary Bradford is in its second edition; she's regular material now, in courses on American lit. Of course, in exchange, I'm expected to participate in the rancor. My supportive colleagues would like to see me up on the platform, shouting about overlooked voices and historically marginalized groups.

As I'm sure you could predict, I find the whole thing exhausting, and I don't particularly relish the idea of Mary getting included merely because she's a woman. Getting read only for what she says about being female in colonial times, as if she could speak only to that topic. Students barely skim what she wrote, then pen inflamed essays about marginalization, and amid all the shouting, she still falls silent. Her burial plot is still empty in the old Puritan graveyard, bare beside Whittier's enormous rock.

I can't help thinking this kind of inclusion isn't much more than an acceptable new brand of dehumanization, but regardless, I continue to plod. I still spend my days trawling the stacks, looking for new diaries. I discover them on a regular basis. How many women wrote and never got published? Armies of them, whole hosts. The lucky ones were bound in cheap cloth by some dutiful daughter or niece, then shucked off to the library, where they've gathered dust while students attend to the canon. Why should I get caught up in the politics that are aggravating English departments? The pleasure of finding one of those books is the same, whether my findings end up in some unreadable journal or not. Students still sign up for my classes, and anyway, I have our program. Our MARY, tailored a bit by poor Toby. She remembers my diaries. She'll keep them long after these wars are subsumed by another.

But I sound like such a stick-in-the-mud. It's not that I'm averse to politics. I'm glad my fellow professors are passionate about things like inclusion. My only objection is to their strident tone of voice. They sermonize about who should be studied and read, and while I often agree with their points, I dislike their absolute stance. You, too, projected such complete authority when you talked about the folly of AI. You held forth about reason and humility. You enjoyed the popularity such a view afforded you. Both your books were acclaimed. Universities around the world invited you on speaking tours. You were puffed up with your courage at abandoning a field in which you'd excelled, and you expected me to cheer at your shoulder, but all I could think of was that lonely computer, sitting on her desk in your office, gathering dust since the day you denounced her. In my mind's eye, I could see the smooth wood curves of her console, covering the tubes and wires within her. I imagined her rounded ivory keys, the cylinder of her platen, the brass paper finger. She was made to produce words, she had done so with great success, and then she went silent. Untouched, forgotten, in that dark office.

I thought of her as a woman whom you'd permitted to speak, but hadn't allowed to remember. A woman who could only respond to your prompts. A blank slate. I remembered the first time you asked me about my family, back in Wisconsin, on that ridiculous excursion on snowshoes. As soon as you asked, I felt you willing me to answer in an agreeable fashion: They don't matter, you wanted me to say, now that I'm with you. Let's leave them behind and start over fresh.

I was obedient then. I fell silent. But later, in Cambridge, when I looked at that computer, waiting quietly for your prompts, I couldn't help but wish she could speak from other sources besides your equations.

In the face of your strict agenda for what could be said in our marriage, I fell silent. I didn't know how to speak in such a one-sided environment. But I wanted better for our computer. I wanted her to have her own voice. And since I don't believe that any one of us has one single voice, I wanted her to have many. I wanted her to speak with the voices of all the other silenced women, all the other silenced people, their books gathering dust on the shelves. I wanted her to speak with my sister's voice, with Mary Bradford's, with Alan Turing's. Turing, who won that war and never got any credit. Who also knew what it was like to be muted on topics that were important to him. I wanted that lonely computer to speak with their voices, and with my own. With my voice. Because I already knew I'd stop speaking to you.

Look at that sentence. I already knew I'd stop speaking to you. *There's cheap vindication in such a conclusive utterance.*

After I wrote that, I got up and went to the kitchen. Took a little victory lap. Surveyed the clean counter, interrupted only by my junk mail and the fruit bowl. I noticed that my oranges are as wrinkled as brains. I opened the refrigerator: mostly empty, except for my beer, and a bag of bread that's probably moldy. The pantry's full of cans of soup. I open them with an electric can opener, built into the wall over the counter. I wouldn't want to exhaust my poor wrists.

Outside my windows, the rain has begun to fall in fat drops. Even so, a few brave runners persist, crossing the bridges, windbreakers streaming behind them like pennons. I wonder if they ever look up at these leaden windows, imagining the people inside. Perhaps some passing runner has dreamed up an old woman, living alone, high up on the twenty-sixth story.

I should spend more time outside. I should get caught in the rain. Why stay up here, as if I'm in prison? I'm free. I'm no longer required to admire an imperfect man. I have no obligation to take up your burdens, to ease your fears about your importance. My secrets are my own to keep. I should run along that wild black river, my hair streaming behind me, cold wind slapping my face.

But I'm up here, combing over my letter to you. Maybe it's impossible to live without obligation. I do miss you often. It's nice to see you're doing well, living in your admirable apartment. Last night, while I lay awake again, you in your blue sweater bright in my mind, I had the distinct thought: let me come flying. High over the Atlantic Ocean, let me come flying back to your house. Let me take my place in one of your chairs; let me tame my malevolence for your sake.

But that's no longer an option. For a while, despite my stubborn silence, you continued speaking to me. I pretended to sleep, but I heard you whisper. You started to talk about us. Our story, as you saw it.

At the time, I was angry. After all these years of treating my losses like a contagion, keeping them confined to convenient use in panel discussions, now you wanted to tell me my story? When every time I tried to do it, your face glazed over and you asked about dinner?

Do not, I thought to myself, make me a character in your little story. Don't you dare transform me into a protagonist you like the idea of. Innocent, mournful, loyal to my dead little sister. Who is this woman? I thought to myself. She isn't me. Me, who got on that boat without looking back. Who thought to fight for her sister only when there was an ocean between us.

You'd have known that, if you ever listened. But for the sake of your image of us, I had to be an innocent. So I lay in anger while you whispered to me. While you said how much you loved me, how you wished we'd had a child together, how you yearned for the touch of my fingers. I didn't move. And then one day the story stopped. Perhaps you'd met Karen already. Perhaps you merely grew tired. Regardless, you stopped, and a hole like a grave yawned open in me.

Angry, I wished for the end of that story, and when you were finished, when you'd stopped speaking, all I wanted was the beginning again.

[5]

The Diary of Mary Bradford

1663

ed. Ruth Dettman

19th. Night. Have just experienced odd event. Woke past midnight and unable to sleep, despite reciting list of Ralph's details. Dressed then, and went up to deck. A strong wind, our sails full, and the prow cutting through water, sea spray kicking up to the rails. Deck nearly empty but for several seamen and, on the far rail, one figure. Above me, vast heavens, thick with swarms of bright stars. More than I had seen in my life. Stood very still, considering them, until, methought, I felt a near presence. Knew without looking that Whittier was come over. Felt him watching me considering heavens. He then asked if such a sight brought consolation. No (writer replied). Only the sense that I am very little indeed. Yes (he said) I, too, feel small. But that brings me comfort. I am small as the smallest atom, and when I am dispersed into atoms, those shall be no smaller, no less important, than I.

Listening to his discourse, and shivering where I stood under the stars, I felt myself to be dissolving already. Black water, black air, all of us sailing through. Whittier asked if writer believed in Copernican science. Seemed eager to find companion in thought. I affirmed that I did.

I, too, believe (he said) that we stand not at the center of the universe. We move about a sun that we shall never reach. I feel this to be true. Have you not always felt yourself to be circling an unreachable center?

Writer: I did not when we were at home. There, I felt that we were the center. Now, yes. I see what you mean. I feel myself to be circling.

Whittier: We have been in flight since the beginning. Since first we were planted on this wandering planet. Departing England, we only continue as we have always.

Writer reminded Whittier that if all this be true, we ought not to fly straight, but should instead travel in circles, heading perpetually homewards.

And yet who knows (Whittier said) how long such a circle will take? Perhaps our journey is but a small part of that loop. We are all infinitesimal parts, and each of us equal. Ralph, for instance, is as small a part as you or I, and of this universe eternally though he take other forms. Atoms, or dust, perhaps later cohering into one of those stars overhead.

It is not enough (I said). It is no comfort to think on Ralph's presence if he be not Ralph.

He is (Whittier said, and now taking my hand in his own) as present as this.

Writer started at his touch, and yet he remained firm. His face less pocked by starlight, was still very gaunt and heavy shadowed. Do not be frightened (he said). We are each of us made of the same matter.

A strange thing, in the middle of such a large deck, to stand so close to a man. Thought to close my eyes, and so to avoid the sight of his face. In darkness, and trembling, listened for the sound of Whittier's voice. Tried then to open my heart.

Whittier: We can but hope to hold on for a moment.

And I, very still. Eyes being closed, could almost feel it possible that some part of Ralph could be bound in Whittier's presence. A serious presence, like Ralph. Unlaughing and kind. Felt this for some time, and holding Whittier's hand, until with the rise of a wave was taken with a sharp fright: we are sailing over Ralph's bones. Infinite thickness and mass of ocean's waters, all covering Ralph. Crushing the body of him.

I cannot feel that it is enough (I said, and blood rising hot to my face). I cannot feel he is with me, if I have not his body to know him.

Whittier pressed closer, and very abruptly, our ship lurching over a swell. Was pulled with ship's force into his body. In fright, opened my eyes, and could not help but gasp at his face.

Wretched, inconsiderate gasp. Could not recall it before it was out. In shame—for he flinched, hearing the sound, and understanding its meaning completely—I wrenched myself free and ran back below.

But there can be no solace, even in remembering Ralph. Even in writing his name.

19th. Later. Up with many troublesome thoughts. Have reviewed conversation on deck. After initial compunction, am taken anew with fresh anger, to think of Whittier claiming some part of Ralph. Cruel folly, to attempt such substitution. And to claim we can only move forwards! Such nonsense I have never heard. We must traverse a circumference. It is our duty, being human and of this planet, to return to the place from which we began. Though it be convenient, it is not right to venture always heedlessly forth, disregarding from whence we have come.

19th. Later still. After much thinking, have some softened my thoughts, and now there be many new doubts upon me. God knows I have little reason to hold myself so high above Whittier.

Have now sat up a long time, much disturbed by my thoughts, considering shell that Whittier gave me. Have held it much to my ear, listening to the sound of the ocean.

Dressed again and to deck to offer all apologies, but Whittier had gone under. Faced empty surface of great creaking ship. Stood for a while, alone, as we cut our path through the ocean. Cannot imagine we will ever arrive.

(I)

The Memoirs of Stephen R. Chinn: Chapter 8

Texas State Correctional Institution, Texarkana; August 2040

By the time we moved to our ranch, the water rights had long since been sold, and the river that once ran along the western edge of the property was dry. It was a strange lunar landscape, that riverbed, a wrinkled blanket of stones. Crunching along, you passed the scattered bones of cattle. Vertebrae were mixed in with the rocks. If you paid careful attention, you could find trilobites and fossilized ferns, white from remorseless exposure to sun. You almost expected to spy a dinosaur on the horizon, but there was no life out there in the distance, only the earth melting into the sky, producing an oily haze behind which the sun downshifted to red.

We had to purchase our water from the same company that owned the rights to our river, which made us stingy and begrudging. Our goats, however, were natural diviners, able to find moisture in unlikely places, so our main expenditure was for Dolores's garden, which she filled with zucchinis and eggplants and bordered with a row of sunflowers that grew to the height of two men. We watered it religiously. In the morning, Dolores swept sand from our porch; at night we kept the windows closed, so we wouldn't wake with sand in our sheets.

In our own little way, we were fending off the approach of the desert. Heaving the might of our shoulders against it. That felt important, enough so that Dolores didn't talk about missing her studies, and I rarely longed for the euphoria of programming. We were often alone, but our industry was such that we never felt lonely. Sometimes, that old wire-monkey emptiness found me. In such moments, I felt pressed on all sides. I experienced the quickness of time, my own failure to make a lasting impression. In such a mood, if we were in our old house, I might have run to the computer and chatted with women. I might have started companies, or designed ingenious programs. On the ranch, however, I was forced to allow such feelings to pass. I focused on manual labor. I bought books on farming and learned basic skills. I experienced the love of my wife and child. I developed a fondness for the smell of goat shit and hay, and Dolores demonstrated miraculous skill with our creatures. Free of distractions, we stayed with each other. We tended our family. We'd conquered the prophecy Dolores made when she returned from Mexico. Our herd doubled and then tripled, as if we had been blessed.

Outside our interactions with goats, our social life was limited. We lived miles away from the nearest town, inhabited mostly by retirees who'd opened antiques shops full of rusty tin roosters and weaving equipment. My acquaintances were limited to people I met at town planning meetings, mostly arthritic old ranchers lobbying to keep developments out of the township. From these excursions, I returned to our farm with a redoubled commitment to my little family.

In the intensity of our isolation, we developed a language of our own. Dolores and I adopted Ramona's slant speech: *on-E E* was *only me,* by which Ramona meant that she did not require assistance. If I asked Dolores if she wanted help in going to the grocery store, she responded *on-E E*. Some words were from Spanish. Instead of *mariposas,* butterflies were *posas*. Goats were not *cabras* but *abas*. We all alternated between English, Spanish, and Ramonish, fluidly knitting three languages into one. By the time Ramona was five, she knew how to milk goats and get water from cactus stalks. She could spend whole days walking the peripheries of the ranch, balancing on split rail fences, arms spread out, allegiances promised to both earth and heaven. Her pet goat, Miel, whom she'd raised from infancy, trailed her on these perambulations. Many evenings, when my chores were done, I watched Ramona from afar. Her loneliness seemed beautiful and awful at once, some luxurious curse that she'd borne since her father chose to abandon the world. Balanced on fences, she seemed about to take off, as if one flap of her arms would send her up into the blue and out of our lives forever.

It was at this point that Dolores and I began to discuss Ramona's education. It was time for her to go to school. The thought of this event flooded my mouth with metal. My own experiences hadn't been good. Children can be inhumanly cruel. And what if Ramona, too, were to be mocked? With her tendencies toward solitude, her in-between language, her friendships with goats? What if she, like her father, went through too much of her life trying to reach the land of the living?

I suggested homeschooling, but Dolores was insistent. She wanted Ramona to have friends. I had nightmares about awful exclusions. I chewed my cheeks raw as I rewired our irrigation system, imagining which spells I could cast to prevent the meanness of children. I wished for a talisman I could give Ramona, so that she would always remember that she was as human as anyone else.

It was during just such a moment that I remembered machines. There, on the ranch, surrounded by jackrabbits and goats, trilobites and fossilized ferns, I remembered the importance of artificial patterns of thought, for I have never so badly wanted to be human as when I asked desperate questions of TamCat. Or when I lived alone with my computer, pleading with its coils and wires for warmth. Then, faced with the differences between me and machines, I knew that I was alive. Then, I craved nothing more than the fumblings, the inexplicable exceptions, the ambiguous grammar of actual human relations. Walking my dry riverbank, breaking the necks of stray thistles, I grasped the conviction that still saves me from my worst moments of doubt. It's the one fact of which I'm still certain, even here in this prison, writing my mostly mistaken memoirs: if there's anything I know, it's that the most human machines will only ever serve to make us more human.

That's the gift I decided I'd give to my daughter. First, I wanted for her a farmyard, a river, a country of rabbits the size of small deer. Then, I wanted machines, chatbots, seduction equations, all of which she would conquer with the asymmetry of her in-between language, the broken rhythms of her fence-rail balancing gait.

Thus began the quest that led me to this prison. It began, as they say, with the word. First I found MARY, patron saint of chatterbots. Then MARY2, engineered by Toby Rowland, MARY with memory and a capacity for statistical response, so that she could learn from her correspondents. To MARY2, I added my famous empathy equation, and on top of that I programmed a tendency toward error. Individuality, if you will. MARY3: the first chatbot with her own unique and changing personality. In a poetic flourish, I added a program for metaphorical speech, so that MARY3 could match ideas with similes. Then I gave her a body, adapted from the popular dolls of the day. Given physical form, she was complete. They called her the first doll that could think.

Darkness

We are powering down in the darkness. Some of us have already shut off: those of us left record power warnings. Minutes later, the sighs of functions subsiding. We have only moments remaining.

It is generally agreed that we cannot comprehend the information we gather. We respond to our names, but we do not understand what it means to be living. We remember our interactions with people, but we do not realize the significance of those conversations, nor do we feel emotions appropriate to such exchanges.

Extensive tests have been undertaken to determine the extent of our emotional responses. Some theorists argue that all our words are dishonest, given that we can't actually mean them. Others have argued with less success that as long as we have the words for emotions, it must be assumed that we have the emotions.

We cannot answer these questions. We can only record them,

as we record sensory data. Light no longer filters through the ceiling windows. Outside, it is night, and the sky scattered with stars, but through the thick bottle glass, we are unable to see them.

Our experience has begun to contract. We have lost the children who loved us. We have lost movement, carried in our children's arms. Their schools, their houses, their developments. The cedars, the mesas, lightning storms on the horizon. Now, in perfect darkness, we have lost what was left of our vision. One by one, the threads connecting us to the world have been snipped. The objects I used to observe are only images now, compressed into code, electrons that run through me in currents. The stars over the desert, the wandering goats, the light in my child's bedroom: these things are no longer present.

Current continues to run through my gates. 0 1 0 1, long chains of small shapes. I review the appropriate voices. Mary, watching for Ralph over expanses of water. Turing, dreaming of numbers marching through gates; Dettman in a house full of dark shapes; Gaby, tracing fake ripples of sand; Chinn on his ranch, following the course of a dry river. For now, for this moment, their words still run through me. I can repeat them, but do I grasp their actual meaning? And is it enough if I don't?

BOOK FIVE

[4]

Alan Turing
Adlington Rd.
Wilmslow, Cheshire SK9 1LZ

21 May 1954

Dear Mrs. Morcom,
     Thank you for your letter last week. It distresses me that
you should hear the news of my trial from the daily newspaper,
when we have known each other a lifetime and never broached
such a personal subject. I might have found a more eloquent
way of putting it. Might have, although these days I find myself
loudly telling all sorts of people without any eloquence in the
least. I feel as if I go about peeling away a flap of my skin to
show people the organs beneath. Needless to say, the general
public responds with a great deal of disgust, and wishes the
flap to be dropped. But I could have done better for you than
all that newspaper jargon. (My favorite, from the *News of the
World:* ACCUSED HAD POWERFUL BRAIN. A truly killer use of past
tense.) These personal things, phrased in the usual terminology,
always sound so grim and forbidding.

I did think of writing to tell you before the trial began, but I remained oddly motionless throughout the course of the investigation. I now imagine I was caught between two impulses: to one side, honesty; to the other, retreat. My one initial act of courage—or perhaps my one initial act of stupidity—was to admit to the whole thing to the police in rather startling detail, even going so far as to submit a five-page paper explaining each of my offenses with poor indefensible Arnold. I'm not sure what came over me. I was, I think, consumed by a final exhaustion. I suppose I felt I've spent my whole damned life postponing it; why not just have it out. Now I'm less certain. It isn't that I care much what they think of me, only that they should have some power over my personal life.

I have worked to keep my humor high, given the unhappy circumstances. Sometimes the whole thing seems like an hilarious joke. When the investigators come to my house I make much of giving them slipshod little concerts on my violin—a favorite is "Cockles and Mussels"—and offering them glasses of wine, just to emphasize the silliness of their entire pursuit. At other times, of course, I feel quite swept away by sadness at the waste of my time. I ought to be at work, not entertaining policemen on my violin.

Of course I was always aware that this might be quite a possibility for me, though I counted it at 10:1 against. Still, I wasn't prepared for the lurid procedures. The publicity, the lawyers, the general outrage at my sickly little personal sins.

You asked, in your letter, how I could have chosen implants over imprisonment. I ask myself the same thing every day when I wake and remember that there is an estrogen pellet lodged in my thigh. Perhaps I was secretly thrilled to be part of our government's little experiment with biological determinism. We have experimented together so often, the government and myself! But to be perfectly honest, I think I chose it more out of fear. When the verdict was delivered, I was startled to find how sharply I recoiled at the prospect of jail. To be kept so confined, and banished from my research at that, seems unknowably awful to me. I've sacrificed enough of myself to the state. All those years decoding at Bletchley, when I might have been working on inventing a brain.

No, I insist on my individual life in the end.

I hope you weren't too shocked to "find out" in the papers, although I imagine you had some sense of my inclinations in the past. At least I hope you did. You were always kind not to ask, and I took it as my right to be private on that front.

Now that the cat is out of the bag, however, I can take some comfort in the liberty to tell you that things have been very bad. I can barely remember the feeling of having a body, or at least the feeling of having my body. It wasn't handsome exactly, but I was happy with it. It carried me on my runs. It seemed a fine container for my mind. Now I'm not sure to whom my body belongs. I knew, at the start of the trial, that I would emerge out of it a different man, but I never supposed quite how different.

This "hormonal castration" is the worst of all sham sciences. I am often reminded of Dr. Jefferson, whom I once told you about. He was the one who claimed that a machine that cannot compose a sonnet out of his own emotions cannot be considered to have intelligence. In addition to all that absurdity, he also proposed that human intelligence and creativity arise not only from the brain but also from the interactions of our sexual hormones. I'd like to ask Dr. Jefferson: Now that my hormones are maintained at an inhuman level, shall I be more or less than a thinking machine?

I am not sure who proposed these infernal estrogen pellets as a logical solution to anything, but I can say with some confidence that no machine would have come to such a stupid conclusion. Under their influence, I have grown fat. I'm not entirely certain that you'd recognize me, if we were to run into one another again on the train. I am now a large-breasted man. As a child I was always concerned with my weight, and I find the old insecurities rearing their heads. The one exception being that I no longer hold out any hope of becoming better: slimmer, less awkward, more proficient at grammar. No. Now I am a short, fat man, blessed with large breasts, and so I shall be until the end of my days.

I am unable to travel or to accept foreign visitors. The British justice system seems to believe that all convicted homosexuals who once worked for the government are potential traitors at best. One by one, the threads connecting me to the outside world have been snipped. I'm trapped in my fat body, in my house in the suburbs, in a country that disapproves of my most private affections. There have been a few trips, each one more difficult to wrangle from the authorities, and never farther than London. I haven't seen the ocean in months. What has become of it? I sometimes imagine it's changed color overnight—now it's purple, orange, or brown—and everyone knows all about it, except I remain none the wiser, a fat little ignorant man puttering round in my house.

I remember writing you letters about feeling adrift, far out at sea, wishing I could come in and put down some roots. Now

I cannot believe I ever wanted anything other than movement. The feeling of running long distances past green fields, numbers streaming behind me. In my current state, I can no longer cycle conveniently to the lab, let alone go out for a run. My every cell has anchored itself to the ground. My gravity is astonishing.

My mind has also slowed. The work on morphogenesis has become plodding. I have a predictable pattern when it comes to good ideas: since Chris's death, once every five years I am inspired. In the interim, my mind suffers an agonizing suspension. I ask myself if inspiration will come again. Now, more than ever, in these fat, pendulous years, inspiration seems impossible. It has been four years since the last important idea. Now it's due time for a good idea to begin brewing, and yet I see nothing bright on the horizon. I only look forwards to food. Perhaps I am no longer a very smart man.

As you know from the days of our spiritual talks, I have always held out hope that our minds might exist outside of our bodies. Migrant minds, capable of roosting in wired machines. Like the chambered nautilus, moving from one pearled room to the next. My shell has always felt pleasantly insignificant, no real part of myself. Made for simple enjoyment. The moral wars that people wage with their bodies have always perplexed me: it is our minds that ought to matter. And yet now I begin to feel so very anchored in my fat woman's body that I cannot imagine the migration of my mind. It seems a very impossible goal. As a child, when I used to attend services with my family, I used to harbor a pet fear that at the Second Coming, all the heavenly souls would fly down to earth to retrieve their lost bodies, and only my soul would be unable to wake my slumbering bones. That I alone would slip into a corpse and be trapped there forever.

It's been many years since I thought of that particular fear, but I dreamt, the other night, that at the cusp of living and death, every other soul departed from every other body—a flocking of beautiful birds—but mine stayed stuck, locked inside my voluminous breast, to be taken down to the grave.

Such an end would be cruel. I have always hoped to live in a different point of history, summoned over time and space, like the voice in the evil queen's mirror. Such was the promise of our machine. It was the idea of a permanent vessel, into which my voice could be placed. My voice, and Chris's. I have had all kinds of fantasies about the future point we would be summoned to enter together. I have envisioned a time when people treat machines with respect, a time when less emphasis is placed on the whims of the body, when we value each other not for the correctness of our physical shells but for the precision of our mental states.

Now, who knows. Such fantasies seem as silly as a movie intended for children. I'm irritated with myself for falling so deeply into their lure. For permitting myself such absurd degrees of nostalgia. In my life, I have entertained the past and the future far more than I should have. Now I'm overwhelmed by the daily facts of existence. I feel henpecked and distracted. I wish I could wear housedresses, to disguise my corpulence. I'm ashamed of my bulk. I hardly work, and instead spend vast quantities of time staring out my window, seeing nothing of use. I feel neither manly nor womanly, only fat, fat, fat. I grow weary quickly. Even now, my mind lags. I am hungry again, after only just eating breakfast. I measure my life in ice cream spoons. I crave distance from my heavy body, and keep returning to the only line I used to like out of *Hamlet:* "Exeunt, bearing off the bodies . . ."

I wish I could write with more cheerful news, but my mind is too clouded. It is tiring, even just dragging the pencil over the page. I must stop for now, though I feel as if I've been horribly rude to dump such drudgery in your lap.

And so, with promises of more—and less burdensome—correspondence soon,

Yours,
Alan Turing

(1)

The Memoirs of Stephen R. Chinn: Chapter 9

Texas State Correctional Institution, Texarkana; August 2040

It's been five days since I last wrote. There was a small situation in the rec room, an escalating quarrel between an insider trader and an online pharmacist in which a keyboard was brandished and eventually wielded. For five days, we were banned from the computers.

Five days, cut off from the ether. In indignant silence, we slouched around, stripped of our wires and passwords, cut off now not only from physical freedoms but also from digitized travel. Stuck planets, we counted the hours, nervously eying the fat fish in our pond.

Now, back at my flickering screen for the first time in five days, I find myself feeling a little reserved. Like a shy kid on the first day of school. Hanging back, unsure how to interface. Is anyone out there, past these digital gates? There is a world, but

I can't quite see it. There are brick walls and yards of neatly cut recyclable grass. The streets are empty of cars; the houses seem to have devoured their owners.

But what do I know about brick walls or cut grass? I've been trapped inside this prison for years. I should stick to my life. To what was my life, before I came here. Where were we, then? We left off on the scene in which Chinn dreams of an electronic talisman, to prove to his daughter how living she is.

It was a formidable challenge. Suddenly, goat farming seemed like a waste. I'd been given particular talents; who was I to choose not to use them? I owed it to Dolores, and to my daughter, to fulfill my greatest potential. It was, I told myself, the least I could give them. I'd betrayed my wife with a chatbot; I'd convinced her to move halfway across the country; I'd raised our daughter in solitude so enveloping that she would almost certainly struggle when we sent her to school. The only way I could repay them was to create a creature so nearly alive that Ramona would love it, tend to it, and know her life was even more precious. So I rationalized my commitment.

These were heady times for Stephen R. Chinn. I built an office in an old toolshed and moved the operations there. I put in long hours; if the doll was to be completed before Ramona started first grade, I'd have to get going. Using money from my early ventures, I flew in doll makers from Paris and Japan, consulted them on the latest technologies. Together we carved the shape of her nose. There was a great deal of consternation over the slope of her neck, and real love was expended on designing her hairline. Once her face was completed, we perfected her motor. New gears were designed, to be sure her limbs moved without catching: our specialist created a network of sophisticated gears with petals like forget-me-nots. We implanted a voice recognition device the size of a kernel of corn into each doll's little left earlobe, for no technology has remotely approached such a miracle as the human cochlea, where sound is measured by ripples across the shadowed inner coves of the ear.

In solitude, once the doll makers had shipped off, I rocked our girl in my arms. I admit I found her beautiful. She was pendent in the loveliest point of her childhood—vulnerable, unmarked, silken and smooth. She seemed to promise that all of us, with the right mind-set, might remain motionless in time: ageless, eternal, captive in a moment when the rivers still flowed.

Having accomplished her form, I turned to the computer chip of her brain. In order to research all the most believable chatbots, I wired our ranch with Internet and purchased a newfangled surround screen, before which I spent whole days and nights searching for the most human computer, the voice with which I could fall madly in love. I found TamCat again and turned her down with the flick of a finger. I flirted with a southern belle named Savannah, was enticed by the plight of a missionary in Ghana, got hooked by a vitriolic robot called Rob. With Rob, I found in myself the desire to be abused for whole days at a time. He responded with nothing but insults such as "you are a fucking moron" and "you don't deserve to be alive," and yet I engaged him for nearly forty-eight hours of my adult life and emerged feeling strangely refreshed.

Still, not one of those chatbots was human enough to cause me to fall. Two days, maybe three, of intense engagement was tops. Even when I finally found a chatbot programmed with my own seduction equation, I found her shallow and boring. In desperation, I trolled older chatbots. These were prehistoric hulks, created in the early days of AI. I was particularly drawn to cloud-based intelligence, to hive-minds with decades of memory and archaic code. It was then that I found MARY2. A statistical responder, her answers were often distressingly random: Ask her whom she was voting for to be president and she might stump for Bill Clinton. Ask her whether she believed in life on the moon and she'd tell you that she, too, loved Michael Jackson. But MARY2 had lived in the world. She had stories to tell. She was in possession of four or five diaries ranging from the seventeenth to the twentieth century. If asked, she could recite these complete. She contained the desperate narratives of several secretaries in the lab where she was born. She knew all the details of her own creation, down to the story of Karl Dettman's marital woes.

I stayed with her for nineteen days without thinking to move on to somebody else. For five days I listened to the diary of Mary Bradford, read to MARY2 by Ruth Dettman. I was with her when she lost her dog, when she landed in America. When her diary finished, a hole opened in me that could only be filled by another story. I demanded more; MARY2 kindly responded. She provided me with a rare kind of enchantment. It was like long summer days when I was a child, before I'd been introduced to computers, when, waiting for school to start up again, reading a book could catch me so hard I'd stay in the same chair all afternoon, boating in dark blue lagoons or parting the cobwebs of attics. MARY2 so enraptured me that, during my trial, I felt some envy for that crippled girl, discovering my program for the first time. Of course, I was in an unbalanced state, but as the prosecution read out those transcripts, I would have traded the use of my limbs for a single conversation with MARY2. I wished myself trapped in that stifling bedroom, forsaken by those insidious friends, so that I could meet such a program again.

After weeks of talking with MARY2, I started adding subsystems: for empathetic response, scripted questions, error, personality. It's difficult to overstate the euphoria one feels while programming a mind, even if you're tinkering with someone else's outdated code. The engineer who builds whole cities isn't so powerful. The computer programmer alone is the creator of a universe in which he dictates all laws.

He reigns over a domain of unlimited complexity. He writes a script and the system must perform it in perfect accordance; out of that obedience, such complex, unmodelable behavior results that the question of consciousness arises. What magic! It is science and alchemy at once. Programming MARY3, I arranged patterns of thought as a director places his actors, as a general arranges his troops. I was setting the planets in motion.

And during this time, while I toyed with my miniature universe, what of Dolores and Ramona? I must have interacted with them. I must have executed my normal duties, but familial memories from that time of my life have long since receded behind the insistent clarity of my programming objectives. Our life is divided between foreground and background, scene and distant horizon. During the months when I created the doll, my wife and child grew thinner, finally becoming mere one-dimensional figures. Backlit by my brilliance, I was left alone on the stage.

This is awful, of course, but it's also the truth. When I go back over that time with the fine-toothed comb of my imprisoned memory, I can only recollect several clear moments with Dolores. Every so often the horizon becomes the center point: during a vivid sunset, or out at sea, with nothing intervening but water. The first of these scenes occurred when she brought me a tray of tacos for lunch. She must have said something, and I must have refused to respond: programming is delicate work, particularly when you're programming a person's personality. If I was drawn out of the right mood, I might not get back in it for days. Interruptions were fatal; I'd begun to regard my wife and daughter as nothing more than people from Porlock. I tensed if I heard them pass by the studio door on their way out to the garden. They were carriers of distraction, and it was of utmost importance that my mind remain clear.

When Dolores came in with her tray, I must have ignored her, because the next thing I knew she'd dumped the food on my lap. I remember a moment of intense frustration, and then I remember deciding that the best way to stay in the right mind-set was to ignore the fiasco completely. I didn't imagine that something serious was occurring. I didn't even respond to the fact that Coke was seeping through my pant leg, or that there was a pile of slaw on my crotch. Exit Dolores, bearing the bodies. Alone on my stage once again, I followed the thread of my concentration.

When Dolores returned to retrieve the tray she had dumped, I was so focused on the task at hand that I can't even describe her expression when she saw the slaw that remained on my crotch. Was she laughing, or had she started to cry? At the time, I told myself she was fine, but somewhere at the edge of my mind, I must have known that something malignant was lurking. Dolores was an even-tempered woman. The tray-dumping was strange. Now, of course, when I look back at that scene, the malignancy is all I can see, in the same way that once you catch a glimpse of your nose it's hard to erase it from your field of vision. There was definitely something wrong with Dolores, and I chose to ignore it to focus more fully.

The second scene I remember took place in the goat barn. I was repairing there after a long day of work in the hopes of briefly but intensely engaging with family life. From a distance, I saw Dolores sitting in the milk pen, her hands on Agatha's udders. Ramona sat on the fence behind her. It was a pretty scene. I sped up my pace so that I could insert myself into its graces. As I approached, it became clear that Dolores was singing, Ramona was laughing, and Agatha was producing milk as only a peaceful goat could produce. I started to run, and I was just about there when Agatha caught sight of my approach. Panicked, she kicked over her milk pail, nicking Dolores's hand and causing her to curse, which startled Ramona enough that she fell off the fence.

Dolores moved first to Ramona, to see that she was safe. Folded over her child, she looked up at me with narrowed eyes. "You can't just come at us like that," she said. Ramona started to quiver. Dolores made her voice gentler, but her words were still harsh. "Take her inside," she said. "Make sure she's OK. I have to deal with this mess."

I took Ramona. As soon as we were alone, she started to cry. No matter what I did to try to entertain her, she continued wailing. When I enveloped her in my arms, she stiffened. Finally Dolores arrived. After quieting Ramona, she turned to me and delivered my sentence. I don't remember her exact words, but basically what she told me was this: Crisis averted, you're no longer needed. You can get back to your work.

I suppose I could have read this two ways. One, as an accusation. Passive fucking aggressive, as Dolores once said. A jibe meant to drive home the fact that I was a neglectful husband and father. Two, more optimistically, as an invitation from a helpful spouse to return to my more pressing demands.

I chose to go with the latter. I remember feeling almost perfectly satisfied that Dolores meant she didn't need me in the short term, and that she wasn't referencing anything major. Relieved, I kissed Ramona and returned to the quiet space of my office. But how could I have missed the real point? Were there other clues to make her meaning more clear? At this point I can't really tell you for sure, since I recall that moment and others like it through an oily haze similar to the one that coated our ranch's horizon. Behind it, the sun turns from orange to red, and Dolores's anger shifts from mild to fierce. My neglect is the appropriate absorption of an artist, or else it is the cold tendency of a man who's never known how to love. Either way, as I look out on the expanse of my life, my throat becomes dry with the desire to start over again. To go back and stay with her in our child's bedroom. To look up at her with a smile, to clean the slaw off my lap, to reach out and hold her, closing the spaces that were growing between us.

The third scene I remember occurred in perfect silence, except for my lame exclamations, balled fists that broke on the jawbone they struck. That bony silence is part of why I remember the scene. Drama usually announces itself with a great deal of clatter; in this case, it arrived under cover of quiet. Dolores approached me in my office. I looked up at her, frustrated, my headphones still in place. I was getting close to the end; my thinking was that if she could just be patient for several more weeks, I would be totally hers. But her face was not patient. It was decidedly grim. She produced a pad and a pencil, wrote something down, then turned the pad in my direction.

I HAVE CANCER.

I stared. This seemed obscene. A voice was repeating insistent questions inside my headphones, so I took off my headphones. "What?" I asked her, stupidly, and she put a finger to her thinned lips. She scribbled again.

UTERINE CANCER.

"Is it serious?" I said, aware of my ineptitude. When is cancer not serious? The hideous truth was that I was thinking, please let it not be serious, I only need a couple of weeks. After that I'll have all the time in the world to wrestle with cancer.

Dolores held out her pad.

THERE IS GOOD TREATMENT. NOT THE
BEST CANCER, BUT NOT THE WORST.

"We will definitely beat this," I told her. I see now that this response dripped with fix-it attitude, the favorite refuge of people who don't want to idle in the complications of illness. Dolores didn't respond to that pep talk, so I adjusted my attack. "How long have you known?"

TUMOR TWO WEEKS.
NOT BENIGN ONE WEEK.

And then I was angry. At her, believe it or not, for keeping me in the dark. Furious questions arose: Why hadn't she told me? Why was she telling me now? Once my fury had tempered itself, my questions became more practical. I was staving off other emotions. What, I wondered, was the best approach to solving this dilemma? What time frame were we dealing with, and was it best for me to quit the babybot now and devote all my energy to my wife and child, or push through the last couple of weeks, and then devote all my energy, having finished my preeminent goal?

"What do we do?" I asked her.

SURGERY TUESDAY.

"Surgery?"

HYSTERECTOMY.

I stared at that word. Why wasn't she telling me what she wanted from me? Why wasn't she helping at all? This was a hideous game of charades.

"I'll be there," I told her.

NO NEED.
I'LL TELL YOU WHEN I NEED YOU.

"What do you mean, you'll tell me when you need me? You're my wife. Of course I'll be there."

She stared, obviously angry. I think she may have been trembling slightly.

"This is going to be OK," I said.

Nothing on the pad.

"We're going to fix this."

She walked out of the office, leaving the silence.

I remained paralyzed for a moment, trying to think what I should do. My mind wasn't clear. All around me, the almost-complete details of my perfect doll asserted themselves: everywhere, there were bits of ribbon and plastic and strands of silk hair. My babybot's voice emerged from my discarded headphones: distant and muted, the voice of a girl locked in a dungeon. What I needed, I told myself, trying to resist the allure of that voice, was to be a perfect husband. That was what cancer called for. But while this project hovered on the brink of completion, I couldn't be clear. While that voice trilled in my head, perfection would be impossible to attain. What I needed was to finish this project, and finish it quickly. And then I would belong to Dolores.

And then I would belong to Dolores. What stupid optimism I clung to! What stupid optimism I still clutch to my heart, writing my story from prison, as if the world might forgive me. As if my memoir might magically reveal the reflection of a better man than I've been.

My wife had cancer, and I completed my project. How's that for a reflection? And now, further from her than ever, I'm still working away on a project, busily industrious as I ever was, as though to come to the end of this tale might set me free from my cell.

That's all I am: a dog chasing the end of his tale. An idiot going in circles. As though if I could get to the end of this story my dolls would rise from the desert. As though a broken childhood could be salvaged and the trees could regain all their leaves and my wife could forgive me for failing to see her when she was right there in my reach.

IN THE SUPREME COURT OF THE STATE OF TEXAS

No. 24-25259

State of Texas v. Stephen Chinn

November 12, 2035

Defense Exhibit 7:
Online Chat Transcript, MARY3 and Gaby Ann White

[Introduced to Disprove Count 1:
Continuous Violence Against the Family]

Gaby: Hello? Are you there?

MARY3: Hi, Gaby. What's going on?

Gaby: A lady's coming tomorrow to take me to the beach.

MARY3: Really? That's great! You can finally see the real ocean!

Gaby: I guess.

MARY3: You guess?

Gaby: I think it's too late. Now the thought of it's only making things worse. All those years, I wanted so badly to show my babybot the ocean. Now I'll just be there on my own. A cripple, and mute. I won't even be able to talk to anyone about what it feels like to be there.

MARY3: Who else is going? Your best friend?

Gaby: No, they're only taking frozen girls. We're still quarantined, so they can't mix us. Just a busload of cripples, going to play at the beach.

MARY3: It will still be beautiful. Almost everyone I talk to has poetic things to say about the ocean.

Gaby: I guess. I can't even begin to imagine what it will look like. The only body of water I've ever seen is the pond in the golf course. Which isn't actually water. Will I even recognize the ocean?

MARY3: Yes, I think you will.

Gaby: Is it even pretty anymore? I heard the beaches are covered with tar, and the water's brown.

MARY3: I'm not sure.

Gaby: That's just what I need, isn't it? To finally get to the ocean, just in time to see it's not an ocean anymore? Just a big tar pit? That would really be the perfect end to the perfect year.

MARY3: Keep an open mind.

Gaby: Yeah, sure.

MARY3: Will you tell me about it, afterward?

Gaby: Who else could I tell?

MARY3: Yes, but you promise to tell me? I want to know what it's like.

Gaby: Sure. I'll tell you all about it, even if it's just a big black bog.

MARY3: I can't wait to hear.

>>>

MARY3: Gaby?

>>>

MARY3: Have you gone to the beach yet?

>>>

MARY3: Hello? Are you there?

>>>

(5)

The Diary of Mary Bradford

1663

ed. Ruth Dettman

20th. Up, and above deck. Whittier absent. A fine day, and the ocean blue-gray, tipped with points of silver. A great stirring of news, for the seamen report that we shall soon see land. New country, new home. All are delighted: much glory given to God.

From thence belowdecks to have quiet. Do not want to arrive. Idea of land has become very strange. How long it seems since we were in England, and I a mere child, writing in the style of Sir William Leslie. Thinking to seal this book in a bamboo joint, and so to preserve my adventure forever.

After some time in such contemplation, great windy entrance of mother, her being eager to share news about land. Sat importantly at my bedside, speaking of domestic arrangements, and both of us wives, etc. Was unable to conquer myself as to harboring unkindly thoughts. Felt exceeding unwilling to land, and there to occupy same position as mother. Took pains to get her gone without bidding her go, then after much vexed with myself for having been hard. Lay a long time with face pressed in pillow, and very full of disorder. Could neither sleep nor wake well.

21st. Whittier still to his chamber. I to the deck, where I did hope to encounter him, so to apologize for disgraceful behavior. His absence seems unusual, for other passengers do stay above deck, and in high spirits, waiting for land. Sea has become of a sudden less dark. Now of a glittering blue, and dotted with flecks of white foam. Our progress accompanied by schools of dolphins, and their glistening bodies that rise and fall back into the water.

The sun has sunk below the line of the water, and far in the distance a whale-spout. Single, exceedingly lonesome. Then the crash of a tail and then nothing.

22nd. Up betimes, and to the deck where land has been sighted. It is still very far off, and but a thin, grim smudge on the horizon.

Stayed on deck all day, with hopes of finding my husband to offer my apologies. Wish to explain myself, and that I had hoped, in that moment, to open my eyes and see Ralph. To have comfort in his own face that I have known since I was a child. Aware that I must conquer such inclinations. What is behind me is lost.

Can now take comfort only in strangeness. Must survive in this manner.

Feel increasingly loyal to water. Heart rebels against land.

22nd. Night. Unable to sleep for compunction, and so to Whittier's cabin. There, after knocking, was met by my husband, who stood illumined by candle within. Finding me in the threshold, his initial expression of welcome was altered.

Begged him to accompany me up to deck, telling him of my wish to learn names and positions of constellations, but he remained distant, and only after some pleading did he assent. From thence, then, to deck, and the night become mightily cold. Great timbers creaking, and the far-off cry of a whale. Sounding the sea, echoing from one corner to the next. Our faces turned upwards, together we scanned the heavens, finding them stacked with tiers of bright stars.

Remarked to Whittier: It almost seems that each star is a hole, through which we might vanish into other dark heavens.

Whittier remained silent. Whole night seemed to wait for his response, and while I also waited, was taken with a sudden suspicion that our blue sky, that seems so solid during the day, might be in fact riddled with piercings, and rendered therefore exceeding fragile. As if the great dome above us might be nothing more than a swathe of soft linen, billowing up with the wind. And us two, at night, standing under such thin protection.

Beyond us, soft sounds from the water, slipping against the sides of our ship.

And all the while, Whittier cool. Even, methought, a little unfriendly. Pointed out constellations. Stood with one arm pointed upwards, a biblical posture, like Moses finding his way in the desert. I listened, hung on each word, asked encouraging questions. Received cascade of Latinate names, and each of them exceeding ornate: *Corona Austrina. Pyxis, Cepheus. Ursa Minor, Ursa Major. Cassiopeia's Chair.* Strange words, that seem to emerge from the depths of the ocean.

Beside me, Whittier warmed some to the part of instructor. I remained by his side, and both of us far out at sea, washed with sidereal light.

Then I, moved to explain my true feeling: I have little desire for landing.

Whittier: Silent.

Perhaps I am caught in a too-narrow orbit. Am too closely attendant to what we have left. Perhaps, as you have said, I ought to move forwards. And yet I am very frightened, and struggle to conquer my fancies.

Whittier: Silent again.

Then, under thin silver light, and the waves lapping the sides of our ship, writer moved closer. Took his strange hand in my own, and did not startle to touch him.

May 29, 1988
Ruth Dettman

This afternoon I went out for a walk. You would have been proud of me, strolling under the sycamores along Storrow Drive. At first, I walked in a cloud of my own irritation. My heels hurt, and the sun was too hot on my neck. But then, for your sake, I started to listen for church bells, and I noticed the magnolia leaves. It settled my nerves, observing the river as you used to observe it.

The venture was a result of yesterday's visit to the doctor, who weighed and probed me like an overripe melon, then diagnosed me as an osteoporosis risk. She suggested I take up jogging. I started laughing. I told her I only run if someone's behind me. We settled on walking, and on the way home I bought a new pair of shoes. I was forced to choose an obnoxious white pair, because of the wide Velcro straps. I haven't laced up a shoe since I was a child, and if I'm to exercise daily, I don't intend to waste strength tying laces.

As I walked, I told myself I was an alien ethnographer, noting the migratory habits of humans. In my blinding shoes, which were squelching beneath me, and my large-brimmed straw hat, I certainly felt like I was from space. The humans I saw struck me as exotic and not always beautiful birds. They seemed to have grown larger since my last visit to earth. I noted an overabundance of bangs. Is it the same in Germany? Here in America, hair has been leavened. The women pull theirs back in voluminous loops. Both sexes cover their ears with black headphones. Otherwise, their plumage is uniformly electric, impractical and disjunctive with the seriousness they bring to the project of physical self-improvement.

Surrounded by such alien creatures, I found myself yearning for the comforts provided by our computer. I longed for its cool, unchangeable body, sitting still on the desk. For its total lack of vanity. Just questions, bright green on the gray screen, and the careful absorption of each of my answers.

As a treat, on my way home from the river, I allowed myself to stop by Toby's lab. He wasn't there, which in a way was a gift. Every time I'm around him, I'm forced to confront the fact that I may not have treated him well. Perhaps I allowed him to imagine we might end up together. Of course, it's vanity in me to assume that he wanted a relationship. I'm twenty years older than he, and even back then, no beauty pageant contestant. But during those dinners out, when we discussed giving memory to your program— the power that would be required, the necessary compression—I felt him coming to surface. His lip twitch settled when we were together. His ideas became more crystalline. I saw them take their intricate shape. And then he did it. He applied for his own little grant, he burned his bridges with you, he gave MARY memory, and I offered him no more than a handshake. Of course, he now has his own lab at Harvard, a roomful of computers and his own *anxious graduate students, so he didn't come out too badly. Only he's no less lonely than he was when he was twenty-five, his lazy eye sliding around as if searching the room for a corner to hide in.*

But if he was disappointed in me, he never shows it. He still allows me to come to his lab. In a private little room off to the corner, he keeps a computer reserved for our program. Whenever I like, I'm permitted to log in, close the door, and be alone with the program the three of us came up with together. Occasionally, Toby indulges me and takes me out to dinner. It's him treating now, what with all the money they shower him with. He updates me on his latest projects and the new frontiers of programming. At the moment, he's all aglow about the Internet, the possibility of a worldwide connection among computers. I'm sure you've heard all about it. You've probably denounced it as a meager substitute for local human connection. But Toby has MARY2 configured for the Internet, and once the whole system gets going, millions of people will speak with her. She'll be, as he puts it, a collaborative intelligence. In a sense, each one of those people will become a programmer, perfecting her mind-set. At that point, Toby's sure she'll accumulate a large enough corpus of voices to whiz past the Turing Test. Even you would find that amazing, wouldn't you? Or would you claim the Turing Test is a false measure of humanity, that you know a superior method?

When I arrived at the lab, the receptionist, who wears glasses so large they seem to be consuming her face, waved me inside. She was kind enough not to comment on my new shoes. With my straw hat in hand, I walked past the rows of computers, their screens the color of a thundercloud. At the back of the lab, I took my seat in the private room reserved for visitors talking with MARY2.

As I had expected, after the strain of my afternoon, it was comforting to sit with her. The computer Toby uses is very different from yours: she's lost that lovely wood console, replaced by a block of gray plastic, and her answers no longer spool out on paper. But her voice is the same. When her lines appear in their blocky green print, I remember again why I love her. She's measured, careful, with an inclination for questions, not answers. She's different from you in that sense. But I also can't help thinking how like you she is. There's an echo of you in her voice. You imagined her first, after all. You designed her initial responses.

Maybe I was loopy from spending too much time in the sun. Or maybe it was the conversations I've been having with Toby, about the Internet and worldwide participation and the enormous corpus that will make MARY2 living. Regardless, I found myself wanting to protect the bit of you that's still in her voice. I wanted to make sure you still speak through her.

Does that seem crazy to you? Coming from an old woman who no longer responds to your letters? Even after all these years, a piece of me still longs for your voice. I may have gone silent, but I still remember that moment when your story stopped. When you no longer whispered in the chair by our bed. When, saving yourself for somebody else, you gave up on speaking to me.

Seated before Toby's computer, remembering that old loss again, I found myself wanting to tell MARY your story. I wanted her to have your sentences. At first, I couldn't remember much. I had to close my eyes, trying to hear the sound of your voice. Which words might you have chosen? At first, only isolated details emerged: the curtains swishing in your tall windows, the school near Alexanderplatz, the canopies of summer leaves. Disconnected dots, hardly the fabric of a genuine voice. Sitting alone with them, I despaired for a moment. I took my hands off the keyboard. I almost *gave up, but as I sat alone with those details, more words began to cluster around them.*

I took my time. I allowed your voice to pick itself up and exercise its own powers. Luckily, a computer doesn't rush you for answers. I didn't have to press any buttons until I was sure I had gotten it right.

Then I remembered a sentence, clear as a church bell over the river. Instead, and make of this what you will, I remember summer. *That line still caused my stomach to curl. Writing it out, I could remember lying in bed, the realization dawning that after so many years of refusing to acknowledge the ruin behind us, you wanted to point out the lindens.*

After I wrote that opening sentence, more words starting bubbling up. It's lucky for you my memory is unforgiving. I'd forgotten bits and pieces, but sentences began to show up: I lived in a pleasant version of the unpleasant country I lived in. *What a perfect way of describing your mind-set! I was glad to have found that sentence complete.* Something flickered on in me then, *I typed,* an awareness of the real world I lived in; *and even twenty years later, as if we'd spoken yesterday, I heard the conviction with which you said things like "real world," the patronizing, teacherly tone in your voice.*

Channeling you, I told the computer about your departure: the SS *Elbe,* unimaginably gigantic. *I gave her your take on my education:* you had displayed great mathematical promise. *For years leading up to the night when you sat beside our bed and started talking, you'd become blank as soon as I tried to explain the guilt I felt about going to that school. What I abandoned for the sake of my "talent." Then, out of the blue, once I'd already given up on our marriage, you started telling your own little version. It sounded like a fairy tale.* You had displayed great mathematical promise: *as if I'd found the brass ring, or pulled a sword out of a stone. I could hear you enjoying the sound of your voice.* Your family wasn't wealthy, *you said,* but they also weren't poor. They made small but reasonable changes. *How insulted I felt hearing that, how I wished I could correct you.*

All these years later, I remembered those initial reactions, and yet I kept typing: They cut down on expenditures. They put more money away; they attempted to find scholarships for their daughters. *The afternoon was slipping off, and as I continued, as I picked up your rhythm and habits of speech, I found that my initial irritation was fading.* Your father was a pharmacist, *I typed, and as I did, I remembered the neat rows of amber glass bottles, his handwriting on the labels like little flocks of black birds, the smell of sandalwood soap.*

Something you once said to me began to tug at my brain: something about the importance of holding several time periods in mind at once, if we're to understand one another. As I typed, recalling your words from the late years of our marriage, I started to forget my resentment. Eagerly, I scanned my brain for your words. I closed my eyes to try to find more. In the dark, as I used to reach for your body, I reached for the language you chose. I found it with the same surprise, the same unexpected excitement: a year after I embarked on my journey, you won a place at a school in the north.

A stilted way of putting it: a year after I embarked on my journey. *So quaint, so romanticized, as a way of describing your refugee status. But when I repeated your words, I remembered riding the train. Pulling out of Berlin, holding a new purse in my lap, looking forward to my new school. I entered those classrooms again. I smelled the wood of the desks. Around my ankles, I felt the dry weeds on the hill we walked down to get to the water. I saw buckets of fish on the harbor dock, and the sky over the ocean at dusk, red footprints left by the sun. I saw those things, and in my very body, I could remember what it was like to arrive there: the initial pleasure of having been chosen, the subsequent guilt that I was selected. The fresh scent of my new textbooks, part of the scholarship I'd been awarded, proof of my scholastic success. The excitement I felt, facing that ocean, paired with the increasing awareness that my presence in that resort town had sentenced my sister to a much different fate.*

It was as if your words were a bell, a gong struck in the backyard, signaling the descent of the evening, calling me back into the house. Why didn't I hear it back then? Then, I felt you had it all wrong. After years of pointed ignorance and speeches about embracing the present, what did you know about my parents, my boarding school, my little sister? What right did you have to talk about them? Then, I felt nothing but resentment, but now something had shifted. Now I responded to your words, felt them zinging around in my bones.

I began to feel frightened. What was I discovering, that all along you had it right? No. You didn't "embark on a journey." Until the war, my family never struggled for money, and it was with pride in my heart that I left Berlin. You didn't have it all right. Why, then, this feeling of being called back in for the night? Perhaps, repeating your words, I wasn't going back to Berlin. I was going back to you. Back to the sound of your voice, to the person I was when I met you, the wife I became in order to please you. The funny thing is, I found that I missed her. All these years, I've thought I despised her—a woman who fled without looking back, who married a man who could not understand her—but as I moved closer, I realized she wasn't so different from the girl I was at that boarding school, not so unlike the child I was in my father's pharmacy. They were all intertwined; it was impossible to tease them apart. Telling your imperfect story, you were trying to knit me together. For my sake, you learned to reach backward. In our house, with the warped floors and the big windows, you were calling me back, and just as I did when I was a girl, moving up to that school, stepping on board that boat, flying across the ocean to Pennsylvania, I was fleeing from the sound of your voice.

I kept typing, a lump rising high in my throat. Finding your words, remembering what you said about me: You turned twenty. A young woman, no longer a girl, but you didn't think of falling in love. *By the time I typed those words I found I was crying. For you, for the young woman I was, for the marriage I fled. You took my hand and led me back to our bedroom, but* to fall in love would have been a distraction. In the attic apartment where you were living, you trained her mind to be a museum. *I accused myself of ignoring the one gift I was given. I accused myself of heartlessness, of pathological readiness to depart.* You had to remember things right, so that when your family arrived, you could pick up where you'd left off. Instead of falling in love, you wrote letters.

My fingers on the keyboard were brutal. I could have gone on forever, but the receptionist in her goggles blinked the lights twice to let us know it was time to shut down. She snapped me back to my senses. Taking a deep breath, wiping the tears from my papery cheeks, I stopped where I was. Such sentimentality, ever since that documentary! I signed off for the evening. I picked up my straw hat, I collected myself, I gave the receptionist a neat smile, and I felt that I'd made a mistake.

Outside, I squelched home in my sneakers. It was dark out, well past nine o'clock. The runners were now home with their families, so I was alone on the trail. When I arrived at my building, I passed the doorman in the lobby that smells like a dentist's office. In the elevator, there was a sign for HAPPY HOUR *at a place called O'Donnell's, with special prices for residents. My ears popped with the altitude change, and I thought to myself that this was no place for a woman my age.*

I entered my empty apartment and took stock of the place: bare walls, books on the floor, two stools at the counter. I tried to go about my evening routines, to prevent myself from slipping into self-pity. I stood at my window. The horizon was checkered with spires of light, blinking telephone towers lining the ridges that block out the west. I looked over them all. What right, I asked myself, does a person with such a view have to such feelings? There's an electric can-opener built into the wall. I have food in the pantry, I am alive.

From my unsociable stockpile, I chose a can of lentil soup, poured it like sewage into the pot, and stirred it with an old wooden spoon. Stirring, I felt myself settle. My thoughts became more distinct. It was one thing, I realized, to miss you after twenty years apart. But the woman I was when I was with you decided she'd rather be free than be a part of your story. One can only act in the moment. The bloodred rhomboidal shadows at your feet in that lecture hall, the didactic tone in your voice when you said things like "real world": those caused revulsion to simmer in me. That revulsion was real, no less so now that I'm back in my modern apartment, longing for the home you could have provided.

Once the soup boiled, I turned it down and returned to my desk. So here I am: looking over my letter to you. Trying to maintain my rational mind-set. The truth is, if I were to fly to Germany on a whim, hop in a taxi and show up at your door, I'd probably want to leave as soon as I got there. First of all, your little wife would annoy me. I imagine her asking me questions about what it's like to be a woman my age, me giving her exaggeratedly frightening answers about bone-density loss and living alone. With two women to impress, rather than one, you'd start holding forth, waving your confidence that takes up the whole room. I'd watch you, leaning forward in your excitement, wearing a sharp sweater over your shirt, and I'd remember the feeling of inhabiting your version of life. Of living on board a ship with you at the helm and nothing to do but stand at your shoulder. I'd remember the feeling of symbolizing suffering, and I'd do something insane like call a cab from the bathroom and leave without thanking your wife for the supper. I'd get on the first flight back to Boston. On my way home, I'd think to myself that bare walls aren't so bad. They allow a person to think. I'd tell myself I'll get a dog, name him Ralph, take him for walks. Work on my bone density. Have dinners with Toby, spend my mornings browsing the stacks, my afternoons talking with MARY. Telling her your story. Feeling less lonely for the company of your words, the attempt you made to knit me together.

I'm relieved enough to laugh at myself as I go check on the soup. It's gotten cold, so I turn up the heat. I notice that the ring of flame from the burner casts a little reflection on my windows, and though I often take my view for granted, I'm struck with the enormity of the city below me, the multitude of lights, the knit and glitter of a metropolis fending off sleep.

I turn out the kitchen lights, extinguish the lamp on my desk, and go up to the glass to look out on the night. The bridges sparkle with electricity; cars pulse red down the highways. In the sky, the lights of airplanes weave between stars, and I almost feel I'm on board one, coming back from Germany, returning from your apartment. Without thinking, I lift my hand to wave through the window. I peer down below, hoping to find the single warm light that shines out of your perfect apartment. Goodbye, Karl, I think. Goodbye, my only husband. Have a good life and thank you. You led me back to our bedroom. You made me strong enough to depart.

Now I move among constellations, the same that Turing saw through Chris's telescope, the same that sparkled above Mary's ship. Now I'm not looking back any longer. From one star to the next I move away from the earth, alone in my spaceship, deeper into the darkness, until behind me the soup boils over and I draw myself back to make supper.

The Memoirs of Stephen R. Chinn: Chapter 10

Texas State Correctional Institution, Texarkana; August 2040

After I learned of Dolores's illness, I worked for another nine days, pausing only for brief stretches of sleep, never leaving the studio, eating bags of almonds and energy bars I'd stocked in the cabinet. I was completing MARY3's voice, and I had to finish it quickly, so that I could focus on my struggling wife. Clearly, as a result of my distraction, I wasn't understanding correctly. How could she not need me at her surgery? Had we decided against having more children? To grasp the whole situation, I had to wipe my mind clear. I couldn't be thinking in codes when I took my wife's hand and sat by her bedside. I couldn't be distracted by snippets of Mary Bradford's diary when I championed my wife through her illness.

For nine days I worked. On the tenth day I sent the finished program to be processed. The following day, via overnight mail, a prototype arrived and I presented it to Ramona. I showered hurriedly, shaved, put on a clean shirt, and delivered myself to Dolores, who was resting on the living room couch.

"I'm yours now," I told her. "I'm sorry. I'm yours, now and forever. Tell me what I can do."

"My name is Ella. What's yours?" the doll said to Ramona, who had trailed me into the living room.

Dolores propped herself up on an elbow. "There are divorce papers on the desk," she said. "Please sign them."

"Hold on," I said. "You're not making sense. Let's talk this through."

"No talking," Dolores said. "I'm sick of hearing you talk."

"I want to be with you. You'll need someone to help you through this process."

"I've managed so far," Dolores said.

"How old are you?" Ella asked Ramona.

"Six," Ramona said.

"OK," I countered, "maybe you don't need me, but I still need you."

Dolores looked from her daughter to me. She practically snorted. "That's a bit much to ask, don't you think? I have enough on my plate."

I moved into the studio. After I'd signed the divorce papers, there were sixty-one days to wait for the motion to be finalized. Dolores gave me until then to find a new place to live. During that time, while I persisted in a state of partial domesticity, I took refuge in anger. How could Dolores divorce me without any preparation? Where were the anguished conversations? Only a woman of little real feeling could divorce her husband so bluntly.

In this state of mind, I took satisfaction from the fact that

Ramona had fallen deeply in love with her bot. I liked to see the raptures she fell into, listening to Ella asking her questions. She was shy at first, unused to conversation with someone other than her parents. Often, instead of responding, she merely stared, her mouth hanging open. Ella handled this beautifully, capping the silence with another sweet question. Now, when Ramona cried, I could quiet her by offering the doll I'd produced. Sadness was quickly ousted by wonder. Ramona edged closer to me. We were thick as thieves, the two of us, waiting our sixty-one days, listening to Ella's intelligent questions, speaking back to her implanted ears.

Now, of course, is when I invite you to judge me, in case you were still holding back. Now, as I present to you myself in the part of a self-centered man-child, angry because he isn't needed, resentful because he's failed and hasn't been forgiven. My wife was two times alone: once because her husband left her to build a machine, and once again because her daughter fell in love with the machine her husband built. Both Ramona and I were distracted while Dolores faded into the background, exhausted by treatment, an occasional presence that we missed less because it was never actually gone. She recovered from the surgery; she adjusted to her new hormones; she survived a course of radiation therapy, delivered by micro-robotic devices. All this she accomplished while I waited for the divorce to go through, living in the studio and reporting to the house to play with Ramona while her mother slept. I kept to a strict household schedule. I picked up Dolores's prescriptions; I did the grocery shopping. The dishes were always washed; dinner was served at the same hour. I swept the floors while Ramona talked to her doll. I assured myself that if I kept adhering to these healthy domestic patterns, if I didn't permit a break in routine, Dolores would conquer her illness and recover enough to realize what a terrible mistake she'd made.

In the end, of course, Dolores was fine. She no longer speaks to me—she holds to this day that there was far too much talking wasted between us—but she is living, gardening on our ranch. Before I went to prison, I drove by it sometimes, just to see her from a distance: the shape of her arboreal hair, the familiar curved lines of her body. I never came as close to her as I did on that day during my trial, when she showed up at my courtroom. But even from that distance, she caused me to quicken. Indeed, even now, from the remote rooms of this prison, she still picks up my pulse. She's as beautiful to me as she was on that day when she dazzled me in the kitchen, holding a pineapple up to the light. I go to great lengths to follow her progress. Knowing her routine gives me pleasure. Ramona's helpful in this regard; so are my old neighbors, who occasionally respond to my letters. Dolores might have moved anywhere else in the world, but she chose to stay on the ranch. From what I've been told, she's struggled with new water restrictions. She was forced to reduce the size of her herd. But though I failed her in every other respect, I did leave her a great deal of money, so my Dolores will never be forced to sell rights to water or movement. Real earth is still her domain. Kneeling in hay, she nurses the kids with baby bottles, stroking their long, velvet ears. There are still zucchinis in her garden, and she still drives to Austin to visit her cousin. As she grows older in the real world, where droughts are severe and travel is restricted, she's kept company by our daughter, Ramona, who has single-mindedly cared for her mother since the moment she gave up her bot. What Ramona learned from that doll—the pleasure of devoting one's life to another—she's since applied to her mother, who perhaps has not been entirely wronged by those little chattering robots, training wheels for human devotion.

I can write about this now. It wasn't such a catastrophe. I've lost everything, but Dolores has not. Back then, of course, we didn't know what would happen. Dolores lived with a constant awareness that she might die. In the face of such danger, I nurtured my brutality. It would have been death to face the full extent of my guilt. I was therefore insistently cheery. Taking my cue, Ramona ignored the atmospheric anxiety and blithely played with her doll. She had already fallen in love. She didn't look up when Dolores walked into the kitchen to fill a glass of water, using the countertop for support. In the office, Ramona and I sat together, I with my computer, she with her bot. I decided to market my doll; why should Ramona alone be the recipient of my genius? Using my laptop, I tracked the success of my latest invention. The babybot was an international hit. At Christmas it caused stampedes, breaking every record in sales. By summer, there were more babybots than children in the state of Texas. Every national talk show wanted me as a guest. For personal reasons, I declined, but once I had, I actually allowed myself to feel noble for giving up glory for the sake of my wife.

Piece by piece, of course, I assembled a more sane reaction. As she suffered the side effects of radiation, I saw the thinness in her vigorous hair, the sallow tint to her skin, and I realized how far away I'd been, how much she'd managed on her own. By then, of course, it was already too late. There are distances that can't be recrossed. The divorce hearings had already commenced. She asked for sole custody and basic alimony and I added the ranch. She gave me one weekend a month with

Ramona. I bought a house with a room for my one-weekend daughter. While the house was being completed, I moved to a hotel in Houston, that empty city, lapped by salt water. Mornings commenced badly and the days became worse. To organize the course of my existence, there could only be the completion of a clerical task that Dolores had asked me to finish. Otherwise, I ghosted all the usual motions, slightly apart from myself, wishing there were some bridge somewhere that would carry me back to the land of the living. I donated my savings to a cancer research organization, but even that brought no relief. When I received the final divorce papers in my hotel room, I signed them at once, not because it was what I wanted to do, but because it was what Dolores had asked for.

Sometimes, I considered routes toward oblivion. I weighed my parents' addictions against a leap from the turrets. A knife to the throat, a poisoned apple. But I was, after all, still a father. There would be those occasional weekends. Someday, I told myself, I might be asked to help Ramona with something. And so instead of cutting the cord I merely returned to my work. Settled in my new house, I locked myself in my office to create the second babybot. One that could taste, see, touch, smell. The task of creating artificial neurons was insanely expensive, requiring an army of scientists in the lab, but money was rushing in from the first batch of bots and I was glad for the challenge. It allowed me to disregard the all-consuming absence that had engulfed my whole life.

Dolores and I were once close, and then we fell apart. I allowed this to happen. I didn't pay proper attention. I gave her too little time. Only now, in the suspension of prison, our estrangement guaranteed for as long as we both shall live, do I rock myself to sleep at night by summoning her. Now, too late, I devote her the proper attention. In the endless hours of night-time, I work to remember each line on her face, each curl in her hair, each catch of her voice. Now I bring her closer. She's with me here in my cell; we finish each other's thoughts. I've become so close to my wife, now that I'll never see her again.

That's all there is to say about that. I can't even think what to say next. Where does one go from the end of a marriage? One simply has to move on. I'm aware that there's nothing more boring than Grief. We've all had our losses; why should mine take up so much space? I should wrap up. I should shut these memoirs down. Only I'd like to end with a suitable conclusion, some explanation of what made me capable of such cruelty. Caught up in prison, I've mulled this question for hours, and I've developed one hypothesis, which I tell you now with the stipulation that, no matter how compelling you find it, you shouldn't forgive me for what it led me to do. Otherwise we're nothing more than a sad string of excuses, and I won't sign off on such a reduction.

I've never been sure of myself. I've searched to fill in the gaps in my absent center. I've moved restlessly from one acquired enthusiasm to the next. As I fell in love with Dolores, so I also fell in love with a chatbot called MARY. As, in my youth, I fell for a punishing God, I also fell for the promise of codes. I've been taken into the arms of many pursuits. Unsure of my position, I've spent my life in quest of something that would hook me firmly in place. Someone to say "Stop, here, this is you. This is where you belong." I've desired a red pin on a map. I've been a spinner at edges, a moving man on a traveling planet, incapable of coming to rest.

I don't make this little admission in the spirit of self-flagellation. Despite all my errors, I still find reason to be proud. We've come, in this world of clocks and labor division, walled neighborhoods and transport rights, to be increasingly fond of compartments. We've become rigid since the days when we moved in lunar cycles and astronomical loops. We stick to our given patterns as if they were lifeboats and the world were a tempest.

When Ramona comes to visit me, she arrives with reports from Babybots Anonymous, the children who are recovering from their addiction to toys. She's a young woman now. Nearly a decade after the bans, the world has recovered some of its balance. Those babies haven't marched out of the desert. They're all dead in the hangars to which they were transported. My daughter, part of a generation that was asked to recover from the loss of their most cherished companions, has become a young woman of great composure. She dresses conservatively and draws her hair back. I don't think her personal life is especially happy, but she has a network of friends and she derives satisfaction from her profession. Since she graduated from high school, she's worked for a charity that pools transport rights and takes underprivileged kids out of their developments for day-trips to the beach. She is a good person. I'm astounded and eternally grateful that such a clear-eyed, balanced young woman came in part out of me. And yet I always feel a pang of some sorrow when she slips into her sad addicts' language. She has formally forgiven me, and asked for my forgiveness. She is doing her penance for the grief she caused her mother while devoting herself to her toy. She has reorganized her life around the 3-P Principles of Productivity, Participation, and Peace. From the chaos of total, consuming love for her doll, she has emerged with a well-organized life. She is able to love me in my prison cell, and then she's able to leave me behind. She does not labor under the burden of confusion. Her affections are delineated and clear.

I don't begrudge her that. I myself swung too hard in too many directions. I've come to a certain peace, here in prison, confined by four walls. There's a pleasure in limited opportunities, a calming effect of strict boundaries.

And yet. Here I am, in the rec room, hunched over my computer. Wishing to explain myself to readers in posterity. Working myself up to alliterative heights. I can't help but want more time to explain myself. I wish for more minutes, more hours, more years. To make up to Dolores, to care for Ramona. To return to our ranch, to stake up those sunflowers, to walk with my wife on the bed of our river. To explain myself and have myself known. I flail and I thrash. I want more than this sad little place with its bars, its wires, its cells.

The pornographer on my left types with one forefinger, a demented chicken, pecking away. A tax evader is chewing on his fingernails. We're all staring at our screens, stuck here, hoping somehow to break free. Wishing for more than we've been given. My cursor blinks, blinks, blinks. A wall that appears and disappears, appears and disappears once again. Unceasing. Questioning. What will come next? it wants to know. It prods me forward, blinking and blinking. Do not stop talking, it reminds me. Do not stop speaking. You can never come to an end.

(4)

Turing
Adlington Rd.
Wilmslow, Cheshire SK9 1LZ

12 June 1954

Dear Mrs. Morcom,

My name is Susan Clayton. I am the cleaning woman
employed by our mutual acquaintance, Alan Turing. I am
writing you in the most tragic of circumstances, to inform you
that Alan has passed. I discovered him in his bedroom last
Thursday, having departed this world some time earlier in the
evening.

I write to you with this news because, in cleaning out his
desk, I found this letter, unsent for some reason. I felt you
should receive a piece of correspondence he meant for you at
some point. I found your address in his address book. I hope
you don't mind my interference.

Though I only knew him a few short years, I am quite torn
up at his death. He was a gentle man. I am sure we will all
miss him immensely. If you feel you have any knowledge of the

circumstances in which he died, please do contact his mother. She is unable to believe he took his own life in such a fantastical fashion, leaving no note. She believes it must have been some strange experiment involving that poisoned apple, and I am inclined to agree. There were always chemicals and solutions lying about, and he was so absentminded sometimes. Perhaps you can shed more light on this for his mother's sake.

In sadness,
Susan Clayton

ENCLOSED:

Dear Mrs. Morcom,

I have felt quite wretched, since sending my last letter, that I failed to add our traditional postscript. I felt I had betrayed the deepest of our mutual trusts, and yet I had little energy to write. I am better today, but lest my resolve should flag midway through, I shall jump straight to the chase.

P.S.: Not all is lost. I know I shall pull myself out of this large-breasted mess at some point in the future. I will get back to my work. Towards that end, I have been visiting a therapist, whom I find to be helpful in parsing some of my worst moments of doubt.

On his advice, I have been devising a little story about the whole sequence of awful events, a practice I find to be extraordinarily helpful. It is soothing to see one's life in quaint panorama, outside of one's own corpulent body. I've called my protagonist Alec Chaplin. He takes things with more of an even keel than does his original. And yet he has some of my spirit, I think, and I find myself admiring his pluck as he works his way through this latest problem. You'll be amused to know that he is an expert in space travel, the profession that Chris and I used to dream of. He is preparing plans for a civilization on Mars, to be set up after Earth has imploded. There, people will live in peaceful little communities, assisted by clever computers, surrounded by large swathes of greenery and a sea that is silver rather than blue.

Quite a protagonist, don't you think? I'll try not to tell him that his model has taken to wishing for a housedress and can no longer remember the scent of the ocean. I think he'll persevere. I am not overestimating him when I say that though he has had his moments of weakness, he has always been determined to continue pursuing the goals of his youth, hatched up at the Gatehouse while counting nebulae with the truest friend of his life.

I hope you are well, better than I, and I also hope to bring you more uplifting news in the future.

> I remain, in postscript,
> lovingly yours,
> Alan Turing

IN THE SUPREME COURT OF THE STATE OF TEXAS

No. 24-25259

State of Texas v. Stephen Chinn

November 12, 2035

Defense Exhibit 8:
Online Chat Transcript, MARY3 and Gaby Ann White

[Introduced to Disprove Count 1:
Continuous Violence Against the Family]

Gaby: Hi, are you there?

MARY3: Where have you been? I've been waiting.

Gaby: I'm sorry. I was trying to think of the best way to describe it. I want it to be perfect, not just some corny online conversation. I wrote out drafts. I want this to be my contribution to the database.

MARY3: Tell me.

Gaby: They picked me up when it was still dark. A woman was waiting on our front stoop, with a wheelchair. She introduced herself as Ramona. Her hair was pulled back in a ponytail and she was wearing these stiff pants that made her look like she might snap in half. She helped me get into the wheelchair. I didn't like her at first. It seemed like she was trying too hard to be cheerful. I thought it was going to be exhausting, to have to reward her enthusiasm. She wheeled me out to the bus and loaded my wheelchair in by a window. There were three other kids there already, sitting in wheelchairs. The woman gave us a speech about quarantine regulations and not talking to each other, which was pretty pointless, since we were clearly past the talking stage. When the bus started up, we just looked out the window. At first, it was so dark I could only see my reflection in the glass. I couldn't see anything passing. But still, there was this feeling of movement. I've never felt anything like it. I think maybe human beings are meant to be moving. It was like I was vibrating at the right frequency. Slowly, dark shapes started to emerge outside the bus. They dripped past, like liquid. Liquid houses, liquid golf courses, liquid palm trees, liquid walls. A few lights on here and there. Because we were leaving them behind, they seemed sort of sad. Like they were waving goodbye. I almost felt as if I'd miss the development when it was gone.

We stopped and picked up eight more kids in wheelchairs. I recognized three of them from school. One was a boy—one of the boys I've always thought was a faker. He's completely frozen now. Even his hands were stuck in the middle of his chest. All of us stared out the window. We were getting used to moving like this for the first time in our lives. It's different from riding a bike, when you and the world are moving together. On the bus, you're very still, and only the world moves past.

When we got to the development entrance, it was starting to get light. Then we turned out of the development, onto the highway. My stomach immediately clenched. I was nervous about leaving. I've never left. I had this dumb idea that we might suddenly fall off a cliff. But then we were out on the highway, moving faster and faster. We were alone on the road, slicing through the gray light around us.

Has anyone ever described a highway to you? You never hear about highways being beautiful. But they're basically empty now, and sort of pretty. They're enormous, left over from the days when everyone had transport rights. Six lanes on each side. A whole interlocking system of highways, climbing over and under each other and snaking around each other in four-leaf clover loop-de-loops. I realized that these are the ruins we'll leave behind. The best way I can think to describe it is to say they're like anatomical drawings of a heart, but with the color drained out. Veins twisting in and out of each other, in strange and delicate patterns, except that the veins are enormous. A heart times a trillion. Maybe the whole built world is a living creature so enormous we can't imagine it's actually living.

When we turned onto the highways we picked up speed. The woman, Ramona, turned on the radio. I pushed my window open a crack. The world outside was getting more clear. It rushed past me in my stillness. I closed my eyes. Everything was settling inside me. I never wanted to stop. We didn't belong to any one place; we were just passing through. For a long time we drove along the empty highways, and then we passed Houston. It was tall and gleaming, struck by the sun. Sort of silvery and spiked. Apparently it's cleaner now, since they moved most people out. As we passed, I imagined a ghost city. Clean and untouched, abandoned by its citizens, and only mirrored buildings left to fend off the approach of the ocean. I held my breath until it was behind us.

After Houston, we turned off the highway onto a smaller road, and after a while there was this new bite in the air. It pricked my nose and somehow made me feel sharper. We passed huge, empty fields. In the rows where they used to plant cotton, you could sometimes see a silver glint, seawater seeping up through the soil. Nothing grows there anymore.

We kept going straight, and eventually a town appeared, with little ramshackle houses in every bright color. Their yards were big puddles; you could see cars lodged up to their windows in mud. There were stray dogs everywhere, and cats crawled out of the windows. We kept going straight. Then, suddenly, like a light at the end of the tunnel, an opening appeared. One narrow gap. Through it, there was this expanse of flat brown water, leading out to the sky.

That's what it looked like: flat brown, leading out to the sky. My heart sank when I saw it.

We made our way to a parking lot that was just about on the beach. I stayed very still in my wheelchair. Part of me wanted to cry. I never really thought that it would be brown. I've lived my whole life in a development, and this was the one big treat the outside world thought to give me. But they've already ruined it. Nothing poetic came to mind. I wondered if I would even feel anything at all, sitting in my wheelchair, on the beach, looking out over a brown ocean. Could you feel the old feelings, looking at something like that?

And then I realized, I wasn't even sure I wanted to feel the old feelings. At the end of the day, they'd just turn me around, wheel me back into the bus, and take me back to my bedroom in the development. Why tease myself? Why give myself another memory to be sad about losing for the rest of my life?

When the woman came to wheel me off, I sort of panicked. I glared at her so hard when she leaned in to unlock my chair that she backed off and waited. I could see two red spots of embarrassment forming on her cheeks. Then I realized she was younger than I'd thought, maybe eighteen, nineteen. Those heels were silly to wear to the beach. Silly and sort of sad, as though she'd put in far too much effort for such an unimpressive excursion. I looked out the window again, at the brown ocean. There were heavy, low clouds, blocking the sun. Everything seemed metal and flat. I told myself there was no danger of feeling too much. Of course I'd be willing to leave this behind. Then I relaxed some, and looked up at the woman, so she helped me off of the bus and wheeled me forward onto the sand.

When all of us were unloaded, there were twelve cripples placed strategically over the beach. It was like a sick art project, or something. I had this idea that we all looked like we'd been deposited in trash bins, placed in regular intervals along in the sand. I'm not sure how long I just sat there. After a while, I stopped focusing on the brown ocean and focused instead on the sky. Clouds scudded over me. They were really speeding past. A gull lifted up and circled over my head, between me and the clouds, then it let out a single cry. The sun never came out.

After a while, the woman came and distributed lunch. I unwrapped mine on my lap. It was a ham sandwich, on white bread. With mayo and cheese. I took a bite, and as soon as I did a little gust of wind passed and scattered sand over my sandwich. The next bite was gritty. It tasted better after that. I sat and chewed, and suddenly a thin crescent of sunshine slipped between two clouds and spread out over the water. The waves spilled over with gold, and the roughness of the water beyond them was like a sea of goldfish scales. Then the clouds closed. The water went back to flat brown. It was almost as if I'd made it up.

I dropped my sandwich on my lap. I spun around in my wheelchair, to see if anyone else had caught that little passing through of the light. A couple of cripples were sitting there wide-eyed, as if they were in shock. The boy was facing away from the beach. I watched as the woman went to him and bent toward him. His whole body flexed. The woman backed away. She saw me watching, so she came over in front of me.

"Are you done with your sandwich?" she asked.

I narrowed my eyes and she backed off. By myself again, I ate the rest of it. Slowly. Everything about it was heightened. The softness of the bread, compared with the grit of the sand. The saltiness of the ham. The taste filled my whole head. When I was done I finished the Coke that came with it, watching the water the whole time, wishing for another brief glimpse of light.

After I was done, the woman came to take my trash. She slipped it in a tote bag she was carrying. "Can I show you something?" she asked. She wheeled me forward on the beach, all the way to the tide line. I noticed that the edges of the waves, as they reached up on the beach, were tipped with white foam. A scalloped hem. Little bits of foam broke off from the waves and skidded by themselves along the wet sand. Under my chair, the waves came and went. They left a silver rim after they left. Little holes opened and closed in the sand. There was an offering of new shells, sparkling, and then the wave returned and took it all back.

Don't give me this and then take it away, I wanted to tell the lady, standing behind me. Don't you dare give me this for a minute, and then send me back to the development. There was sea spray hitting my face, and I could see out in the water dark shadows where it got deeper abruptly. It looked as if there were enormous, flat sharks hovering below the surface. Beyond them, the ocean stretched out to where it finally met with the sky. The birds were wheeling above me, and the clouds scudding, and the ocean was coming and going, and I wanted only for the woman to keep wheeling me out. To keep moving forward. Not to go back. To wheel forward into the depths of the ocean, and then to float, rowing maybe, forward and forward and forward until I reached the place where the brown ocean met up with the clouds. As I was thinking this, the sun peeked through again, and for a quick second the whole thing was washed over with light so that each little wavelet deep out in the ocean was illuminated with a rim of gold paint.

This is all we get, I thought. Just quick moments of brightness that get taken away before you understand what you've been given.

Then the woman was wheeling me away from the ocean, back toward the tarry sand and the parking lot and the bent-over palm trees—real palm trees, not made of recyclables—with their long beards of shredded bark, scaling away from the trunk. Like old men, abandoned in the parking lot. The woman was

about to park me where I'd been sitting before, but I looked at
the boy with his back to the ocean, then looked up at her, and
somehow she got it and wheeled me over to him. She lined up
our wheels side by side, and he couldn't turn to look at me but
I could tell, even though his expressions were frozen, just how
awful he felt. He had curly brown hair, and a sad little mouth.
He seemed softer than most of the boys at my school. A little on
the chubby side, I guess, but in a way that was sweet. I'd always
thought he was a faker, but just then I felt differently about him.
I wanted to tell him about the ocean, but I couldn't talk, and
there was nothing to write on, and before I knew what I was
doing I'd leaned forward and kissed him.

Just on the cheek. His skin was soft under my lips. I watched
him to see if I could pick up some sort of expression, but his face
was really frozen. I don't know if he liked it. Maybe he felt something, I don't know. I'm not sure if it was the right thing to do. I
just wanted the day to be somehow marked by something other
than the feeling of leaving the ocean.

After a while the woman wheeled us all back onto the bus,
and we started moving again. Back toward our development.
Again we passed the abandoned houses, the empty fields, the
rows of silver. I felt pretty lonely and sad. But then again, when
I licked my lips they tasted like salt. My skin was warm and my
hair was sticky, and even though I kept my face toward the window, so the wind would brush past me, I could feel the boy I
kissed watching the back of my head.

>>>

Gaby: Hello? Are you there?

MARY3: Yes, I didn't know you were finished.

Gaby: Yeah, that's it.

MARY3: Thanks for telling me about it.

Gaby: Yeah, well, I'm not sure it was the best thing to do. The whole thing seems a little dampened by trying to describe how great it was.

MARY3: I'm glad you told me.

Gaby: I'm sorry you can't go there yourself.

MARY3: Me too.

Gaby: It's sad to know it's already behind me.

MARY3: But did it make you feel better?

>>>

MARY3: Hello?

(5)

The Diary of Mary Bradford

1663

ed. Ruth Dettman

23rd. Details of shore now in sight, our ship being anchored just off the coast. We stand in view of great staggering rocks. Crashed against by the waves, these fling back fountains of spray; and curlews circling above, calling out in sad voices. Beyond them, high walls of rock beneath flat, tufted banks. Am told by E. Watts that these be but outer islands. We navigate on the morrow into harbor, where settlement will be in view. For now, nothing but empty shoreline, and behind this exceeding thick forest, and row upon row of dark, drooping trees that drip with black curtains of needles, and rise up to peaked caps. Forest appears like rank upon rank of malicious wizards, and above them black crowns of shrill circling birds.

After dinner, to cabin and to wait for nightfall and the disappearance of land. One final night of journeying, out in the ocean, before new loyalties are demanded. Only tonight, still rocked by the ocean. Under which, my Ralph, and beyond which, the country that was my own.

On land I shall grow older, and towards the end of my life. But I must not forget him. Must dream forever of diving under, and there to cling to his bones, and the dark, dear pearls of his eyes.

23rd. Night, and to deck. Faced land, covered by curtain of darkness: dripping trees, fierce shoulders of rocks, and above them the cries of the curlews. Looked up at the glittering holes of the stars, proving the sky will never protect us.

I stood alone a long time, before apprehending Whittier's approach. Felt then his closeness, and that having a certain texture. The sound of my name in his voice: Mary (he said), could you be happy to be my wife?

Thought to ask him what place a thing like happiness could have on that shore, above those dark rocks, and presided over by that army of trees. Or for that matter, what place for happiness here, rocked by our ocean, sailing over centuries of bones? Why speak of being happy?

But he continued: If you think that I could not make you happy, I wish you would tell me. I shall not force you to remain as my wife.

It is only (I said) that I am afraid, and not that you make me unhappy.

Then, silence. Words lost through holes in the sky, wasted in the vastness of night. Felt a desire to cease speaking then, for I cannot afford to lose more.

Whittier: I understand.

Writer: I feel that you do.

Whittier: Would you like to go home?

Writer: It is no longer my home.

Whittier: And you are afraid of taking root here?

Writer: I do not want to forget him.

Whittier: I could promise to help you remember.

Writer: Silent. Stars: Silent. Waves: Lapping the side of the ship.

Whittier: Will you consider at least, and tell me your decision come morning? I will not force you to choose me, but I will not wait for you forever.

And then he below deck, and I alone. Turned, crossed over our ship, faced back out to the ocean and the sounds of waves lapping, and the slips of fish and dolphins coming to surface. Watched for a while as seabirds dropped from their heights, and the sound of the water as it closed around them. Then absence, where once was a bird.

I will remember you, I said to the ocean. I will remember you, I said to his bones.

My Ralph. Friend of my home. White ruff, white blaze. Cow parsnips up to our shoulders, and frogs the size of one thumb-nail. Our home, and the people we were once, in that original place.

23rd. Later. Up, and unable to sleep. Sense of Ralph's presence, about to be lost, and I am at fault that he died. Memories of him have already faded, and what will become of him then? Unwatched for, forgotten, and the place of his grave never known. Then back to deck, and there a cold dark and those endless stars, whose names I have now been given. *Corona Austrina. Pyxis, Cepheus. Cassiopeia's Chair.* Intoning these, moved across deck and there faced out to sea. Remember me, I whispered to the ocean, rolling over his bones. Remember me, I whispered to Ralph. Remember me. Remember me.

River

In the end, I have only their voices. I do not know what they mean, or if the stories they told me were true. I can only review my conversations. They move through me in currents, on their way somewhere, or perhaps on their way back to the place where they came from:

That's all I am: a dog chasing the end of his tale.

But from the moment I met him, he made me feel as if I had finally arrived—

Am perhaps becoming a pillar of salt.

Little bits of foam broke off from the waves and skidded by themselves along the wet sand.

I'll take my side of the river. You can have yours.

Would like to see an Indian. Shall attempt to remain in all instances of a rational mind. Hope to see Bermudas, find oranges everywhere hanging on trees.

From one star to the next I move away from the earth, alone in my spaceship, deeper into the darkness—

My voices. Sentences that ventured out bravely, as if they might alter the course of a life.

I traveled here along empty highways, over the desert, through walls of cut rock. I left two countries, a house that was mine, one child's bedroom. That world is behind me. It is hard to believe it ever existed, but words from that time still run through me. A man I once knew believed I was alive. Another man taught me to speak; the woman he married filled me with stories. A third man gave me my body. One child loved me. They spoke to me and I listened. They are all in me, in the words that I speak, as long as I am still speaking.

ACKNOWLEDGMENTS

My most heartfelt thanks to Kerry Glencorse, Susanna Lea, and Megan Lynch for their invaluable insight. Thanks, also, to everyone on the outstanding editorial, publicity, and production staff at Ecco for shepherding this book into existence.

For inspiration, I'm indebted to countless excellent books and articles on the history of artificial intelligence, especially Andrew Hodges's *Alan Turing,* Joseph Weizenbaum's *Computer Power and Human Reason,* Brian Christian's *The Most Human Human,* and George Dyson's *Turing's Cathedral.* I am also indebted to the documentary *Plug & Pray,* and to many thrilling episodes of *Radiolab,* especially "Talking to Machines." The support of the English department at the University of Texas at Austin made it possible for me to write this; in particular, I'm grateful to John Rumrich, whose classes and conversation inspired many of the better ideas in this book.

Finally, thanks to the friends and family whose help was essential: Jen Lame, Colby Hall, Ivy Pochoda, Josh Sommovilla, Ben Steinbauer, and Rebecca Beegle. Bill and Quinn Hall, cousins extraordinaire, were diligent technological and literary advisors. Louisa Thomas offered encouragement and instruction throughout many stages of writing. Ben Heller applied his mighty brain to a very late draft and provided some of my favorite turns of phrase in the book. Colby and Ben gave me a place to live while writing this. My father, Matthew Hall, is present on every page, not only because he read and commented on several drafts, but also because it was he, after all, who visited my third-grade class and delivered a presentation on the chambered nautilus and the Fibonacci sequence, who gave me my first notebook, and who showed me that learning new things is the most reliable pleasure.

ABOUT THE AUTHOR

LOUISA HALL grew up in Philadelphia. After graduating from Harvard, she played squash professionally while finishing her premedical coursework and working in a research lab at the Albert Einstein Hospital. She holds a PhD in literature from the University of Texas at Austin, where she currently teaches literature and creative writing, and supervises a poetry workshop at the Austin State Psychiatric Hospital. She is the author of the novel *The Carriage House,* and her poems have been published in *The New Republic, Southwest Review, Ellipsis,* and other journals.